Lucas took a deep breath. "Unfortunately, there's no record of how it was done. All we know is that Leforte was captured trying to sneak out of Paris dressed as an old woman and thrown in the Bastille. The Scarlet Pimpernel took credit for his escape. It would've been nice if they could have clocked back to see how it was done. But however it was done, we're going to have to be the ones to do it."

"Sure would be nice if we could hop on a plate and jump ahead a few hours so we could see how we did it," Finn said. "But then, we'd have to do it first before we could see how it was done. Ain't temporal physics wonderful?"

"It's times like these that make me wish I'd kept my old job," said Lucas.

3 TIMEWARS

THE PIMPERNEL PLOT

BY SIMON HAWKE

ACE SCIENCE FICTION BOOKS
NEW YORK

THE PIMPERNEL PLOT

An Ace Science Fiction Book / published by arrangement with
the author

PRINTING HISTORY
Ace Original / September 1984

ISBN: 0-441-66409-1

Ace Science Fiction Books are published by
The Berkley Publishing Group,
200 Madison Avenue, New York, New York 10016.
PRINTED IN THE UNITED STATES OF AMERICA

For Rob, Pete and Debbie Siegel,
with friendship and gratitude

An End to War . . .

On April 1, 2425, Dr. Wolfgang Amadeus Mensinger, professor emeritus at Heinlein University on Dyson One, discovered time travel. Already hailed as the greatest scientist of his time for his formulation of the Unified Field Theory at the age of eighty-five, Mensinger had been in disfavor with the scientific community for thirty years as a result of steadfastly maintaining that time travel or, as he preferred to call it, temporal translocation, was theoretically possible. When he made the announcement on his one hundred and fifteenth birthday, he promptly became the darling of the media. Had anyone else come forth with such a theory, he would have been just another mild and amusing curiosity, but when the man who had relegated Einstein to the league of the also-rans made such a pronouncement, people listened.

Access to the media had never been a problem for Dr. Mensinger. He was a garrulous, highly articulate, and charming man with an empathy for the nonscientific mind, which resulted in his being able to explain complex ideas in a manner that the layman could easily understand. He also understood what, traditionally, most scientists did not, that scientific research was to a large degree a game of politics.

Initially, his theory was received with great excitement by

the media and the masses, while his colleagues in the scientific community reacted with a degree of skepticism that bordered on derision. Most of them felt that the venerable Dr. Mensinger had already done his best work and that in reaching for a still greater achievement, he had overextended himself and irresponsibly turned to cheap sensationalism. The media, always anxious for an entertaining confrontation, provided countless opportunities for his critics to attack him, which attacks were made more feasible by the simple expedient of Dr. Mensinger's lacking any proof to back up his assertions.

Furious at the treatment accorded him by the media and his peers, Mensinger went into semiseclusion at the university on Dyson, where the administration was more than happy to provide some limited funding for his research in exchange for having the famous Dr. Mensinger as a lecturer on its faculty. Professor Mensinger married the daughter of the dean and settled into the academic life, all the while driving himself with superhuman energy to complete his research. As time wore on and results failed to appear, his budget was steadily whittled away and his health began to decline. He began to grow derelict in his academic responsibilities and the only reason he was kept on was the value of his name and his relationship to the dean. His fellow professors liked him, but they looked on him with pity as a tragic case of burnout. Then, in his hundred and fifty-second year, he developed the first working model of the chronoplate.

When Mensinger died, fifteen years after he made time travel a reality, his work was continued by his son, Albrecht. Unfortunately, by this time, Albrecht was only able to refine his father's work. He no longer had control of the discovery. The politicians had stepped in.

On June 15, 2460, the Committee for Temporal Intelligence was formed. Agents of the committee, after careful training and conditioning, began to travel back through time for the purpose of conducting further research and testing of the apparatus. In the beginning, many of these agents were lost in transit, trapped forever in a temporal limbo some government official had nicknamed "the dead zone," but those who returned came back with often startling information. Historical records had to be revised. Some legends turned out to have been fact. Some facts turned out to have been legends. Historical events that previously lacked documentation were verified. Other events were brought to light. The Theory of Genesis was refuted and there followed a revolution in the Church, which culminated in a radical proposal made by Cardinal Consorti that agents be sent back through time to determine if Christ actually arose after his crucifixion. A restraining order was placed on the Committee for Temporal Intelligence to prevent them from attempting such a thing and Cardinal Consorti was excommunicated.

On January 25, 2492, in a historic meeting which became known as the Council of Nations, taking place in the capital of the United Socialist States of South America, a proposal for an "end to war in our time" was put forth by the chairman of the Nippon Conglomerate Empire. Though Dr. Albrecht Mensinger, invited to the council as a guest of honor, argued passionately against the resolution, it was passed by an overwhelming majority when he was unable to offer conclusive proof that the past could be affected by actions taken by time travelers from the present. The past, argued the members of the scientific community invited to the conference, cannot be changed. It had already happened. It was absolute.

On December 24, 2492, the Referee Corps was formed, brought into existence by the Council of Nations as an extranational arbitrating body with all power to stage and resolve the proposed temporal conflicts. On the recommendation of the newly created Referee Corps, a subordinate body named the Observer Corps was created, taking over many of the functions of the Committee for Temporal Intelligence, which became the Temporal Intelligence Agency. The TIA absorbed the intelligence agencies of most of the world's governments and was made directly responsible to the Referee Corps. Within the next ten years, temporal confrontation actions, presided over by the Referee Corps, began to be staged. The media dubbed them the "Time Wars."

In September of 2514, Albrecht Mensinger published the work that was to establish him as an even greater genius than his father. The conclusions he had reached were also to result in his eventual total nervous collapse a few years later. These conclusions, which resulted in the hastily reconvened Council of Nations and the Temporal SALT Talks of 2515, were published as "Mensinger's Theories of Temporal Relativity." They were as follows:

The Theory of Temporal Inertia. The "current" of the timestream tends to resist the disruptive influence of temporal discontinuities. The degree of this resistance is dependent upon the coefficient of the magnitude of the disruption and the Uncertainty Principle.

The Principle of Temporal Uncertainty. The element of uncertainty expressed as a coefficient of temporal inertia represents the "X factor" in temporal continuity. Absolute determination of the degree of deviation from the original, undisrupted scenario is rendered impossible by the lack of total accuracy in historical documentation and research (see Heisenberg's Principle of Uncertainty) and by the presence of historical anomalies as a result either of temporal discontinuities or adjustments thereof.

The Fate Factor. In the event of a disruption of a magnitude sufficient to affect temporal inertia and create a discontinuity, the Fate Factor, working as a coefficient of temporal inertia, and the element of uncertainty both already present and brought about by the disruption, determine the degree of relative continuity to which the timestream can be restored, contingent upon the effects of the disruption and its adjustment.

The Timestream Split. In the event of a disruption of a magnitude sufficient to overcome temporal inertia, the effects of the Fate Factor would be canceled out by the overwhelming influence of the resulting discontinuity. The displaced energy of temporal inertia would create a parallel timeline in which the Uncertainty Principle would be the chief governing factor.

Mensinger appeared once again before the Council of Nations and he formally submitted his publication, along with its supporting research and conclusions, to the world leaders. Once again he argued passionately, this time for the immediate cessation of the Time Wars. This time, they listened. Resolutions were made, voted on, and passed. However, the one resolution Mensinger most wanted to see passed was tabled, due to the lack of agreement among the members of the council. Mensinger left the meeting in despair, a broken man. The Time Wars continued.

PROLOGUE ═══════════════

The city square was utterly silent as the crowd waited in tense, almost reverential anticipation. The only sounds that broke the stillness were the praying of the man atop the wooden platform, the sobbing of his wife at the bottom of the steps, and the squeaking of the pulley as the blade was slowly raised. The man's prayer was rudely interrupted as he was seized and forced down to his knees, his head jammed into position. The lever was tripped, there was a brief scraping sound as the blade descended swiftly and then a duller sound, not unlike that of an axe sinking into wood. The man's head fell into the wicker basket and the crowd roared its approval.

Joseph Ignace Guillotin's device, proposed in the Assembly by the venerable physician as a "merciful" method of execution, had not been in use for more than a few months, but its blade had already been thoroughly tempered in the blood of the victims of the Revolution. The mob had stormed the Tuileries and the Swiss Guards, who had been ordered to cease firing by the king, were massacred. Louis XVI was held prisoner with his family in the old house of the Knights Templars and the provisional government was in the hands of Georges Jacques Danton of the Cordeliers. Marie Joseph Paul Yves Roch Gilbert du Motier, the Marquis de Lafayette, whose Declaration of the Rights of Man had been hailed and accepted by the National Assembly as the embodiment of the principles of "*Liberté, Fraternité, Égalité,*" had been branded a traitor and had fled for his life to Austria. The bloody September Massacres, in which over one thousand aristocrats would be sacrificed on the altar of the new regime, were underway. The rest of Europe would be deeply shocked at the events in Paris, at Versailles, in Lyons, Rheims, Meaux, and Orléans; however, they were just a prelude to the excesses of the Jacobins under Robespierre's Reign of Terror.

With glazed eyes, Alex Corderro watched the man's decapitated body being dragged off the guillotine. The executioner paused only long enough to give the blade a quick wipe with a red-stained rag before he motioned for the next victim to be brought up. The dead man's wife was frogmarched up the steps. She was incapable of standing and had to be held up for the crowd's inspection. Once again, the mob fell into an eerie silence. A hungry silence. The woman swayed unsteadily and, for a moment, her eyes came into focus. She saw her husband's head being dumped out of the wicker basket and she doubled over, vomiting upon the wooden platform. It was all Alex could do to keep himself from doing likewise. He had thought that he would be prepared for this, but it was nothing like what he had imagined. This was a far cry from Sidney Carton's romantic last hurrah in Dickens's *A Tale of Two Cities*. This was wholesale slaughter and Alex Corderro could not bear to watch it any longer. The squeaking of the pulley was like fingernails scraping on a blackboard and it made him shiver. It would have been, he thought, a far, far better thing had he stayed home where he belonged, in the 27th century, where such things were only to be read about in books and gleaned from information retrieval systems, where their graphic reality did not intrude upon the senses with all the power of a butcher's maul.

Alex was a private in the Temporal Corps. This was his first hitch to be served in Minus Time. France's army, the most efficient and progressive fighting force in all of Europe at the Revolution's start, was in a sad state of decay. The purchase of commissions had been abolished and most of the officers, members of the now-despised aristocratic class, had fled the country. The Assembly was anxious to rebuild the army, since war seemed imminent, and a nationwide call for volunteers went out, which call would soon be replaced by an order for the conscription of all single men between the ages of 18 and 40. This order was to provide, in a few short years, a mighty army for Napoleon. Alex was a double volunteer. He had volunteered for enlistment in the 27th century and, after training and implant education, he had been clocked out to the late 1700s, to volunteer again for service in the Revolutionary Army. It had been determined by the Referee Corps that this would be the most effective way to infiltrate soldiers of the Temporal Corps into the French Army, for service in the War of the First Coalition.

Alex didn't know why he was going to be fighting, why he was about to be placed into the front ranks of the war against Austria and Prussia. Soldiers were never told such things. He knew only that two major powers in the 27th century had submitted yet another grievance to the extranational Referee Corps for arbitration and that temporal units from both sides had been clocked out to the past to fight a "war on paper" on a battleground of history. To those who determined the outcome, it would be a "war on paper." To the Referees, Alex would be just another factor in the point spread. For Alex, it would be a very real war; a war in which the odds of his survival would be very, very low. It was something he had considered when he had enlisted, but at the time he had dismissed the possibility of his being killed as quite unlikely. After all, he was a modern man, demonstrably superior to these primitives. He had thought that it would be a grand adventure. Now he found that he no longer felt that way.

Paris was not the romantic place he had imagined it to be. He had seen the violence in the streets; he had watched aristocrats being wheeled to the guillotine in parades of tumbrels as the *citoyens* and *citoyennes* ran alongside the carts, jeering at the condemned and pelting them with refuse. He had seen the blade descend over and over and he had watched the old knitting women, the *tricotteuses*, trying to clamber up onto the platform to get locks of hair from the decapitated heads as souvenirs. He had seen the children jump up and down and clap their hands with glee as the wicker baskets reaped their grisly harvest. He had seen too much.

Feeling numb, he turned away and began to push through the mob, receiving not a few shoves in return as people angrily repulsed him for blocking their view of the proceedings. Alex heard the dull sound of the blade severing the woman's head and cringed, redoubling his efforts to fight his way free of the crowd. He fought his way clear, stumbling away from the

Place de la Révolution to wander aimlessly through the city streets in a state of shock. War was something he could handle. This callous, systematic killing, on the other hand, this chopping off of heads methodically, like the slicing of so many stalks of celery, was more than he could take. It brought back an image from his survival training, a graphic image of his drill instructor showing the boots how to kill a chicken by biting down upon its neck and giving a slight twist, the head coming off the chicken and still being held in the drill instructor's teeth as he tossed the wildly flapping, thrashing body of the bird into their midst, spattering them with blood and causing several of the boots to faint. As he swayed through the streets of Paris like a drunkard, Corderro imagined the executioner biting off the heads of the aristocrats and dumping their bodies off the platform and into the crowd until the streets were choked with headless corpses lurching wildly about, knocking into walls and splashing citizens with blood.

He lost track of time. It was growing late and only the increasing flow of people past him told him that the gory festivities had ended for the day and that the mass exodus from the square had begun. The entertainment was not yet finished for the day however. There was still more sport ahead, perhaps not as dramatic, but equally significant for the participants. He was caught up in the current of the crowd and carried to the West Barricade, like a paper ship floating in a river. There, the portly Sergeant Bibot of the Revolutionary Army conducted the evening's entertainment.

Each afternoon and evening, just before the gates closed for the night, a parade of market carts lined up to leave the city, bound for farms in the outlying districts. Each afternoon and evening, desperate aristocrats who had fled their homes to go into hiding in some corner of the city tried to steal out of Paris in order to escape the wrath of the Republic. Seeking to evade the clutches of the Committee of Public Safety and the bloodthirsty public prosecutor, Citoyen Fouquier-Tinville, they tried to sneak out past alert soldiers such as Sergeant Bibot and flee the country to find safe haven in England, Austria, or Prussia. Their pathetic ruses seldom worked. Though they tried to disguise themselves as beggars, merchants, farmers, men dressing up as women and women dressing up as men, their lack of experience in such subterfuges invariably resulted in their apprehension. They were arrested and marched off to confinement, to await their appearance before the public prosecutor, which without exception was followed by a humiliating ride through the streets of Paris in the two-wheeled tumbrels and a short walk up a flight of wooden steps into the waiting arms of Madame la Guillotine. To the once-proud aristocrats who tried to sneak out through the city gates, it was a final, desperate gamble. To the citizens of the Republic who thronged to the barricades to watch their efforts, it was a delightful game.

Sergeant Bibot was a favorite of the crowd. He had a macabre sense of theatre, which he applied with great panache to his duties at the city gate. Keenly observant and well familiar with the faces of many aristocrats, Bibot was proud of the fact that he had personally sent over fifty Royalists to the guillotine. He basked in the attention of the onlookers, playing to his audience as he conducted his inspections prior to passing people through the gate. He was a showman with a sadistic sense of humor. If he spotted a disguised aristo, he would draw the process out, teasing his victim, allowing him to think that he would be passed through before dashing all his hopes in a flamboyant unmasking. The crowd loved every bit of it. Sometimes, if he was in an especially playful mood, Sergeant Bibot would actually pass an aristo through the gate, giving him a short head start before sending some of his men to catch him and bring him back, dragged kicking and screaming through the city gate and to his doom. On such occasions, the crowd would always cheer him and he could climb up on his ever-present empty cask of wine, remove his hat, and take a bow.

Each night, after the gates were closed, Sergeant Bibot would remain to smoke his clay pipe and drink the wine that his admirers brought him as he regaled them with anecdotes concerning his illustrious career. He was particularly fond of telling them the story of the day that Citizen Danton had personally come to watch him discharge his duties. He had unmasked six *ci-devant* aristocrats that day and the Minister of Justice had personally commended him for the zeal with which he served the people.

Corderro found himself propelled along by the crowd until he was standing by the West Barricade, where a sizeable throng had already gathered to watch Sergeant Bibot put on his show. A large and heavy man with a florid face and bris-

tling moustaches, Bibot was squeezed into his ill-fitting uni-
form like ten pounds of flour packed into a five-pound sack.
A long line of carts and pedestrians was already cued up, held
back by Bibot's men until such time as the audience was built
up to a suitable size. There was a great feeling of camaraderie
and anticipation in the air as Sergeant Bibot strutted to his
post, taking time to pause so that he could exchange pleas-
antries with some of his regular observers, be slapped upon the
back and, he hoped, admired by the young women in the
crowd, whom he greeted with exaggerated winks and blown
kisses. Corderro thought that he was going to be sick. He felt
all wound up inside and his skin was clammy. He looked down
at his hands and saw that they were shaking.

Sergeant Bibot began to have the people brought up, one at
a time, so that he could examine them and pass them through.
The people in the crowd called out encouragement and suggestions.

"There, that one! That beard looks false! Give it a good,
hard yank, Sergeant Bibot!"

"Why don't you come here and yank it, you miserable son
of a Royalist bootlicker!" shouted the owner of the beard, a
burly farmer.

"I'll do more than yank your phony beard, you bastard!"
yelled the first man as he ran forward and tried to climb up on
the cart, only to be pulled away at the last minute by Bibot's
soldiers.

"Peace, Citizen!" cried Sergeant Bibot, melodramatically
holding up his hand. "All will be settled momentarily!" Turning to the farmer, Sergeant Bibot smiled pleasantly, wished
him a good day and asked him to excuse the zeal of the good
citizen who was only anxious that *ci-devant* aristocrats be
brought to justice. "Purely as a matter of form," said Sergeant Bibot, "would you consent to showing me your hands?"

The farmer grunted and held out his hands, turning them
from palms down to palms up.

"*Merci*," said Sergeant Bibot. "These are the roughened,
calloused hands of a working man," he said to the crowd.
"No aristo would have hands such as these. And the beard appears to be quite genuine," he added for good measure. "A
fine, luxuriant growth it is, to boot!"

He clapped the grinning farmer on the back and passed him
through as the crowd applauded. The process continued as

Bibot intently examined everyone who sought egress through
the gate, making a show of it and striving to entertain those he
examined as well as the people in the crowd.

A large and heavy wagon filled with wine casks came up
next and Bibot made a great show of opening each cask and
checking to see if anyone was concealed inside. His examina-
tion revealed no concealed aristocrats and Bibot passed the
wagon through. Several others he allowed to pass with only
the most cursory inspection, as the drivers were known to him,
having regularly passed through his gate twice a day on their
way to and from the city. An undercurrent of hostility swept
through the crowd as an elegant coach drew up and stopped at
Sergeant Bibot's post.

Surely, no aristocrat would be so great a fool as to attempt
leaving Paris so conspicuously. Several of the people in the
crowd, close enough to see inside the coach, recognized one of
its occupants and word soon spread throughout the mob that
this was no person worthy of derision, but the very beautiful
and famous Marguerite St. Just, that celebrated actress of the
Comédie Française, whose brother, Armand St. Just, was a
leading figure of the Revolution and a member of the Committee of Public Safety.

Citoyenne St. Just had recently caused a bit of a scandal
when she married that wealthy English baronet, Sir Percy
Blakeney, thus becoming Lady Blakeney, but no one could
accuse her of being an aristocrat, much less a Royalist. The
popular actress was well known as an ardent Republican and a
believer in equality of birth. "Inequality of fortune," she was
fond of saying, "is merely an untoward accident. The only inequality I recognize and will admit to is inequality of talent."
As a result of this belief, her charming salon in the Rue
Richelieu had been reserved for originality and intellect, for
wit and brilliance. She had entertained members of the
theatrical profession, well-known writers and famous
philosophes, and the occasional foreign dignitary, which was
how she had met Sir Percy Blakeney.

It came as quite a shock to those within her circle when she
married Blakeney. They all thought that he was quite beneath
her, intellectually speaking. A prominent figure in fashionable
European society, he was the son of the late Sir Algernon
Blakeney, whose wife had succumbed to imbecility. The elder
Blakeney took his stricken wife abroad and there his son was

raised and educated. When Algernon Blakeney died, shortly
following the death of his wife, Percy inherited a considerable
fortune, which allowed him to travel abroad extensively before returning to his native England. He had cultivated his
tastes for fashion and the finer, more expensive things in life.
A pleasant fellow with a sophomoric sense of humor, Blakeney was a fashion plate and a bon vivant, but he made no pre-
tense to being an intellectual. It would have been ludicrous,
since he was hopelessly dull and generally thought to be a fool.
He was totally enraptured with his wife and seemed perfectly
content with remaining in the background and basking in her
glow. Marguerite's friends were all at a loss to understand why
she had married him, unless his slavish devotion pleased her.
However, though Marguerite St. Just might have been found
wanting in her abilities to select a fitting husband, she could
not be faulted for her politics. While the sight of Blakeney at
the window of the coach provoked some unfavorable com-
ments and some jeers, the appearance of his wife beside him
was greeted with a scattering of applause.

"I say there," Blakeney said in perfect, if accented, French,
"what seems to be the difficulty, Sergeant? Why this tedious
delay?"

Bibot appraised him with obvious distaste. The man was
both rich and English, which were two counts against him
from the start, but when he saw the well-known actress, his
manner changed and he removed his hat and gave a little bow.

"Your pardon, Citoyenne," said Bibot, totally ignoring
Blakeney, "but everyone must be passed through one at a
time, so that I may prevent the escape of any aristocratic
enemies of the Republic."

"Aristocratic enemies?" said Blakeney. "Good Lord! Does
this mean that we are to be detained?"

Bibot glanced at Blakeney the way a fastidious cook might
look upon a cockroach discovered in her kitchen. "Your wife,
monsieur, is a well-known friend of the Republic and you,
though an aristocrat, are obviously English, which assures
your safety, at least for the time being."

"Oh, well, thank the Lord for that," said Blakeney, flutter-
ing a lace handkerchief before his nose. "Then we shall be
allowed to pass?"

"I see no reason why you should not be—"

At that moment, a captain came galloping up to Sergeant

Bibot, scattering all those in his way. His slightly skittish horse caused Bibot to back off some steps to stand before the Blakeneys' coach.

"Has a cart gone through?" the captain demanded.

"I have passed through several carts," Bibot began.

"A cart . . . a wagon . . . loaded with wine casks. . . ."

Bibot frowned. "Yes, there was one, driven by an old wine merchant and his son. But I examined each and every cask and—"

"You fool!" cried the captain. "You checked the empty wine casks, but did you examine the wagon itself?"

"Why, no . . . " said Bibot, nervously.

"Idiot! That wagon concealed the Duc de Chalis and his children! They've managed to escape, thanks to you!"

"I say there, Sergeant," Sir Percy said, stepping down from the coach, "are we to be allowed to pass or—"

"How long ago did they go through?" the captain said.

"Why, only a short while—" said Bibot.

"Then there may yet be time to stop them! If they escape, Sergeant, you shall pay for this with your head! You had best pray that I can catch them!"

No, thought Corderro, not children! They can't guillotine innocent children! Forgetting his strict orders not to interfere, Corderro leaped out in front of the horse just as the captain set spurs to the animal's flanks. Eyes rolling, the horse reared and threw the captain, who knocked Blakeney to the ground as he fell. Corderro smashed a hard right into Sergeant Bibot's face and at the same time wrenched the sergeant's pistol from his waistband. He spun around, but the fallen captain had managed to get his own pistol out. Still, Corderro was quicker and he fired first, sending a ball into the captain's chest. The captain fired as well, but instead of shooting Corderro, the ball went through the coach and struck Lady Blakeney.

The shots frightened the horses and they bolted. Corderro leaped up on the sideboard of the coach and the runaway horses hurtled through the city gate. Bibot's men raised their muskets and fired at the coach, hitting Corderro several times. He managed to get the door of the coach open and threw himself inside, where he collapsed onto the floor of the coach and lost consciousness.

The crowd at the gate had panicked at the shots and they scattered, fleeing in all directions. The army captain lay dead in the middle of the street with a bullet through his heart. Clutching at his chest and coughing, Blakeney stumbled weakly through the gate in a vain attempt to follow his coach. He managed about one hundred yards before he sank down to his knees at the side of the road, retching blood. The hooves of the captain's rearing horse had crushed his chest and with every step, his splintered ribs hastened the inevitable. Blakeney spoke his wife's name and collapsed into a ditch. His eyes glazed over. The Scarlet Pimpernel was dead.

1

Biologically, Andre Cross was in her mid-twenties. If her age were to be reckoned chronologically, however, she would be well over fourteen hundred years old. She would grow older still, now that she had been given antiagathic drug treatments. Given all of this, it was difficult for her to accept the fact that by the standards of the 27th century, she was still little more than an adolescent.

If asked, she gave her biological age, which was twenty-six. To do otherwise meant getting into complicated explanations. It would mean revealing that she had been born in the 12th century to a couple of Basque farmers who had died when she was still a child. It would have meant explaining that she and her little brother, Marcel, had gone out alone into the world to become itinerant thieves, surviving as best they could, which meant that they were almost always starving. She would have had to explain that she had learned to pass as a young boy because, as vulnerable as young boys on their own could be, young girls were even more so. If all that did not already strain credulity, there was the matter of their having been befriended by an aging, addle-brained knight errant who had taken them both on as squires so that he would not be alone and so that they could care for him. In return, he had trained them in the arts of knighthood (for he had never suspected that Andre was a female). While Marcel was a bit too delicate of frame and disposition to be very good in the skills of chivalry, Andre had excelled at them. She was possessed of an indefatigable drive and under the doting guidance of the senile knight, she had transformed her young and coltish body into a well-coordinated, broad-shouldered, muscular physique. Nature had not endowed her with a voluptuous figure. She was slim-hipped and small-breasted. A life of hardship and physical toil had given her the sort of shape that was not traditionally associated with feminine beauty. She was wiry and unnaturally strong, which had made it easier for her to carry on her male masquerade into an age when most awkward girls began to develop into graceful women. When the old knight died, she took his armor and, swathing her small breasts in cloth, she assumed the role of a young "free companion," a mercenary knight. She took the invented name of Andre de la Croix and eventually found service with Prince John of Anjou at a time when he plotted to seize his brother Richard's throne.

She found herself involved with time travelers from the far future, although she had not known it then, nor would she have understood it if she had. She knew nothing of time travel and she was ignorant of the Time Wars, a highly dangerous method of settling conflicts in the future by sending soldiers back through time to do battle within the confines of armed struggles of the past. Her first knowledge of such things came from a deserter from the Temporal Corps named Hunter, a man with a stolen chronoplate who helped her to avenge her brother's murder and then took her ahead through time to the Paris of the 17th century. There, ironically, she once again became involved with the machinations of people from the 27th century, this time taking a more active part in their activities on what they called "the Minus Side." If not for her, two soldiers named Lucas Priest and Finn Delaney might have died. They repaid her by granting her request and taking her with them to the time from which they came.

Even explaining that much to people would have meant omitting many details and inviting further questions, so Andre Cross (for that was her name now and, indeed, she could no longer recall the name she had been born with) did not bother with any explanations. A small handful of people knew her true history. As far as everyone else was concerned, she was just an ordinary young woman of the 27th century who had enlisted in the Temporal Corps and been assigned to Lt. Col. Forrester's elite First Division, better known as the Time Commandos.

When she had first arrived at Pendleton Base, at the Temporal Departure Station, she had been completely overwhelmed with future shock. She had understood literally nothing of what she had seen and had been badly frightened, in spite of warnings from Priest and Delaney to expect a world of seemingly inexplicable miracles. Now that she was returning to Temporal Army Command Headquarters, she still possessed an unbridled fascination with the new world in which she found herself, but it was no longer an awesome mystery to her.

Since her arrival in the 27th century, she had been in the hands of specialists, being prepared for her new life at the Temporal Army Medical Complex in Colorado Springs. Firstly, and most importantly, it had been necessary to determine whether or not her temporal transplantation would have an adverse effect upon the course of history. The first part of this question had been settled when it was discovered that, due to an injury sustained in combat at some time in her past, she would be unable to bear children. The second part took a little longer, but exhaustive research and the correlation of findings made by members of the Observer Corps on the Minus Side satisfied the investigators that Andre's removal from her natural time would not constitute a threat to temporal continuity. That opened her way to a new life as a soldier in the Temporal Corps. However, it had been only the first step.

It had been necessary for her to receive immunization treatments, followed by the carefully administered program of anti-agathic drug therapy that would extend her lifespan far beyond what she had believed to be possible. That was followed by a long series of tests designed to establish a psychological profile for her, after which she underwent surgery to receive the cybernetic implants that would enable her to function as a temporal soldier and allow her to be implant-educated to compensate for the knowledge she lacked as a result of her primitive origins. They had viewed her as a blank slate and the programming had progressed in slow and carefully controlled stages, during which she was assiduously monitored to make certain that at no point was there any danger of sensory or cerebral overload.

After the long process had been completed, she had emerged as a full-fledged citizen of the 27th century, computer-programmed to take her place in the modern world and trained to assume her new role as a private in the First Division. She had the lowest rank of any soldier in that vaunted cadre, but she had already participated in one of the most important missions in the history of the unit. While she had still been back in 17th-century Paris, she had worked with Finn Delaney and Lucas Priest, as well as agents of the TIA, to help foil a terrorist plot against the Referee Corps. As a result of her performance, Forrester had personally invited her to join his unit and to be trained to work alongside Priest and Delaney.

As she rode the lift tube up to First Division Headquarters in the Temporal Army Corps HQ building at Pendleton Base, she was looking forward to seeing Priest and Delaney once again. When she had completed her training and preparations at the Colorado Springs facility, she had contacted the First Division administrative offices, requesting that Priest and Delaney get in touch with her as soon as they were able. Shortly thereafter, as soon as they had clocked in from an assignment, she received a message from them.

"Private Cross is herewith ordered to report to the First Division lounge, TAC-HQ building, on 1 January 2614 at 2100 hours. Congratulations are in order. Major Lucas Priest and Staff Sergeant Finn Delaney, First Division, TAC."

She smiled when she saw them waiting for her at a table by the huge window that comprised the outer wall of the First Division lounge. It was at the very same table that she sat with them when she first met Colonel Forrester and had her first taste of a drink called Scotch. It had helped to numb her senses somewhat as she gazed out that window and saw the shuttles floating by like great steel birds while, far below, soldiers massed down in the atrium, looking like insects from the great height at which she gazed at them.

Priest and Delaney saw her coming and they rose to their feet to greet her. Andre saw that there was a sort of center-piece upon the table consisting of a medieval broadsword crossed with a 17th-century rapier. Above the juncture of the two swords, in a little velvet-lined box, was a golden division insignia, a stylized number one bisecting a horizontal figure eight, the symbol of infinity.

She marched up to the table, snapped to attention, and gave them both a sharp salute. Lucas grinned, picked up the insignia, and pinned it to the collar of her green transit fatigues. Both men then stood to attention, returned her salute, and then each of them gave her a most unmilitary kiss.

Though the kisses were affectionate in nature, rather than passionate, she was nevertheless taken by surprise.

"What's wrong?" said Lucas, seeing her expression.

"Nothing," she said, smiling, "except that's the first time either of you have ever kissed me. In fact, that was the first time I've been kissed since I was just a child."

"Well, don't let it go to your head," said Finn, "both of us can do much better. How are you, Andre?"

"Well, thank you, though I still have a great deal to get used to. It hasn't yet ceased to feel strange to come across things that I have absolutely no experience of and suddenly discover that I know all about them."

"It probably never will cease to feel strange," said Lucas. "It's something all of us experience at one time or another. Believe it or not, you'll grow accustomed to it. It's what soldiers call 'subknowledge.' You'll learn to live with it. In fact, you wouldn't survive for very long without it. None of us would."

"You've come through with flying colors," Finn said. "I spoke to that officer who was in charge of your case—"

"Colonel Hendersen," she said.

"Yes, that's the one. He said he was damned sorry to have to let you go. You're the most radical case of temporal relocation in the history of the corps. He said that we've had people relocated further back in time before, on the Minus Side, but evidently no one's ever been displaced and permanently assigned to Plus Time. He was bending over backwards trying to get you reassigned to his unit."

"He wasn't the only one," said Andre. "The recruiters wanted to get their hands on me, as well. Evidently, as an example of the type of woman that soldiers could expect to meet on the Minus side, I'd be a good inducement for enlistment." She laughed. "Never mind that it would be misleading, I found the whole thing extremely funny. Women are certainly treated far better in this time than in the one I came from, but I suppose that some things will never change. The recruiting officer practically turned himself inside out trying to get me to sign some papers and he was quite upset when I told him that anything I did would have to be cleared through Col. Forrester first. By the way, where is the old man? I was hoping he'd be here.''

Lucas grinned. ''Just make sure you never call him 'the old man' to his face! He wanted to be here, but he couldn't make it. Something came up and he was called upstairs, which means that either Delaney's up on charges again or there's a good chance we're going out soon.''

''Does that mean that I will be included?'' Andre said.

Finn flicked her collar up with a finger, the side with the division insignia on it. ''That makes it official,'' he said. ''Meanwhile, there's still a part of your education that's been sadly neglected.''

Andre frowned. ''But I was assured that my programming was quite complete,'' she said.

''All except for one thing,'' said Finn, ''and that's something implant education can't take care of. Now that you're a soldier, you're going to have to learn to drink like one.''

''Are you implying that I'm deficient in that department?'' she said with a smile.

''Well, let's say that you have yet to prove that you are not,'' said Finn, chuckling.

''That sounds like a challenge.''

Finn grinned. ''Name your poison,'' he said.

Andre looked at him with amusement. She knew that Delaney was a prodigious drinker, but she also recalled that there was one drink in particular, preferred by Col. Forrester, that Delaney truly loathed. She hadn't tried it, but she recalled Delaney saying that it took a deathwish and a cast-iron stomach to be able to stand it.

''Red Eye,'' she said.

Delaney looked aghast. ''Oh, no!''

Lucas burst out laughing. ''Ten chits says she drinks you under the table,'' he said.

''Okay, you're on,'' Delaney said. ''Only let's make it more interesting. If you want to collect, you're going to have to match us drink for drink.''

''I think that I can make it still more interesting,'' said Andre. ''It's been years since I've had a man and the last one left a great deal to be desired. We'll all go drink for drink and if one of you wins, I'll take him to bed.''

The two men raised their eyebrows and exchanged glances. "But suppose *you* win?" said Lucas. "Unlikely a possibility though that may be," he added.

Andre smiled. "Then the two of you will pool your resources and purchase me the services of a Class 1 male courtesan."

"A Class 1. . . . Where in hell did you learn about *that*?" Delaney said. "They're putting that kind of stuff in the programming?"

"My therapist at Colorado Springs seemed to think that I'd been sexually deprived," said Andre. "She suggested that as a solution. The idea of a male whore intrigued me greatly and I told her that I would consider it. She said to ask for a Class 1, since they possessed the greatest level of skills."

"Do you have any idea how much something like that would *cost*?" said Finn. "It takes *years* to achieve a Class 1 rating."

"Well, you did say that you wanted to make the wager interesting," she said.

"Of course, you realize that by bringing a Class 1 licensed courtesan into the wager, you're placing a not inconsiderable value on yourself?" said Lucas, with a hint of amusement.

She replied with a straight face. "I always have," she said.

Lucas chuckled. "Very well, I'm game. What about you, Finn?"

"I'm still trying to decide if I can afford it," said Delaney. "A major makes a great deal more than a noncom."

"So who asked you to get busted so many goddamn times?" said Lucas. "I'll tell you what: if Andre wins, I'll advance you whatever you're short, at the usual rate of interest. How about it?"

"This could get very expensive," said Delaney.

"Of course, if you think you'll lose . . . " said Andre.

"All right, I accept," said Finn. "But on one condition. I name the time and place. When I collect, I want both of us to be cold sober."

Finn and Lucas staggered into the briefing room, both of them terribly hung over. Delaney's eyes looked like a map of the city's transit system. Priest was afraid that he had destroyed his stomach lining. They found Andre already in the briefing room, drinking black coffee and looking remarkably invigorated and refreshed. She glanced up at them and smiled sweetly.

"Well?" she said. "Have I learned to drink like a soldier or do I still require practice?"

"That's the last time I ever make a bet with you," said Finn, slowly lowering himself into a chair and signaling the orderly for a cup of coffee. Lucas sank into a chair on her other side.

"I still can't believe she was sober enough to collect last night," he said. He looked at Andre and shook his head, sadly. "Considering how much it must have cost, I hope you were at least clearheaded enough to *remember* the experience!"

"Oh, it was quite memorable," she said, lightly. "It was fortunate for me that there was a female officer in the lounge last night who could assist me in making the selection. I explained our wager to her and she was delighted to help out. She examined your credit discs and programmed the credit transfer, then guided me in making a wise choice. I must say, I found it all absolutely fascinating. However, I had no idea that these courtesans were paid by the hour. It must be an extremely lucrative profession."

Finn shut his eyes. "How long did you keep him?"

"Oh, all night, of course."

Delaney put his head into his hands and moaned.

"Ten-*tion!*" called out the orderly as Col. Forrester entered the briefing room. Andre leapt to her feet and snapped to a smart attention. Lucas took considerably longer to rise and Delaney didn't even bother, remaining slumped over in his chair with his head in his hands.

The massively built Forrester removed his cap from his bald head and looked them over, his craggy, wrinkled features contorting into a grimace of wry distaste.

"As you were," he said, dryly. Andre and Lucas sat back down. "Corporal Fleming," said Forrester.

"Yes, sir, I know," said the orderly. He already had the hypogun prepared. Delaney winced as the corporal pressed the gun against his neck and injected the adrenergen soldiers had nicknamed "nitro" directly into his carotid artery.

"*Christ!*" Finn shouted as the "nitro" hammered into his brain. He jerked violently in his chair. His eyes rolled and he shivered as if with St. Vitus's Dance.

The orderly approached Lucas with the hypogun, but Forrester stopped him, saying, "That's all right, Corporal Fleming. As long as he can stand up on his own, he's sober enough for me. Just bring the major some more coffee."

"Yes, sir." The corporal looked disappointed.

"Delaney?" Forrester said.

"Sir!"

"I swear, I think you're starting to like that stuff. Do you think we can proceed now?"

"Fuck, yes!"

"A simple 'yes, sir' would have been sufficient."

"Yes, sir!"

"Sit down and shut up, Delaney. And try not to shake like a monkey on a stick. It's most distracting."

Delaney sat back down, holding the arms of his chair with a deathgrip. He tried to control the flow of energy, but he still continued to vibrate like an epileptic.

Forrester glanced at Andre and smiled. "Glad you've joined us, Private Cross. Congratulations."

"Thank you, sir."

"Think you're ready for a mission?"

"Yes, sir."

"Good, I'm glad to hear it. This one should provide a decent shakedown for you. I shouldn't think you'd have much trouble, after the Timekeeper affair. This one should be quite simple compared to that."

"I'll do my very best, sir."

Forrester nodded. "Priest, you all right?"

"Just a bit hung over, sir."

"That must have been some celebration last night," said Forrester. "I'm sorry I missed it."

"We'll give you a rain check on another one as soon as we get back, sir," Lucas said. "I'd sort of like to see you and Private Cross hoist a few together. She drinks Red Eye as if it were iced tea."

"Really? Well, it's nice to know that there's at least one person in this unit who can hold her liquor. How much did you lose?"

"I'd rather not say, sir."

"That bad?" Forrester chuckled. "You and I will have to sit down to some serious elbow-bending, Cross. I don't think that these two amateurs are in our class."

"Anytime, sir," said Andre. "It will be my pleasure."

"Good, it's a date. Now let's get down to business, shall we?" Forrester went up to the podium console and leaned against it. "You people will be happy to know that you'll be fairly autonomous on this mission," he said, "meaning that you won't have the Temporal Intelligence Agency to contend with."

"Goddamn spooks," Delaney said, his shaking beginning to subside a little.

"Keep your opinions to yourself, Delaney," Forrester said. "In any case, you might be interested to know that after that last mission, the Referee Corps has seen fit to grant the army eminent domain regarding temporal adjustment missions, which means that the TIA is back to its intelligence-gathering role under the aegis of the Observer Corps. That didn't sit very well with Darrow, so he resigned and there's a new agency director now, brought in from the Observer Corps. I hope this will end the rivalry between our two branches of the service. I also checked on agent Mongoose, in case you should be curious how things turned out with him. He was critical for a while, but he's recovered nicely and his features have been reconstructed. He's also been demoted from field operations director to intelligence evaluation and it's my guess that it will be a long time before he's trusted with another field assignment. Considering how badly he botched that mission, it's nothing but a slap on the wrist, if you ask me, but that's none of my concern. By the way, Delaney, I am given to understand that the two of you had some differences of opinion that you had intended to resolve privately, between yourselves. Needless to say, I don't want to hear about any breach of regulations, but I would not be displeased to learn that agent Mongoose had been temporarily removed from the TIA active-duty roster for the purposes of further medical attention. In this regard, I trust that any 'discussions' between the two of you will be handled with discretion."

"I'll see to it, sir," Delaney said. He was only twitching now.

"You can see to it on your own time," said Forrester. "Right now, there's more pressing business requiring our attention. We have an adjustment on our hands and you'll be clocking out immediately following this briefing." He pressed a button on the console, activating the computer. "Forrester, code 321-G, clearance blue," he said.

"Clearance confirmed," said the computer. "How may I assist you, Colonel?"

"Request general background information on the French Revolution, circa 1789 to 1799," said Forrester.

"Working," said the computer. "Do you require visuals?"

"I'll specify visuals if need be," Forrester said. "Proceed when ready."

"French Revolution, immediate causes," said the computer. "Rapid growth of French industry and commerce in the late 1700s leading to growth of the middle class; inequitable taxation in many cases exempting aristocrats and members of the clergy; weakening of the old regime by the Treaty of Paris in 1763, which gave French possessions in India and North America to the British; consequent loss of revenues to the government; further depletion of the treasury due to expenditures incurred in giving aid to the Americans in their revolt against the British; bankruptcy of the king's treasury in 1787; refusal of King Louis XVI to institute needed social reforms; growth of the *philosophe* movement leading to—"

"That's enough," said Forrester. "Proceed."

"May 5, 1789," said the computer. "King Louis XVI summoned a meeting of the Estates-General at Versailles in order to raise money for the treasury. Representation consisted of 300 aristocrats; 300 clergy; and 600 commons, *tiers état*, or third estate. Immediate debate concerning voting powers led to the members of the third estate assuming the title of the National Assembly, June 17, 1789. June 20, meetings were suspended and members of the Assembly took the Tennis Court Oath, so named after their place of informal meeting, resolving to draft a constitution. The Assembly was joined by members of the clergy and aristocratic classes. The Comte de Mirabeau rose to prominence as principal orator of the third estate. Dismissal of chief minister Jacques Necker by Louis XVI on July 11 and threatened dismissal of the Assembly precipitated the storming of the Bastille by a mob on July 14, the murder of Governor Launay, and the freeing of political prisoners. Neckar was recalled, the Marquis de Lafayette was appointed commander of new National Guard, adoption of the tricolor and the beginning of emigration by members of the aristocratic class followed. Mass uprisings took place throughout France. On August 4, 1789, aristocratic representatives surrendered all feudal rights and privileges, titles were abolished, sales of offices prohibited, guilds were dissolved. August 27, 1789, the Assembly accepted the Declaration of the Rights of Man, drawn from English and American precedents and theories of the *philosophes*. October 5, 1789, an outbreak of mob violence in Paris culminated in a mob consisting primarily of women invading the royal palace at Versailles. The royal family was rescued by the Marquis de Lafayette. The National Assembly adopted a constitution creating a monarchy answerable to a one-house Legislature. The property of the church and of emigrated nobles was seized by the government to provide public funds. The state assumed the support of the clergy. July 1790 saw the abolition of old provinces and governments; France was divided into 83 departments, subdivided into 374 districts and cantons, each with a local assembly. Voting or active citizens paid taxes equivalent to three days' labor wages; nonvoting or passive citizens paid no taxes or a sum less than the three days' minimum. The old judicial constitution was abolished. Civil organization of the clergy, with priests and bishops chosen by popular vote, accompanied the growth of the political power of the Jacobin Club under the leadership of Robespierre, and of the Cordeliers under the leadership of Georges Jacques Danton and Jean Paul Marat. King Louis XVI attempted to flee France with his family on June 20, 1791, was captured at Varennes, and was brought back to Paris. Dissolution of the National Assembly by vote of the membership occurred on September 30, 1791 and election of the Legislative Assembly took place on October 1, 1791, with 745 members elected by active citizens and divided into a Right faction, consisting of constitutionalists and Royalists, and a Left faction, consisting of Girondists, Jacobins and Cordeliers. August 27, 1791, the Declaration of Pillnitz by Frederick William II of Prussia and Leopold II of Austria resulted in the alliance of Austria and Prussia against France in February of 1792 and the War of the First Coalition.''

"Stop," said Forrester. "All right, those are the highlights, you'll get the rest during mission programming. The key point here concerns the fact that the Referee Corps had assigned an arbitration action to take place during the War of the First

Coalition. There was a call for voluntary enlistment in France and soldiers of the Temporal Corps were clocked back to various locales in key municipalities to be infiltrated as volunteers for the French Army of the Republic. Continue, computer."

"August 10, 1792," said the computer, "rioting mobs broke into the Tuileries, killed the Swiss Guards, and forced the king to turn to the Legislative Assembly for protection. The Assembly imprisoned the king and took away all of his remaining powers. There were mass arrests under the provisional government headed by Georges Jacques Danton. September 2 to September 7, 1792, the September Massacres—"

"Stop," said Forrester. "Now by this time, there was total panic among the aristocrats remaining in France. Computer, general overview concerning aristocratic emigration circa 1792."

"Emigration of *ci-devant* aristocrats was forcibly prevented by the provisional government," said the computer. "The Committee of Public Safety, under the leadership of public prosecutor Fouquier-Tinville, appointed to preside over France's internal security, was charged with power to arrest and execute enemies of the Republic. Mass attempts by members of the aristocracy to escape France, some aided by foreign nationals—"

"Stop," said Forrester. "General background on the Scarlet Pimpernel."

"Working," said the computer. "The scarlet pimpernel: a common pimpernel (*Anagallis arvensis*), having scarlet, white or purplish flowers that close at the approach of rainy or cloudy weather—also called *poor man's weatherglass, red pimpernel*. In conjunction with the French Revolution, the insignia and alias of the League of the Scarlet Pimpernel, a group of British adventurers involved in the smuggling of French aristocrats to England, specifically, the alias of the leader of the group, Sir Percy Blakeney—"

"Visual, please," said Forrester.

A second later, a holographic image of Sir Percy Blakeney appeared before the podium. The projection was that of a tall, broad-shouldered, athletic-looking man with fair hair, blue eyes, and a strong jaw. He looked handsome, but he had a look of vague boredom on his face, giving it a slightly sleepy, insipid air. He was dressed in a short-waisted satin coat, a waistcoat with wide lapels, tight-fitting breeches, and highly polished Newmarket boots. His sleeves and collar were trimmed with fine Mechline lace and he stood in an affected posture, one leg slightly before the other, one hand on his hip, the other bent before him and holding a lace handkerchief in a loose, languid fashion.

"There's a pretty flower," said Delaney.

"There's your assignment, Delaney," Forrester said. "In several hours, that's what you're going to look like."

"Why me?" Delaney said, chagrined.

"Because Priest's too short and you're about the right build," said Forrester.

"Hell," said Delaney. "All right, let's have the rest of it."

"The adjustment stems from the temporal interference of one soldier, named Alex Corderro, assigned to the War of the First Coalition arbitration action," Forrester said. "It was his first hitch in the field and subsequent investigation shows that he never should have been accepted in the service in the first place. Too unstable, a high potential of cracking under stress. Unfortunately, the corps is so badly in need of cannon-fodder that we'll take just about anyone these days. As a result of that sterling policy, we've got an adjustment on our hands.

"Corderro violated the noninterference directives," said Forrester. "He attempted to prevent the capture of some escaping aristocrats and, in so doing, he shot a captain in the Army of the Republic. Blakeney and his wife were on the scene and what seems to have occurred, as best as the Observers can reconstruct it, is that Lady Blakeney was wounded in the exchange of gunfire and Blakeney was trampled by a horse. Corderro escaped through the West Barricade in the Blakeneys' coach, but he was shot several times. Evidently, he lost consciousness and bled to death. The Observers found the coach in a wooded area several miles outside of Paris. The horses had run themselves out and had wandered off the road, somehow managing to wedge the coach between two trees. Inside the coach, they found Corderro, dead. Lady Marguerite Blakeney was alive, but badly wounded and unconscious."

"What about Sir Percy?" said Delaney.

"He was left behind in Paris," Forrester said.

"And where is he now?"

"Well, the Observers managed to remove his body—"

"*His body!* You mean he's *dead*?"

"Chest completely crushed by a horse's hooves," said Forrester.

Delaney swallowed heavily. "Wait, now, let me get this straight, sir. You're telling me that my assignment is to be a plant? A temporal relocation?"

"That's right."

"For how long?"

"Well, that remains to be seen," said Forrester. "We have to make certain that the aristocrats who were smuggled out of France by Blakeney and his group don't wind up on the guillotine. He was also instrumental in the fall from power of a certain French official named Chauvelin, an agent of the Committee of Public Safety. Since Blakeney's operations were of a covert nature, we don't have a greal deal of information on him and his group.

"We have since obtained further data, courtesy of our friends at the TIA. At any rate, even though it may not all be cut and dried, at least you won't have anyone from our time working against you, as you did in several of your previous assignments."

"Still," said Delaney, "what you're telling me is that I may wind up taking Blakeney's place indefinitely."

"That's essentially correct," said Forrester, "at least until the TIA can determine exactly what his activities were in the years following his involvement in the Revolution. However, it should not be all unpleasant," he added. "Computer, visual on Lady Marguerite Blakeney."

The holographic projection of Sir Percy Blakeney disappeared, to be replaced by one of his wife, the former Marguerite St. Just. Delaney gulped and Priest gave a low whistle.

Forrester smiled. "I shouldn't think that life with Lady Blakeney would be very hard to take," he said. He chuckled. "Frankly, Delaney, I think you'll have your hands full."

2

Since Delaney would be the only one impersonating a figure of historical significance, there had been no need for the others to submit to cosmetic surgery. Consequently, after they had gone through mission programming and while Finn was being transformed into the image of Sir Percy Blakeney, Lucas and Andre went down to supply, drew their gear, then took the tubes down to the ground-level Departure Station.

As members of a First Division adjustment team, they had priority status, so there was no waiting for their departure codes to be called. Instead, they were shuttled directly to the nearest grid area, to be clocked out together to the 18th century. As they passed soldiers in transit dressed in period, the soldiers came to attention and saluted them. Both Lucas and Andre were also dressed in period, but Lucas' insignia of rank was clearly visible on his armband and the fact that they were in a shuttle normally reserved for officers clearly labeled them for the groups of soldiers waiting to clock out. Those who were close enough as the shuttle passed to see their silver dogtags, worn on the outside of their garments, and their divisional insignia added small, respectful nods to their salutes. From the point of military etiquette, it wasn't strictly proper to give a nod of greeting while saluting, but it had become an informally established practice among the members of the corps to single out those in the First Division in this manner. The silver dogtags stood out in marked contrast to the color-

coded ones issued to the regular troops. Members of the
Observer Corps wore gold tags and only soldiers of the First
Division wore silver. The tags meant that the wearer was about
to clock out to the Minus Side and silver tags meant an adjustment team was on the way to deal with an historical discontinuity. There wasn't a single soldier in the Temporal Corps
who did not know the meaning of those silver tags and the
nods were both a greeting and an unspoken wish of good luck.

Andre still marveled at the sight of all those soldiers dressed
in period, waiting around the sprawling plaza beside their piles
of gear. Some smoked, some drank, others chatted, a few
slept, and the green recruits were easily identifiable by their air
of nervous tension and their restlessness. They passed a group
of Roman legionnaires in breastplates, sandals, and plumed
helmets gathered around a video game machine. They took
turns pitting their skills against the game computer and they
laughed and shouted like small children, slapping each other
on the back and calling out encouragement. A platoon of
Visigoths snapped to attention as they passed, quickly palming
several tiny metal sniffers which they had been passing back
and forth. On past a group of Crusaders, with red crosses on
their chests, among whom was an obvious green recruit who,
in his nervousness, had been swinging a short mace about. At
the sight of the shuttle, the recruit snapped to attention and,
without thinking, tried to toss off a sharp salute. Unfortunately, he had tried to salute with the hand that held the mace
and the resulting "bong" as he coshed himself and fell to the
floor with a clatter of metal brought about hysterical laughter
from his companions.

The ground shuttle brought them to the gate of the departure grid, a large, permanently installed chronoplate that
differed from the portable personal units in that it could
transport whole platoons of soldiers at a time. The Barbary
pirates standing by to clock out next hurriedly made way for
them as they walked through the gate to report to the grid
transport detail. The OC came to attention and saluted. Lucas
returned his salute, then removed his armband with his rank
insignia upon it, surmounted by the divisional pin, and
handed it to the OC along with his silver dogtags. Andre did
the same.

The Officer in Charge separated the dogtags, taking one
each off the chains and then placing the single tags with the

chains along with their armbands and insignia in separate plastic boxes. With a "By your leave, sir," he then proceeded to search Lucas quickly and efficiently, as per regulations, to make certain that no unauthorized effects would be clocked out along with him, either intentionally or unintentionally. Another member of the detail observed the same procedure with Andre. The man who searched Andre came up with her credit disc, to her embarrassment. She had forgotten all about it.

"Sorry, sir," she said to the sergeant. "I must have transferred it to my pocket without thinking when I changed."

"Don't worry about it, soldier. Happens all the time." He placed the computer disc into the same plastic box containing her armband and dogtag.

The OC then took the two tags that he had separated from the neck chains, each containing their respective codes, and inserted them one at a time into a tiny slot in the grid control bank. He waited for a moment, watching the readout screen, then nodded.

"Stand by, sir," he said to Lucas.

A couple of seconds passed and the borders of the grid began to glow softly.

"Staged," said the OC. "Good luck, sir."

"Thank you, Lieutenant," Lucas said. "All right, Andre, let's go."

They walked forward into the field generated by the grid and disappeared from view.

Delaney stepped out of limbo and onto soft, damp grass. An old veteran of time travel, the chronoplates did not affect him as profoundly as they did most soldiers, who usually vomited upon arrival and suffered from temporary bouts of vertigo and myoclonus, as well as double vision and ataxia. He did, however, feel slightly disoriented and off balance. He staggered momentarily, taking several uncoordinated steps and swaying in a drunken fashion until he was able to shake off the effects and become orientated to his new surroundings.

He saw that he was in a small clearing in a forest, more properly, a wood, since he knew that he was not far outside of Paris and he could see the road leading to the city through a clump of trees. The Pathfinders had cut it fairly close with the coordinates. Still, Finn had clocked in with much less room to spare before. One of the nightmares every soldier had from time to time involved a vision of clocking in at the same time and location at which another person or object occupied that space. The Pathfinders were usually extremely efficient at avoiding such occurrences, but there were still the inevitable accidents. The closest Finn had ever come to one was when he clocked into a forest clearing much like the one he now found himself in. The instant before he had materialized, a rabbit had run across the spot. As Finn clocked in, he had stepped forward and his foot had come down upon the running rabbit, crushing it. It gave off a pathetic squeal, a sound strikingly similar to a baby's cry, and for a horrifying moment, Finn had thought it *was* an infant. It had been necessary for him to kill the poor animal to put it out of its misery and ever since, he had felt jumpy at the moment of materialization.

This time, however, it had gone well and as he looked around, he saw the Observer, disguised as a peasant, approaching him. There was nothing to distinguish the Observer from any other peasant of the time; but the fact that he had just seen a man materialize out of thin air and was approaching him purposefully, as if nothing out of the ordinary had occurred, marked him for what he was. He was leading a chestnut mare on a rein as he approached.

"Major Fitzroy," he said.

"Sergeant Delaney."

The Observer nodded. "The coach is about two hundred yards down the road, off to the side," he said. "You can't miss it. It was stuck, but we've taken care of that. Now pay attention, this is where it stands. We've removed Corderro's body. Lady Marguerite Blakeney is all right. The pistol ball grazed her skull, but it was only a scratch and we've patched her up. We applied some plastiskin to her forehead and she'll never know that she was hit. There's a hole in the inside of the coach where the ball went after passing through the window and skipping off her skull, so if she has any memory of being shot, show her where the ball went and tell her that she must have fainted and struck her head. That will account for any pain that she might feel later when the dope wears off. The coach horses must have bolted when the shot went off, so it's highly unlikely that she saw what happened to Blakeney, even if she was still conscious at the time. Your story is that you were knocked down by the horse, but only winded. You took the captain's horse and chased after the coach as soon as you got your breath back."

"What about Corderro?" said Delaney. "What do I tell her if she asks about him?"

"Chances are she won't," said Fitzroy. "She was probably already unconscious when he jumped onto the coach. If she does remember anything about that, you saw him leap from the coach and take off running into the woods as you were riding up. That same story will serve you if there's any pursuit from the city that catches up with you. If that happens, they won't have any reason to detain you, but you might advance the theory that Corderro was a disguised aristocrat. That should spur them on to look for him and let you continue on your way."

"Got it," said Finn. "We're heading for Calais?"

"Right. Blakeney's yacht will be there to take you across to Dover. You'll be picking up your support team at an inn called The Fisherman's Rest in Kent. Let's just make sure you've got their cover straight."

"They're family servants who were looking after my property in Rouen and they've been sent ahead to England to make things ready for us at the estate now that my land in France is forfeit to the government."

"Good. You'll want to be very circumspect with Lady Blakeney," said Fitzroy. "Several months ago, she denounced the Marquis de St. Cyr for seeking support from Austria to put down the Revolution. He was arrested, tried, and guillotined along with his entire family."

"Nice lady," said Finn.

"Blakeney seems to have shared your sentiments," Fitzroy said. "He only recently found out about it and when he did, he turned off to her completely. Their relationship has been a little strained since then, to say the least. Blakeney's been attentive and polite to her, but evidently that's about as far as it went. She's taken to sniping at him in public lately."

"So much for Lady Blakeney not being hard to take," said Finn.

"What's that?"

"Nothing, really. Just thinking about something my CO said."

"Just be very careful around her," said Fitzroy. "Remember that she's a Republican and not to be trusted. If she finds out you're smuggling aristocrats out of France, there's no telling what she might do.''

"Terrific," said Finn. "Got any more good news for me?"

"I'm afraid so," said Fitzroy. "We don't yet have a complete list of all the aristocrats Blakeney smuggled out of France. The TIA's still working on it, but it's a hell of a job and they've got to separate the ones Blakeney's group got out from the ones who got out on their own. We also have to be especially careful that you don't wind up rescuing anyone who wasn't supposed to be rescued."

"That's a cheery thought," said Finn. "How am I supposed to figure out whom to smuggle over?"

"You'll be contacted at the appropriate time," Fitzroy said. "If it isn't by me, then the codeword will be 'wildflower.' That will identify your contact."

Finn grimaced. "That'll work just great unless someone happens to mention wildflowers in the course of a conversation. Do me a favor. Forget the cloak-and-dagger stuff, Fitzroy. If someone should happen to come up to Percy Blakeney and address him as Delaney, I'll assume that it's my contact, all right?"

"I suppose that would work," Fitzroy said.

"It's nice to see you're flexible," said Finn, sarcastically. "What about chronoplate access?"

"Can't let you have one," said Fitzroy. "Sorry. It would be too risky. However, I'll try to work as close to you as possible, within the limitations of our situation. If you get in a jam or have to get in touch with me for any reason, you've got your panic button. I assume you've had your implants checked?"

"Of course," said Finn, impatiently. No soldier worth his salt would clock out on a mission without making certain that his signal implant, located subcutaneously behind his ear, was in proper working order.

"Good," said Fitzroy. "Now there's one more thing. When he was killed, Blakeney had just embarked upon his smuggling career. He'd had a bellyful of the beheadings and he had arranged with two of his friends, Sir Andrew Ffoulkes and Lord Antony Dewhurst, to smuggle the Duc de Chalis and his children out of France. You're checked out on Ffoulkes and Dewhurst?"

Finn nodded. Since both men were known to be close friends of Blakeney's, all available information concerning them had been included in the mission programming.

"Dewhurst is with the boat," Fitzroy said. "Ffoulkes was the one who drove that wagon. One of the duke's sons was on the box with Ffoulkes, the younger boy and the old man were crammed into a hollow section underneath the box. They wouldn't be able to stay in such a cramped space for very long, so Ffoulkes probably let them out as soon as they were out of sight of the gate."

"What about his wife?" said Finn.

"She died last year. You didn't know that? God, they did put this together in a hurry. You'll have to watch yourself. Now we've arranged for another wagon to act as a decoy, since Ffoulkes won't be able to make very good time in that rig. That way, if there's pursuit, we'll have our wagon between the soldiers and Ffoulkes. They'll catch up to a wagonful of empty wine casks, driven by an old man and a boy, and they can rip it apart to their hearts' content and they won't find anything. That should buy Ffoulkes all the time he needs. However, when he planned their escape, Blakeney didn't know that he'd married a woman who had sent an entire family of aristocrats to the guillotine. So obviously, he can't very well expect to take them aboard his yacht along with Lady Blakeney, right? I'm assuming that he made some sort of last-minute contingency plan with Ffoulkes to hide them out somewhere until he and Lady Blakeney had reached England. Then he probably intended to send the yacht back for them. Unfortunately, there's no way of knowing exactly what sort of plans he made or where he intended to hide them. It's all guesswork. You'll have to improvise."

"I'll work it out somehow," said Finn. "Is that it? We're cutting it a little close, I think."

"That's it," Fitzroy said. He handed Finn a little case, small enough to fit inside his pocket and disguised as a snuff-box. "You'll find a signet ring in there. It matches Blakeney's. Slide the bottom of the signet forward and a needle will pop up. Practice with it a few times before you put it on, so you don't stick yourself. You've got several cartridges in there, all color-coded, and there's a key inside the lid. It's loaded for Lady Blakeney now. Stick her when you're ready for her to come around; it should take about three seconds. After that, load it with anything you wish, just don't give anyone a lethal dose unless it's absolutely unavoidable. Those are the red ones, by the way. If you use one of these, it had better be as a last resort, is that clear?"

"Perfectly."

"Right. Get moving." Fitzroy handed him the reins. "Good luck, Delaney."

Finn swung up into the saddle and rode off at a gallop. No sooner had he arrived at the site where Fitzroy had left the coach with the lead horse tethered to a tree, than he heard the rapidly approaching sound of hoofbeats. Moving quickly, he dismounted, dropping the reins and allowing the horse to nibble at the grass. He then loosed the lead horse and climbed into the coach just as a party of six soldiers of the Republic rode into view. Finn took a deep breath. They had cut it very close, indeed.

He opened the box, removed the ring, quickly checked the needle, then slipped it onto the ring finger of his right hand. He bent over Lady Blakeney and pricked her with the needle just as the officer leading the soldiers opened the door of the coach.

"You! Come out of there!"

Finn looked over his shoulder and saw the lieutenant pointing a pistol at him.

"My wife," he said, anxiously. "She's—"

"Never mind your wife, step out of the coach!"

Lady Blakeney moaned and started stirring.

"Thank God," said Finn. "For a moment, I was afraid that—"

"Step out of the coach, I said!"

Marguerite opened her eyes and gave a start. "Percy! Lord, Percy, I've been shot!"

"No, my dear," said Finn, stepping out of the coach slowly. "You only fainted."

The soldier grabbed his arm and pulled him aside roughly, then looked inside the coach.

"If you're looking for that ruffian," said Finn, "I saw him leap from the coach and run off into the woods."

The soldier spun to face him. "Where? How far back?"

"Damn me, I haven't the faintest idea," said Finn, producing a handkerchief and waving it in front of his nose. He hoped his imitation of Blakeney's voice would pass. He had not had much time to practice and he wished he had Lucas Priest's gift for mimicry. "I was hellbent for leather to try and catch this runaway coach and rescue my poor wife," said Finn, with a touch of indignation. "I was far too anxious about her welfare to concern myself with your renegade aristocrat. He jumped off back there, somewhere." He waved his handkerchief in the direction of the road back to Paris.

"You three," said the officer, indicating several of his men, "ride back and comb the woods; he couldn't have gone far."

The men wheeled their horses and galloped off in the direction from which they came.

"Have you seen a wagon," said the officer, "loaded with wine casks?"

"Lord, what do I know of wagons?" Finn said, rolling his eyes. "I was almost *killed* back there! And my wife was almost shot! There's a hole inside the coach where the ball passed through scant inches from her head! It was a dreadful experience, quite unnerving. I fear that I won't sleep for weeks! My insides are all in knots. This is all too much for my frail constitution. All I desire to do is get back to merry England and leave you to your Revolution. I don't care if I never set foot on French soil again!"

"France will survive quite well without your kind, I think," the officer said with a sneer.

"Yes, but I fear that *I* may not survive France," said Finn. He leaned against the coach for support and wiped his forehead with his handkerchief. "Gad, what a horrible experience! That terrible man! I hope you'll catch him and clap him in the Bastille."

"We shall do a great deal more than that," the soldier said. He put away his pistol, satisfied that Blakeney was no threat. "You are bound for Calais?"

"Yes, if we can arrive there safely without being killed along the way," said Finn. "Lord only knows what dangers await us on the road! I would be most grateful if you and your men would see us to our destination safely. I would feel far more secure in the company of soldiers of the Republic."

"Soldiers of the Republic have far more important things to do than to nursemaid weak-kneed Englishmen," the lieutenant said, harshly. "I would advise you to be on your way and not to stop until you've reached Calais. I wish you a speedy crossing of the Channel and good riddance."

The officer mounted and rode off with his two remaining men, heading away from the city on the trail of the wine wagon. Finn took a deep breath and let it out slowly.

"And good riddance to you," said Finn. "Are you all right, my dear? You gave me quite a fright."

Lady Blakeney gave him an arch look. "It would appear that it does not take very much to frighten you, Percy."

"Not much, you say? Why, having my own wife almost shot to death and myself almost being trampled by a horse and then accosted by those rough-mannered brigands who have the temerity to call themselves soldiers—why, I would say that it was much, indeed!"

As he spoke, Finn took her measure. Marguerite Blakeney was twenty-five years old, tall, and very well-proportioned with an ample bosom, a trim waist and long, slender legs, one of which was briefly visible as she descended from the coach. Her bright blue eyes met Finn's as she attempted to effect repairs upon her coiffure, the lustrous auburn hair having been disarranged while she was jostled about inside the coach. She was even lovelier in person, for the holographic image of her Finn had seen had not captured her voice and its inflections, her mannerisms, and it had caught only a hint of her earthy sensuality. There was, however, a certain air of hostility about her, testimony to the deteriorating relationship between herself and Blakeney.

She had a bit of the gamin in her, Finn saw, though it did not detract in the least from her beauty. Rather, it enhanced it. Her facial expressions betrayed pride and stubbornness and, although she hid it well, Finn could see that she had been hurt by Blakeney. Undoubtedly, she felt rejected, though Finn had no way of knowing whether or not the St. Cyr affair had ever been discussed between them or if Blakeney had simply accepted it as a matter of course and, having been satisfied that it was true, had locked it away inside himself like a guilty secret, never to be spoken of or even referred to. He decided, for the sake of prudence, to adopt the latter attitude, unless Marguerite brought the matter up herself. He also decided to play it very close to the vest, for Marguerite's eyes were shrewd and observant as she regarded him with a faintly puzzled air.

"Are you quite well, my husband?" she said, cocking an eyebrow at him. "Somehow, you don't sound quite yourself."

"I'm as well as could be expected for a man who's come so near to death," he said, leaning back against the coach and shutting his eyes as he fanned himself with his handkerchief. "Faith, my dear, you must have the courage of a lion! That pistol ball could not have passed but a hair's breadth from your head and there you stand, calm as can be, asking me if *I* am well! Would that I were made of such stern stuff, my heart would not then be pounding like a blacksmith's hammer on an anvil!"

"Well, then when your heart has stopped its fearsome pounding, perhaps we could continue on our journey," Marguerite said. "We shall not make Calais before tomorrow, even if we drive hard all the way." She glanced up at the empty box and sighed. "I fear that you will have to play the coachman. It appears that our fainthearted driver was frightened even more than you were."

"That's the trouble with these new 'citizens,'" said Finn. "They put their own petty concerns above their duty. Well, it appears that there's nothing for it. I shall have to drive, then. With any luck, we will make Amiens tonight and reach Calais tomorrow. Are you quite certain that you're up to a hard ride? We could travel at an easy pace, but I'm suddenly very anxious to go on with all dispatch. I fear that I shan't feel safe until we're on board the *Day Dream*."

Marguerite smiled, wryly. "Well, then I shall muster up my lion's courage and steel myself for the dangers of our journey." Her voice fairly dripped with sarcasm. "If you would be so kind, Percy, as to assist me back into the coach?"

Finn gave her his arm and helped her up, then closed the door and mounted up into the box. He whipped up the horses and drove the coach back onto the road. He drove at a brisk pace and, within fifteen minutes or so, the coach came within sight of the soldiers once again. There were only three of them, the officer and his two men, the others no doubt still beating the brush for the nonexistent *ci-devant* aristo. Finn saw that the soldiers had caught up to Fitzroy's decoy wine wagon. They had pulled it off to the side of the road, where the old man stood beside his young "son," wringing his hands and wailing as the soldiers tore the wagon apart board by board, searching for the Duc de Chalis. The officer looked up and gave Finn a scornful glance as Finn gave him a cheery wave as the coach passed by.

It was already night when they reached Amiens and the horses were all done in. Finn took a room for them at an inn and saw to it that the coach and horses would be stabled for the night and made ready for them early the next morning. Marguerite went up to the room to freshen up while Finn stayed downstairs and drank some wine.

So far, so good, he thought. Marguerite had accepted him as Blakeney, though there had never really been any question about that. He was, after all, the spitting image of Sir Percy Blakeney now and he had been prepared as thoroughly as possible to play the role. For Marguerite to suspect him of being an impostor was impossible. However, he would take Fitzroy's advice and tread with care.

There was a great deal to be done. Percy Blakeney had spent most of his young life away from England. He would be known at court, of course, since the late Algernon Blakeney had been a peer of the realm and the family holdings were extensive. Blakeney was one of the richest men in England. That, in itself, would be enough to secure his place in court society, but it would not be enough for this scenario.

Finn would have to establish Blakeney's character in such a manner that he would never be suspected of being the Scarlet Pimpernel. He would also have to make certain that a distance would remain between himself, as Blakeney, and Marguerite. Otherwise, he might not be able to function as the Pimpernel. Finn could count on Lucas and Andre to help him in his efforts to join Ffoulkes and Dewhurst as the first members of the League of the Scarlet Pimpernel. Beyond that, he would be working in the dark.

At the height of Blakeney's career, the League had boasted some nineteen or twenty members. History was inexact as to the figure. That, alone, could result in problems. What might happen if he did not recruit into the League someone the real Blakeney would have recruited? What would occur if he recruited someone who had not, originally, been in the League at all? Due to the inertia of the timeflow, he had a certain flexibility; otherwise it would not have been possible to effect adjustments. However, given this particular scenario, there were plenty of possibilities for things to go wrong. It was not the first time Delaney had found himself working in a period that suffered from inadequate prior documentation. He hadn't liked it then and he did not much like it now. He liked being saddled with Lady Blakeney even less.

Unless Fitzroy contacted him with further information, he

could rely on Ffoulkes and Dewhurst to advise him on whom to recruit into the League. But Lady Blakeney could pose a formidable problem in more ways than one. She was intelligent and sharp and, although the place of a woman in the 18th century denied her a role in much of the pursuits of her husband, he would have to act in such a manner that her curiosity would not be aroused. To this end, he could utilize the recent rift between Sir Percy Blakeney and his wife, building upon it so that he would become the sort of husband whose wife found him tiresome and unattractive. That would not be very difficult to accomplish. Marguerite was quite attractive and already had a reputation as a well-known actress and hostess. It would be a simple matter to introduce her into London society, taking a back seat as the fashionably dull and foolish fop while Marguerite had the spotlight to herself. She would quickly become the center of attention in any gathering and in no time at all she would acquire her own circle of friends and admirers, who would keep her busy while he spirited aristos out of France.

Yet, there was the very real problem of his own reaction to Marguerite. From the very first moment he set eyes upon her, Finn found himself irresistibly attracted to the woman. To remain aloof and unconcerned with her would not be easy. When it came to matters of the flesh, discipline had never been Delaney's strong suit. As he sat alone at a corner table in the inn, nursing his wine, he contemplated the possibility of bedding her that night.

After all, he was her husband. She might welcome a sudden thaw in their relationship and the situation was quite conducive to it. They had just been through a harrowing experience together, the sort of thing that raises the adrenaline and leads people to seek pleasant release in sexual activity. One night, when matters of the preceding day led them to rediscover the joys they knew when first they wed, one night, what harm could it do? The next day, he could resume the status quo, acting embarrassed, awkward, perhaps a little angered at having given in to the pressures of the moment. Things like that happened all the time.

But, no. It would not be wise. She already bore resentment toward her husband, whose ardor had so considerably cooled and whose devotion had become little more than a matter of form. To start something now, only to end it just as abruptly, as necessity dictated, would only make matters that much worse. He needed Marguerite to be bored with Blakeney, not furious with him. He would have to put his lust aside, something that never had been easy and would be that much more difficult, due to the fact that he would have to share a bed with her.

"Damn," Finn mumbled softly, to himself, "I should have thought to take separate rooms for us."

"Sir?" said a soft voice at his side. He turned to see a young serving girl who stood hesitantly by the table, smiling awkwardly.

"Yes, what is it?"

"The lady bid me tell you that she is quite exhausted from the journey and will not sup tonight. She begs you to excuse her and to take your meal at your leisure, if you will. She is content to simply rest for tomorrow's journey."

Well, that settles that, thought Finn. She'll be fast asleep when I come up. Now if I can only keep my hands off her in the middle of the night. . . .

He thanked the girl and had her bring him a supper of cold meat, bread, and fruit. He drank more wine and began to feel relaxed for the first time that day. He purchased a clay pipe for a few pennies from the innkeeper, who overcharged him, seeing that he was wealthy, and he settled back in his chair with the long churchwarden filled with Turkish Latakia. He smoked slowly, enjoying the strong black tobacco and sipping the inn's somewhat plebian bordeaux, which was nevertheless quite satisfying after the bumpy, dusty journey. He bought a few more clays and some tobacco to take along with him the following day, so that he could relax and smoke while they crossed the Channel, then he made his way upstairs.

Marguerite was in bed, with the covers drawn up over her. She had left a candle burning for him and the single light bathed the room in a soft and cozy glow. He saw that Marguerite had laid his sleeping gown out for him, along with his nightcap, both of which he appraised with slight annoyance. He did not like to be encumbered while he slept. Still, the character seemed to call for it and he resigned himself to nightclothes. He only hoped that there would be no bedbugs to keep him company.

Moving very quietly, so as not to waken Marguerite, Finn slowly undressed. When he had taken off his last item of clothing, he heard a rustling in the bed behind him and, thinking that he might have made some sound that had disturbed his "wife," he froze for a moment.

"Are you then well fed and rested, Percy?" Marguerite said softly, her voice barely above a whisper.

Finn turned and saw that she had pulled aside the covers and was lying naked in the bed, in a deliberately and blatantly seductive pose. Her hair was fanned out on the pillow and it glinted like red gold in the candlelight. Her soft skin was without a blemish and her perfectly shaped breasts rose and fell slightly as she breathed through parted lips.

Moving quickly, Delaney blew out the candle so that she would not see what he was unable to conceal, then he made a quick grab for the nightgown. He barely stifled a moan of frustration.

"Forgive me, my dear, I did not mean to wake you," he said, adding an audible yawn. "Lord, it's a wonder you're not sleeping like the dead after today's exertions. Myself, I am quite done in. It was all that I could do to make it up the stairs."

He heard a heavy sigh in the darkness. "Come to bed and sleep, then," Marguerite said, flatly. "You wanted to leave early in the morning and you need your rest."

Finn bit his lower lip and felt his way to the bed, then got in beside her and turned on his left side, so that he faced away from her. He yawned once more, for effect.

"Gad, what a day!" he said. "I feel like I could sleep for a hundred years."

There was no answer from her side of the bed.

"Well, goodnight, then," Finn said. He waited a few minutes, then faked the sounds of snoring. Several minutes later, he heard Marguerite get out of bed and slip into her nightgown, then gently get back into bed. Soon, she was asleep. Finn, on the other hand, knew that he would be lucky if he got any sleep at all. And he knew that in the morning, he would hate himself.

3 ─────────────────────────

They arrived at Calais the following evening, having stopped several times to change horses en route. It had been a long, hard drive. Finn was sore and covered with road dust. Marguerite had been shaken up inside the coach, but she issued not one word of complaint. They drove directly to the port and as he looked out into the bay, Finn could see a graceful fifty-foot schooner with a long and slender bowsprit riding at anchor, its twin masts barely visible in the dusk. They left the coach at an inn and hired a small boat to take them out to the *Day Dream*.

It was brisk out on the water and Marguerite shivered in her inadequate cloak as she clutched it around her, but she didn't say a word. Finn had to admire her. She had been shot in the head, had some minor field surgery performed on her, though she didn't know it, been drugged, bounced around inside a coach on bumpy, rut-filled country roads for some one hundred and fifty miles, which they had covered in an astonishing two days, exhausting several teams of horses in the process, and now she was being violently rocked up and down as the small boat pulled out toward the *Day Dream* in the choppy waters of the Channel. The cold wind sliced through her fashionably light hooded cloak as though it wasn't even there and, with the exception of a slight shaking of the shoulders and a barely noticeable tremor of the lower lip, Marguerite remained calm and poised, as though she were out for a row upon a placid country lake.

The boat pulled up to the yacht and one of the crewmen dropped a rope ladder over the side. As the boatman hung onto the bottom of the ladder, trying to keep the rowboat steady in the swells, Finn helped Marguerite up the ladder, staying close behind her and holding on tight in case she should lose her grip and fall. She climbed a bit uncertainly, unaccustomed to having the world rolling all round her, but she hung on tenaciously and in moments, a crewman was giving her a hand on board. She thanked the young man, who smiled awkwardly in her presence, and turned back to look at Finn with a slightly shaky smile.

"Which way to my room, Percy? Oh, yes, it's called a cabin on a boat, is it not?"

"Allow me, my lady," said a tall, sandy-haired young man of about twenty-six or seven, who came up to them and offered her his arm. He flashed a dazzling smile at her. "Lord Antony Dewhurst, at your service, ma'am. You must be terribly fatigued after your journey. I've taken the liberty of having your cabin prepared and your bunk turned down. There's fresh water for washing and Stevens here will bring you supper and a rum toddy momentarily. I think that you will find the bracing sea air quite conducive to deep and restful sleep. We shall be sailing on the morning tide."

"You're most kind, Lord Dewhurst."

"Antony, ma'am," he said with a grin, "or Tony, if you prefer. That's what all my friends call me."

"Thank you, Tony. I think I will retire, if you gentlemen will excuse me."

Dewhurst led her away belowdeck, with a quick glance back at Finn to tell him that he would come right back at once. Finn leaned against the mainmast amidships and pulled out one of his clays. He filled it with tobacco and tamped it down; then, hunching over it and cupping his hand against the wind, he got it lit after several tries and settled down against the teak railing to wait for Dewhurst to return. With the exception of the captain, a weatherbeaten old salt named Briggs, who only bid him welcome aboard and asked if there was anything that he could do for him, the rest of the crew left him to his privacy. Briggs brought him a pewter flask filled with rum and then departed once again to his own cabin. After several moments, Dewhurst returned.

"I say, Percy, she's absolutely marvelous! Beautiful,

charming and intelligent; you'll be the envy of every man in London.''

"I daresay," said Finn, "excepting those who cannot abide the barbarity currently practiced on these shores."

Dewhurst looked suddenly glum. "It's true, then, about St. Cyr?"

"You've heard, then?" Finn said cautiously, to draw him out.

"Aye, news travels fast when it's bad news," said Dewhurst. "What are you going to do?"

"Faith, what can I do? She is my wife, Tony. I am married to her past, as well as to her future."

"What about Ffoulkes? Is he well away? Have you seen him?"

"Aye, he's well away. He got out the gate a bit ahead of us, but we did not pass him on the road. No doubt he pulled off the main road until he was certain it was safe to go on. There was trouble, though. Soldiers pursued him, but they pulled over the wrong wagon. I passed them as they were tearing it apart in search of human contraband."

"He'll make it, won't he, Percy?" Dewhurst said, concern showing on his face.

Finn nodded. "He'll make it. Andrew is no fool. But we must sail to Dover without him. I cannot risk having de Chalis and Marguerite come face to face. It will ruin everything. We shall have to send the *Day Dream* back for them."

"Poor St. Just," said Dewhurst.

"What's that?" said Finn.

"Oh, I said, 'Poor St. Just.' The only one of the Feuillants with any influence left and they appoint him to the Committee of Public Safety, where he's outnumbered by Robespierre's Jacobins. If only it were the other way around. Yet there he sits, teetering on the edge of the abyss, while Fouquier-Tinville pursues his butchery. Without his help, we would never have got de Chalis out alive, yet I fear that it will be a poor atonement for his sister's crime." Realizing, suddenly, what he had said, Dewhurst looked aghast at Finn. "God, Percy, forgive me! I didn't think. That was a frightfully cruel thing to say."

"Yet, nevertheless, it's true," said Finn. So Armand St. Just, along with Lafayette, was one of the moderate monarchists who had separated from the Jacobins. He was sympathetic to Blakeney's cause, enough so that he had taken an active part in it. That was something Delaney had *not* known. It was a very worthwhile piece of information. If the bloody excesses of the Revolution, combined with his sister's part in the fall of the Marquis de St. Cyr, were an affront to his humanistic sensibilities, Armand could be used. Indeed, it appeared that Blakeney had used him already.

"Still, I'm very sorry, Percy. She is your wife, after all. I hope you can forgive me."

"There's nothing to forgive, Tony. The times have given all of us strange bedfellows."

"I say, that's a little crude," said Dewhurst, a bit taken aback.

"These days, I have little patience for the delicacies of polite behavior," Finn said. "It smacks of hypocrisy, what with people being slaughtered left and right in the name of liberty, fraternity and equality. A poet once said, 'If you can keep your head while all about you are losing theirs. . . .' " He broke off, realizing that the poet in question, Rudyard Kipling, would not be born until 1865. "Well, I intend to keep my head," he said. "And to do everything in my power to keep as many as possible from losing theirs. The guillotine is an abomination and I have set myself the task of denying it as many victims as I can. This is the very least that I can do. It won't bring back St. Cyr or make the knowledge of Marguerite's part in his execution any easier to bear, but if I can spare others from his fate, any risk would be worthwhile. It's not enough to simply spirit one aristocrat out of the country. I must try to save as many as I can and then rub Fouquier-Tinville's nose in it!"

"In principle, I'm all for it," Dewhurst said, "but in practice, it would be quite dangerous. Then, too, there is the matter of Lady Blakeney's views, although I hesitate to dwell upon the matter."

"She must never know, of course," said Finn. "I will have to work in secret."

"Then each of those you help will have to be sworn to secrecy, as well," said Dewhurst. "The only thing is, despite all good intentions, secrets do not remain secrets for long when those who share them grow great in number."

Finn nodded. "I'm certain that the Duc de Chalis can be trusted not to speak of his benefactors. As for any others, I'll have to take great pains to conceal my identity from them."

"Any subterfuge along those lines would come to nought the moment anyone inquired as to the identity of the owner of this boat," said Dewhurst. "You cannot hope to use the *Day Dream* in your plans and still remain unknown. She is far from being inconspicuous and she won't be lost among more common craft."

Finn smiled. "Then I shall sell her."

Dewhurst frowned. "But then, how—"

"After all," continued Finn, "I've grown tired of traveling and I'm on my way back to England to take charge of my affairs. I no longer have need of such an extravagant yacht, since I will be staying in London most of the time. As a matter of fact, I've already sold her."

"*What?* To whom?"

"Why, to you, Tony."

"To *me?*"

"Yes, to you. You've wanted her for years, haven't you? You've been after me to sell the *Day Dream* to you for as long as we've known each other."

"What? Percy, what on earth are you talking about? I've never—"

"Yes, I know you've never done any such thing. You know it and I know it, but no one else knows it and that's all that really matters."

"I don't understand this at all, Percy. What the devil are you getting at?"

"Look, Tony, you don't spend all of your time sailing about in the English Channel, do you? Being the new owner of such a fine boat, is there any reason why you shouldn't realize some profit from her? Allow Briggs to take on some small commissions to help pay for the *Day Dream*'s upkeep and keep the crew from being idle? As a matter of fact, the moment we return to England, you'll be offered just such a commission, by an agent whose name you will conveniently forget. You will be very much surprised when you discover that it was for the purpose of helping the Duc de Chalis escape from France. When you discover this extraordinary fact, you'll be so astonished and delighted that, as a gesture of noble idealism, you will instruct Briggs to keep the boat available to this unknown adventurer, whose face no one will ever see. You and Ffoulkes will make a grand show of helping the new arrivals find a place for themselves in England. You'll speak a great deal about this man of mystery whose cause you have elected to support, even though you don't know anything about him." Finn grinned. "Before too long, I'm certain that you'll be receiving contributions from everyone in London to pass on to Briggs, so that he can give it to the agents of this adventurer. If it's managed right, we can make him a folk hero."

"Don't you mean 'make yourself a folk hero'?" Dewhurst said with a smirk. "Why this sudden modesty, Percy?"

"Because it isn't really me," said Finn. "I don't matter, not as Percy Blakeney, individual. It's the principle involved, the idea of the thing. Suppose for a moment that I acted as myself, as Percy Blakeney, smuggling people out of France at great risk to myself. What would the resulting public opinion be? Some would support me, to be sure, others would think I was a fool. As that faction in Parliament who oppose our intervention in the Revolution say, 'Let 'em murder!' I would attract some attention for a while as a man with the courage to act on his convictions, but in due course, the novelty would wear off and people would grow bored with the whole thing. On the other hand, people love a mystery. If we have some romantic, unknown adventurer cheating the guillotine of victims, that would capture the public's fancy. Who is he? Where did he come from? What is he like, this anonymous crusader against injustice? It's not the *man* that counts, Tony, it's the image. You see what I mean, don't you?"

"Aye, I do. It strikes me that you've missed your calling, Percy. You should have been a politician or a dramatist. You seem to have an uncanny knack for understanding public opinion and emotions. As you say, the imagination of the people would indeed be captured by an adventurer such as you describe, a crusader who cloaks himself in mystery. Such a figure would appear to be larger than life and would become a *cause célèbre*."

"Precisely. We can all help to create him together," said Finn. "We can recruit others into our cause, though we must do so with great care. We will form a league together, with this unknown crusader as our leader. The role that you and Ffoulkes must play in public must be that of men who are only involved indirectly with this man. It must be necessary for you to be able to account for your activities at the times when this crusader is at work; this is for your safety."

"Why must we be known to be involved at all?" said Dewhurst.

"Because I shall need my Boswells," said Delaney. "It will be necessary for the public to know something of the activities of this crusader if we are to curry their favor. Publicly, you will attest to his existence, though you will claim to know nothing of him whatsoever. You will be contacted by his league, his agents, by surreptitious means and told when to prepare for receiving escapees from France. Publicly, you will never set foot on French soil. Rather, you will instruct Briggs when to have the *Day Dream* ready, when and where to have her waiting to accept aristocrats saved by our crusader. When they arrive in England, they will then be in your charge and you and Ffoulkes will help them find a place in our society. This will leave you free to speak of this crusader and his league as the two of you, perhaps more than any others, will then be in a position to wonder at his true identity. You can help to fan the flame of public curiosity and in this manner elicit their support."

"What about yourself?" said Dewhurst. "You will join us in this charade?"

"No, I will not," said Finn. "I must create about myself an aura such that will insure that I can never be suspect in this matter. Only then will I be free to act. I shall have to be an even greater actor than my wife, for I will have to fool her, along with everybody else. None but you and Ffoulkes, as well as Briggs, for I must take him into my confidence, must know the part that I will play in all of this."

"What of the Duc de Chalis?" Dewhurst said.

"I shall have to speak with him and prepare him for the part he is to play," said Finn. "As for the rest of it, you are quite right. We must limit the number of those who share our secret."

Dewhurst smiled. "I must say, it all sounds like a great deal of fun."

"It will be very dangerous," said Finn.

Dewhurst shrugged. "It will be fine sport. And what is sport without some element of risk?" He laughed. "By God, I'm really going to enjoy this! I can't wait to get started!"

Finn smiled. "We have already started, Tony. Let's have a drink on it. To the speedy and safe arrival of Andrew Ffoulkes and to the creation of our mysterious crusader!"

Finn took a sip of rum and then passed it to Dewhurst.

"What shall we call him, then?" said Dewhurst. "He will have to have a name, this flower of English manhood pitted against the *fleur-de-lis* of France."

"Yes, he shall," said Finn, "or he will be a common flower, indeed."

Dewhurst chuckled. "Even a common English wayside flower smells sweeter to me than any of those that grow in France."

"A common English wayside flower," said Finn, musing. "Say, like a pimpernel?"

"The pimpernel," said Dewhurst, considering. He grinned. "The Scarlet Pimpernel!"

Finn raised his eyebrows. "It has a sort of ring to it."

"I like it," Dewhurst said. He raised the flask in a toast. "To the League of the Scarlet Pimpernel!"

The Fisherman's Rest in Dover, in the county of Kent, was a warm and pleasant sanctuary from the damp and piscatory air of the cliffside town. They came in out of the mist to be greeted by the welcome warmth and glow of Mr. Jellyband's fireplace. The proprietor, a jovial, well-girthed innkeeper with a balding pate and a hail-fellow-well-met air, bowed to them as they came in and immediately dispatched his serving girl to the kitchen with orders for the help to snap to, as obviously well-heeled patrons had arrived.

The inn had more of the air of a country hostel than a "fisherman's rest," for it was clean and bright, with a red-tiled floor that was kept spotless and dark oak rafters and beams. The tables, though marked with the ancient circles of many pewter mugs that had overflowed, were well polished and there were pots of scarlet and blue flowers in the windows. They hung up their cloaks and made themselves comfortable at a long table Jellyband ushered them to.

"Your pardon, gentlemen," said Jellyband, wringing his hands in his obvious anxiety to please, "would one of you happen, by any chance, to be the honorable Sir Percy Blakeney?"

"I have the honor to answer to that name," said Finn.

"Ah, yes, well, there is a young woman here expecting the arrival of your lordship," Jellyband said.

"Indeed?" said Marguerite.

"One of his lordship's servants, I believe," Jellyband added, hastily. "A young woman of a most peculiar temperament, if you will excuse the observation, she was most insistent that I—"

"That would be Andre, I believe," said Finn.

"Andre?" said Marguerite. "I thought you said that it was a young woman?"

"Andre *is* a young woman, my dear," said Finn. "Her family has served the Blakeneys for years. She was part of the serving staff at my estate in Rouen. I sent her on ahead with Lucas to make certain that all was in readiness for us at Richmond. Regrettably, they were the only two of all my staff there who have shown me the least bit of loyalty. The others were all so full of revolutionary zeal that they all elected to become free citizens and, as such, could hardly be expected to continue in the service of a despised aristocrat such as myself. Go and fetch her, my good man," he said to Jellyband. Then, turning to Marguerite, he added, "She is of Basque origin, I believe, and possesses the roughness and independent spirit of those people. She is, however, loyal, and makes an admirable servant."

"Is she pretty?" Marguerite said, archly.

Finn frowned. "Pretty? Faith, I can't say as I've ever noticed, really."

"How singularly unobservant of you," Marguerite said.

"Well, at any rate, you may judge for yourself," said Finn. "She will doubtless be here momentarily."

The innkeeper returned, with Andre following behind. If Marguerite had expected to see a well-turned-out serving girl in a clinging bodice darting bold glances at Sir Percy, she was disappointed. Andre was dressed in riding boots and breeches. She had on a plain brown jacket with a matching waistcoat; a white shirt not altogether clean; a bit of lace adornment at the throat, begrimed with road dust; and a simple tricorne, which she carried in her left hand. Her blond hair was worn loose and was considerably shorter than the style of the day dictated.

"I say," said Dewhurst, "there's a manly looking wench. Shoulders like a farmboy's and a manner like a soldier's."

Marguerite sat silent, appraising Andre. Finn had the feeling that Lady Blakeney would just as coolly and as carefully take the measure of everyone and everything involved with her husband and her new life in England. It was the actress in her. She wanted to be thoroughly familiar with the set, to know where every light and prop was, where every other actor was to stand and what lines he was to deliver. Perhaps "Percy" hadn't noticed whether or not Andre was pretty, but he could bet that Lady Blakeney noticed everything.

"Well, then, Andre," Finn said, "is everything in readiness for us at Richmond? How stands the old estate? I trust that it has not fallen into disrepair?"

"Oh, no, milord," said Andre. "The estate has been kept up most admirably and Master Lucas is there presently to make certain that all are prepared for your arrival. The news has caused a good deal of excitement. There has been a great deal of scurrying and cleaning and polishing and several of the neighbors have already sent servants to inquire as to when you and Lady Blakeney would be arriving."

"Ah, you see, Dewhurst," said Finn, "the Blakeney name still stands for something. It appears that we have not been forgotten."

"Or your money has not been forgotten," Marguerite said, dryly.

"My name, my money, what's the difference?" Finn said, with an airy wave. "If I were a pauper, I would not be a Blakeney, nor would you be, my dear, for chances are that I would then never have set foot in France to be captivated by your charms. What, I see our food's arriving. Andre, have you eaten? No? Innkeeper, Jellybelly, whatever your name is, see to it that my servant's fed, there's a good man. And Andre, after you have eaten you may ride ahead and inform Master Lucas that we shall be arriving at Richmond this evening, lest something should happen to delay us. Lord, there have been enough adventures on this trip already! I pray that the remainder of our journey will be safely dull and devastating in its boredom. I've had enough stimulation these past several days to last me a lifetime!"

"If you don't mind, Percy," Marguerite said, rising, "I think that I will take my meal in my room. I fear that the effects of the Channel crossing have not quite worn off and I should like to be refreshed and rested before we continue on our way." She turned to Dewhurst and smiled. "I will leave you gentlemen to discuss the pressing matters which no doubt await us all in London. Since the neighbors are inquiring as to our arrival time, doubtless they plan some entertainment and, in such a case, if Lady Blakeney is to be shown off to her best advantage, it would be well that she were rested. You may send for me after you have had your port and pipes and are ready to continue."

She curtsied and departed.

Dewhurst shook his head. "Faith, Percy, if you are out to encourage Marguerite's indifference, it would seem that you are making a good start."

"Oh, there is one thing more, milord," said Andre, "that Master Lucas bid me bring to your attention."

"And what would that be, pray?" said Finn.

"A minor matter, surely," Andre replied, guardedly, "and nothing that should overly concern your lordship. Rather, it is a matter for the gamekeeper, though Master Lucas wished me to inform you of it in the event that it required his attention and he was not there to greet you when you arrived."

Finn frowned. What on earth was she getting at?

"Why should Lucas be concerned over something that would be the province of the gamekeeper?" he said, genuinely puzzled.

"Well, milord, it seems that some animal has been hard at work butchering the grouse on your estate," said Andre. "The gamekeeper has been at a loss to trap it and he keeps insisting that it is some exotic creature not native to these parts. Master Lucas has resolved to look into the matter personally, in case the gamekeeper has been drinking overmuch or doing some poaching on the side and blaming it on this unlikely creature."

At the mention of the words, "not native to these parts," Finn came fully on the alert.

"What sort of creature does the gamekeeper say it is, pray tell?" he said, feigning only mild curiosity.

Andre stared at him steadily. "A mongoose, milord."

"What, a mongoose, did you say?" said Dewhurst. "Surely, you must be mistaken. A weasel or a ferret, perhaps, even though such creatures do not normally kill grouse, but surely not a mongoose. There are no mongoose in England. Such creatures are generally found in India and thereabouts. You're quite certain that he said it was a mongoose?"

"Quite certain, milord," said Andre. She glanced again at Finn. "As I said, a creature not native to these parts."

"How very interesting," said Dewhurst. "This servant of

yours, Percy, would he know a mongoose if he saw one?''

"Most assuredly," said Finn. "Lucas was a sailor once and he has also been a tracker. He has hunted all over the world."

"He sounds like quite a fellow," Dewhurst said. "I'm looking forward to meeting him. Still, a mongoose! Well, I suppose it might be possible. I have heard that these creatures are frequently captured and domesticated in the east. Perhaps someone brought one into England and it got away, reverting to its wild state."

"Well, I shall hope that Lucas catches it, whatever it may be, before the creature spoils the shooting," Finn said. However, he knew that Andre was not referring to an animal. The only mongoose they all knew was human and he was highly dangerous. Moreover, he was supposed to be confined to the 27th century, barred from field work. Finn met Andre's gaze and saw by the expression on her face that he had guessed correctly.

So they had not seen the last of Mongoose, after all. That worried him. It worried him a great deal.

4 ――――――――――――――――

The Blakeney estate in Richmond was an elegant testimony to the fortune amassed by Sir Algernon Blakeney before his wife was struck down with her unfortunate malady. Having exhausted all hope of curing her in England, the elder Blakeney had sought the advice of countless physicians abroad, all to no avail. She died, hopelessly insane. Algernon Blakeney could not bear to return to his estate, where everything reminded him of the life he shared with his beloved wife, but he could not bear to sell it, either. Leaving the estate and the management of his fortune in capable and trusted hands, he lived out what life was left to him traveling abroad. His solicitors looked after his interests back in England, knowing that young Percy would one day return to claim his rightful place and title.

Percy, or Finn, was now returning to discover that his wealth had increased tenfold due to shrewd management and that, as a result, there was now a great deal of interest in him. What little was known of him filtered back to England from Zurich, Genoa and Brussels, news of him brought back by travelers and friends such as Ffoulkes and Dewhurst, wealthy scions both, who had spent time with him abroad.

The coach turned into the drive leading up to the entrance of the palatial red-brick mansion, which dated back to the Tudor days. The grounds covered some 2500 acres and encompassed a wooded area that teemed with deer; a number of

ponds ranging in size from small tree-shaded pools to little
lakes, all stocked with fish; several immaculately maintained
parks with graceful gardens; white gravel paths and ivy-
covered gazebos and guesthouses; and smaller cottages reserved for the serving staff who did not reside in the mansion
itself, these being the gamekeeper, the stableboys and master,
the houndkeepers, and the gardeners and woodsmen. All were
supported by the Blakeney fortune and the patronage of less
well-heeled gentry, who were allowed the use of the grounds
occasionally for the purposes of shoots and riding to hounds.
This practice, initiated in Blakeney's absence by his solicitors,
helped to support the estate and keep the serving staff in trim,
as well as the hounds from growing fat and lazy. Now, with
the return of Blakeney, the tenure of such usage was in doubt
and many among the local bluebloods were on tenterhooks,
anxious to curry favor with young Blakeney so that he would
not, by his resumption of the tenancy, put an end to their
recreations. Finn found a large number of calling cards awaiting him and no small amount of invitations to parties, balls,
and dinners. Among these were invitations from personages
no less illustrious than Lord Grenville, the Foreign Secretary,
and His Royal Highness, the Prince of Wales.

Marguerite was quite obviously taken aback by the splendor
of the estate. She had known, of course, that she had married
an extremely wealthy man, but it was not the palatial representation of that wealth that so impressed her so much as the
sheer beauty of the grounds. Finn, on the other hand, affected
boredom and leaned back in his seat with his eyes half closed.

The coach pulled up in front of the Elizabethan entrance
hall, stopping between the steps leading up into the house and
a huge sundial on the beautifully trimmed lawn. Andre had
ridden on ahead, as directed, and now a small platoon of
grooms stood by to receive them and the coach. As Finn and
Marguerite disembarked, the coach was taken to the stables
some distance away and servants busied themselves carrying
their things into the house. Dewhurst had remained behind in
Dover, to await the arrival of Andrew Ffoulkes and his
charges and to deliver a message to the Duc de Chalis from Sir
Percy Blakeney.

Both Lucas and Andre stood by inside the hall to greet
them, Lucas having obviously established himself as chief
whipcracker with the staff. He was attired elegantly in a dark

green jacket with a high collar and wide lapels, black breeches, clean stockings and shiny buckle shoes. Andre had changed into a simple dress and, though Finn knew well that she despised it, she had put on a wig to create an air of subdued femininity. She looked well enough, but she was obviously uncomfortable and it showed in her manner.

Finn noted that Lucas had already arranged things so that Sir Percy Blakeney and his wife would occupy two separate suites of apartments above the reception rooms, each separated from the other by the width of the entire house. Marguerite made no comment concerning this arrangement and allowed herself to be shown to her suite by Andre. Lucas directed the other servants to take Finn's portmanteau and chests up to his rooms and then waited until they had all departed and he was alone with Finn.

"She's a hell of a fine-looking woman," Lucas said, nodding in the direction Marguerite had taken. "Considering the way things stand, I hope you've kept your hands off her."

"I have, but it hasn't been easy," Finn said.

"She could cause some trouble."

"I know. But forget about Marguerite for now. What's this about Mongoose? Are you telling me he's *here*?"

Lucas nodded. "Yeah. Surprise."

"You're *sure*?"

"I'm sure," said Lucas, taking his arm. "Come on, let's take a walk. I don't feel especially safe discussing this inside. Everyone here is mighty curious about you and I wouldn't want us to be overheard."

They went outside into the growing darkness and followed a gravel path that led to a garden at the side of the sprawling mansion. Here, after they passed through a gate of hedges, there was privacy for them where they could either stroll through the maze of immaculate hedgerows taller than a man or sit and talk in one of several green enclosures in which marble benches had been placed, as well as marble urns for the knocking out of pipe dottles.

"A guy could get lost in here," said Finn.

"He could, if he didn't know the trick," said Lucas. "You can see into the maze from the upstairs terrace. It looks deceptively simple until you get down here. Algernon Blakeney had a prankster's sense of humor. From upstairs, you can see people muddling about down here, trying to find their way out. You can see which way they have to go, but they can't. I memorized the sequence of the turns you have to take, but it wasn't until I actually got down here that I discovered that there's a key to the maze that'll guide you out in case you forgot the way. Notice how the benches are placed? There's a bench near every key branching off point. The placement of the marble urns, whether on the right or left hand side of the benches, tells you which way you have to go.''

They came to a bench and sat down, hidden from any prying eyes except those which might be watching from the upstairs terrace. However, in the growing darkness, they were almost invisible.

Lucas took a deep breath and let it out slowly. "The other day, one of the grooms came up to me and handed me a note, addressed to Sir Percy Blakeney. Thinking it might be yet another invitation or some such thing, I didn't open it right away. I should have. It was from Mongoose. It seems that he's our contact. Oh, and by the way, the groom was a tall, dark-haired fellow with a beard. I've since discovered that none of Blakeney's grooms wear beards. Mongoose still likes playing games with cute disguises.''

Finn shook his head. "I don't believe it. How in hell did he manage to pull field duty after screwing up so badly on the Timekeeper case? I thought Forrester said he'd been demoted to the TIA's evaluations section? How did he wind up in the Observers?''

"He does have the necessary qualifications," Lucas said.

"I know that. I just can't believe that the Observers would accept him after he almost blew an adjustment. Besides, doesn't it strike you as one hell of a coincidence that our paths just happened to cross again?''

"No more of a coincidence than our meeting up with Andre in 17th-century Paris," said Lucas.

"Maybe," said Finn. "Back when I was in RCS, we did a whole year on coincidence as it relates to the Fate Factor. We used to call it 'zen physics.' But I somehow doubt that temporal inertia had anything to do with Mongoose's showing up here at the same time as we did.''

"You're thinking that it's too much of a coincidence.''

"That's exactly what I'm thinking. In fact, I've thought of little else since Andre gave me your message back in Dover. I just can't see him being given an assignment in the field after what happened. I can't believe it's on the level. It occurs to me that if he had spent some time in evaluating TIA data, then he had access to the records. He might have indulged in some kind of creative programming."

"That occurred to me as well," said Lucas, "but I wanted to hear you say it, just to convince myself that I wasn't getting too paranoid. Still, what we're talking about is computer crime. Unauthorized access and alteration of classified information would carry a sentence of life imprisonment. No re-education, no parole, just hard time in confined social service. Would Mongoose chance something like that?"

"We've already established that he's several cards short of a full deck," said Finn. "He's a megalomaniac who thinks that he can get away with anything. But that's not what worries me. We're the ones who caused his fall from grace as the TIA's number-one field operative. We're also the ones who blocked the agency's attempt to muscle in on the army's jurisdiction in adjustment missions."

"Mongoose brought what happened on himself," said Lucas.

"You don't really expect him to see it that way, do you?" Finn said. "Not our boy Mongoose. His ego couldn't handle that. You been in touch with Fitzroy about this?"

Lucas shook his head. "I didn't want to do anything until I talked to you first. According to the note I got from Mongoose, Fitzroy's set up a safehouse in Paris so he can be close to where the action is. Mongoose is our contact in England, which means that if I push the panic button, he's going to respond and not Fitzroy. At least, that's the way it should work in practice. You think he'll answer if we signal?"

"I'm not sure what to think," said Finn. "It doesn't look good."

"The first year of RCS includes some heavy courses in advanced computer science, doesn't it?" said Lucas. "You take that and add it to the fact that Mongoose had to have top clearance to work in the evaluations section and you've got all the necessary ingredients for his figuring out a way to program an unauthorized transfer. Still, I don't see how he could possibly hope to get away with it. He might be smart enough to have figured out a way to beat the safeguards in the TIA databanks and to have interfaced with the Temporal Corps personnel files, but the records could still be cross-checked against the Referee Corps' databanks.''

"But there would be no reason for anyone to run a cross-check on him unless someone specifically brought the matter up," said Finn. "The refs have too much to do to bother running routine checks on personnel records. Hell, maybe we're way off base and someone just screwed up and approved his transfer."

"You think maybe Darrow might've covered for him?" Lucas said. "Mongoose was his top agent, after all. He had a good record until he got in over his head. The fact that Darrow didn't bust him out of the agency proves that he was protective of his people."

"But Darrow resigned as director after that whole Timekeeper flap," said Finn.

"So?" said Lucas. "He resigned because his position gave him the luxury to do so. Mongoose would've been stuck in an administrative job. Forrester might have considered it a slap on the wrist, but Mongoose loved field work. We both know he got high off taking chances. For him, a desk job would've been slow death and with a new director coming in, a black mark like endangering an adjustment mission might have cost him even that job in a periodic review. Darrow might have done him one last favor before he left."

"It's possible," said Finn. "In any case, there's no way I'm going to work with him again. I'm going to have to lay the law down to Fitzroy. Either Mongoose gets pulled off this mission or the Scarlet Pimpernel goes on strike for the duration."

"Don't be ridiculous," said Lucas. "You know you can't do that."

"Yeah, you're right. That's wishful thinking. Still, we can do our damnedest to convince Fitzroy that Mongoose represents a threat to this operation. We're not exactly his favorite people. He's got it in for us, I'm sure of it. This is all just a bit too serendipitous."

"You don't suppose he'd purposely jeopardize an adjustment just for his own personal. . . ." Lucas's voice trailed off.

"Yeah, funny thing about that," Finn said. "That's exactly what he did the last time. He almost blew the mission just so he could fight his own private war against the Timekeepers. It wouldn't be out of character for him. I've got this feeling of *dèjá vu* and I don't care for it one bit."

"Well, all this guesswork isn't going to get us anywhere," said Lucas. "We're going to have to find out for sure what the situation is. I think I'd better send Andre back to Paris to see Fitzroy."

Finn shook his head. "No, you go. Besides, I need her here to keep an eye on Marguerite. You could do a better job of convincing Fitzroy to check him out than Andre could. The fact that Mongoose is here and apparently acting like nothing ever happened has me extremely nervous. If we're wrong about him and everything is on the level, you're going to have to make Fitzroy understand that Mongoose is a bad risk. If we're not wrong, then we've got trouble and we're going to need some help."

"I'll leave right away," said Lucas. "I'll get back as quickly as I can, but meanwhile, watch yourself, okay?"

"Count on it," said Finn.

The social pecking order had to be observed, which meant that the invitation of the Prince of Wales had to be accepted first. However, when the prince's invitation was replied to, he responded by saying that he would be most pleased to welcome Sir Percy Blakeney back to his native England officially and that he could think of no finer way to mark the occasion than a shoot at Richmond with a group of boon companions, followed by a housewarming dinner. In this manner, the future King George IV of England invited himself and most of London society to Richmond, which made it incumbent upon Finn to crack the whip in Lucas's absence and personally see to it that the Blakeney estate would be prepared for the invasion.

In a way, it was advantageous for him in that it took up a great deal of his time and Marguerite, as hostess, also had a great many preparations to make. As a result, she and Finn did not see very much of each other during the next several days. Finn did not complain. She made him feel very ill at ease. They hardly spoke to each other beyond the necessary polite exchanges and the strain of it, as well as her obviously growing disenchantment and resentment, was wearing on him. Entertaining the Prince of Wales would naturally mean that anyone who mattered in the proper social circles would be in attendance, which would give Finn an excellent opportunity to establish the character of Sir Percy Blakeney in precisely the manner he intended. It would also provide an excellent opportunity to introduce the Scarlet Pimpernel to England.

Sir Andrew Ffoulkes had returned from France, along with the old Duc de Chalis and his sons. On a trip to London to see Blakeney's solicitors, Finn had a chance to look up Ffoulkes, who had already been briefed by Dewhurst concerning their forthcoming plans. Delaney found Andrew Ffoulkes to be an amiable, easygoing young man in his late twenties, tall and slim with dark hair, a clever look about his angular features, and a charming, deferential manner. Ffoulkes, like Dewhurst, was a wealthy young man, although his personal fortune paled into insignificance when compared to Blakeney's. Ffoulkes kept an elegantly understated suite of apartments in London and it was there that they all met to begin planning out the activities of their creation, the crusader who would shortly become known throughout all of England as the Scarlet Pimpernel.

They began to form their league. Ffoulkes and Dewhurst would, naturally, be the first and senior members, taking their direction from Blakeney. Lucas and Andre would act as their links to Blakeney when he could not contact them himself. Together, the three of them discussed the possibility of recruiting fellow adventurers to their cause.

Dewhurst proposed five members, whose personal qualities and qualifications were discussed at length; Ffoulkes brought up four names. They talked about it late into the night and it was decided that all would make good candidates, providing that they could take direction without question and never be informed of the Pimpernel's true identity.

"All right, then," Finn said, when they had finished for the night, "I suggest that the two of you begin approaching those whom we've agreed upon discreetly and sound them out as to their feelings on this matter. Be very circumspect initially and if you have any doubt as to the degree of their commitment, let the matter go no further. Are we agreed?"

"Agreed," said Ffoulkes.

"Agreed," said Dewhurst.

"Good," said Finn. "In that case, we shall meet again at

Richmond. Confer with de Chalis once again and make certain that he knows what to do. We've made a good beginning, gentlemen. Now let's start gathering momentum."

Andre felt sorry for Marguerite Blakeney. She couldn't help it. Since Lady Blakeney had arrived at Richmond, Andre had been spending a great deal of time with her, both to help keep a distance between her and Finn and to keep track of her so that she would not inadvertently cause any element of the adjustment to go awry.

Although she knew that Marguerite St. Just had been instrumental in sending the Marquis de St. Cyr and all his family to the guillotine, it was difficult to believe that Lady Marguerite Blakeney could have been involved in such a thing. Andre wanted very much to question her about it, but she could not bring herself to do so. For one thing, as a servant, it was not her place. For another, it was not a topic of conversation that could be easily brought up. She had no idea how Lady Blakeney would react if she asked her about St. Cyr and she didn't want to risk doing anything that would interfere with Finn's work in the slightest. She had to keep reminding herself that she was a soldier and that she could not allow her personal feelings to enter into the situation. There was far more at stake than the welfare of one woman.

However, on the other hand, she wished that there was something she could do to ease Lady Blakeney's burden. She herself was far from being unblooded. Andre had killed many men. Sometimes, the cause had been just, but other times, it had not been. Marguerite Blakeney had the blood of a family of French aristocrats upon her hands. When compared to the amount of lives that Andre had taken, it was a small thing, indeed. Andre could not bring herself to feel guilt or to bear blame for anything that she had done, although she had a few regrets. Given that, it was difficult to take the attitude that Marguerite Blakeney deserved no pity for having sent St. Cyr to the block. She did not know the circumstances attending the St. Cyr affair. Perhaps there was a reason, some explanation for why Marguerite had done what she had done. Certainly, it was hard to believe that she could have acted coldly in the matter, without remorse, having condemned an entire family simply because her society had determined that aristocrats were enemies of France. After all, Marguerite St. Just had married an aristocrat, albeit an English one, and now possessed a title herself.

As the wife of a baronet, Marguerite Blakeney was more than entitled to act the part, to treat people of a lesser social class as inferiors, to act as though the servants were nothing but possessions or menial employees, part of the woodwork. But Marguerite was kind and considerate to all the members of the household. Within days after her arrival at the Blakeney estate, she had won the love and unswerving loyalty of all the staff, who went out of their way to see to her comfort and to make her feel welcome. The stablemaster saw to it that she had the gentlest horse and he was thrilled beyond all measure when Marguerite, though vastly inexperienced in such things, came to assist him when one of the mares was throwing a colt. The gamekeeper shyly brought her a baby thrush that had fallen from its nest and helped her nurse it back to health. Within the week, she had learned the Christian names of all the servants and she had made it known to them that if there was anything they needed regarding their own personal matters, they were free to come to her for help. The servants, so far as Andre knew, were ignorant of the part that Marguerite had played in St. Cyr's execution and she was convinced that if they were told of it, they would not believe it. She had a hard time believing it herself.

Andre, perhaps much more than Finn or Lucas, was in a position to understand the fervor of the French revolutionaries. Finn and Lucas had traveled throughout all of time and they had seen the cruelty of the "haves" to the "have-nots," but Andre had lived it. She had been born a peasant, she had been a knight, and she had served a king, or a prince who would have been a king. John of Anjou had been a tyrannical, ruthless ruler and his brother Richard had not been much better. When Richard died and John became the king, his own barons had rebelled against him, forcing him to sign the Magna Carta. From what she had learned of the history of France, the treatment of the French peasantry by the aristocrats was not much different from the way that the invading Normans had treated the Saxons in the time from which she came. Leaving aside the right or wrong of it, Andre could understand why the crowds in Paris cheered each descent of Dr. Guillotin's deadly blade.

In spite of her effort to maintain a personal detachment, Andre's heart went out to Marguerite Blakeney. She was a stranger in a strange land who did not yet know anyone but the servants in her own household, with the sole exception of Lord Antony Dewhurst, whom she had met only once. She had no friends, this woman who had commanded the respect and admiration of the finest minds of Paris, and she believed that she had married a man who no longer loved her. Perhaps, with Percy Blakeney, that had been the case. His love for her might well have died when he found out about St. Cyr; but Blakeney was dead now and Finn Delaney had taken his place. Andre had little doubt about Finn's feelings. They had fought side by side together and they knew each other very well. Perhaps Andre even knew Finn better than he knew himself, despite the fact that he was several lifetimes older than she was.

She knew that Finn Delaney was strongly attracted to Marguerite Blakeney. She had seen the way he looked at her when Marguerite's face was turned away. At first, she had thought that it was merely lust and perhaps at first it was. Marguerite Blakeney was extraordinarily beautiful and Finn Delaney was a rampant specimen of manhood. Andre had often thought of bedding him herself. However, lust was a thing that was easily satisfied and when lust was unrequited, a convenient substitute would often do. Finn displayed none of the distemper of a rutting male. Moreover, he displayed no inclination to redirect his urge. They were close friends as well as comrades in arms and Finn knew well that Andre would be more than willing to give him an outlet for his tension, but that was not the problem.

Perhaps Finn did not love Marguerite, at least, not yet. However, he obviously liked her a great deal. He admired and respected her, and Andre knew that he was having the same difficulty reconciling Marguerite with the St. Cyr affair that Andre was having. She knew that playing the part of an uncaring, alienated husband was having its effect on him. He was finding the role increasingly more difficult to play and they had only been together for a brief length of time. To complicate matters even further, Marguerite perceived a change in her husband, a change beyond the distance that had grown between her and Percy Blakeney before Finn stepped in to take his place. She knew that her husband had become a dif-

ferent man, though she would never know just how literally
true that was.

No amount of research or preparation, even in a case that
was exhaustively detailed, which this one was not, could ever
account for every slightest detail. Even though Marguerite had
not been married to Percy Blakeney for very long, she was still
his wife; prior to becoming his wife, she had been courted by
him for some length of time. It was only inevitable that she
would notice some inconsistencies in the behavior of her husband and Marguerite was at a loss to account for them.

At dinner on the second night of their stay in Richmond, she
had watched with puzzlement as Finn enjoyed three helpings
of roasted chicken and it was not until Finn had finished the
last portion that she remarked upon the fact that he had
always hated chicken, avoiding it because it gave him hives.
Finn had mentioned the matter to Andre afterwards when he
instructed her to stay close to Marguerite and gain her confidence, so that he would be kept informed if he suddenly ex-
hibited any other uncharacteristic behavior. To which end,
Andre was soon able to tell him that Marguerite was mystified
as to why he had taken to wearing a gold eyeglass, when he
had always ridiculed the affectation previously, and that
Marguerite was astonished at his sudden capacity for wine
when he had always partaken of it in moderation before,
claiming that it "gave him quite a head" whenever he had
more than three glasses.

Andre was able to settle her bewilderment in some degree
after discussing it with Finn and arriving upon a suitable
rationalization. As one who had "served Sir Percy since her
childhood," she was the logical person for Marguerite to turn
to with her questions. Andre had explained to Lady Blakeney
that "Sir Percy could be mysteriously changeable." She said
that he had always been given to caprice and that he sometimes devised elaborate justifications for his fancies or dis-
likes. At one time, she said, he grew bored with eating chicken
and so elected to tell everyone it gave him hives, undoubtedly
because it seemed a better reason to abstain from it than a
simple change of taste. The same thing with the wine, she said.
Sir Percy had always been a fine judge of good wine and, as
such, extremely hard to please. In order to avoid giving offense, she said, he often partook sparingly of an inferior vin-
tage, claiming that he had no head for it as an excuse for

avoiding further irritation of his educated palate. As for the eyeglass, she merely shrugged and advanced the theory that perhaps Sir Percy, anxious to make a good impression in London society, thought it made him look "a bit more baronial."

"Sir Percy has always been most concerned about appearances," she told Lady Blakeney. "But then, of course, you would know that very well, my lady."

"Oh, Andre, surely when we speak in confidence like this, you can call me Marguerite," said Lady Blakeney. "After all, you are the only real friend I've made thus far in England."

Andre felt a twinge of conscience at her remark and hesitated briefly before continuing. "Well, Marguerite," she said, "I do not think that there is any reason to concern yourself about Sir Percy's sometimes unpredictable behavior. He is not ill or anything at all like that. Rather, much like his father, he likes to indulge his whims and passing fancies."

"Ah, well," said Marguerite, sitting on her bed and gazing down upon the floor, "I fear that I was such a passing fancy."

"Oh, surely not," said Andre. "Anyone can see that Sir Percy's most devoted to you and that—"

"As you said yourself, Andre," said Marguerite, glancing up at her and smiling a bit sadly, "Percy seems most concerned about appearances. Oh, it's true, he was always so, a scrupulous follower of fashion, always attempting to decry affectation while he himself was so vulnerable to whatever was in style, always striving to be the bon vivant and the witty conversationalist when his attempts at repartee were so pathetic and amusing. You should have seen him at my salon in Paris with the likes of Beaumarchais and Saint-Pierre, valiantly trying to hold his own and floundering in water leagues over his head! None of my friends could understand what I saw in such a fool, but he seemed to worship me with a curious intensity of concentrated passion which went straight to my heart. He waited on me hand and foot and followed me about like an adoring puppy. But all that is over now. I suppose that I was just another of his whims, a passing fancy, a victim of his changeability. He wanted a pretty, clever wife, someone he could show off to his friends and, having attained his goal, now he has lost interest in all save those appearances of which we speak. I am like that chicken. He has grown bored of the taste and all that I can do is wait and hope that one day he will crave it once again. He seems so different now in so many little ways. . . ." Her voice trailed off as she stared out the window at the setting sun.

"Sir Percy is a very busy man," said Andre, feebly. "If it appears that he has little time for you these days—"

"He has *no* time for me these days," said Marguerite. "You are right to defend him, Andre, it is loyal and admirable of you, but the truth is that Percy no longer loves me. How else can I explain the distance which has grown between us, a distance even greater than that which separates his bed from mine? I can think of nothing I have done to deserve such treatment except, perhaps. . . ."

"Except?" said Andre in an attempt to prompt her, knowing that she was on the verge of bringing up St. Cyr.

Marguerite shook her head. "I'm tired, Andre, and I weary you with my self-pity. Go now and let me sleep. I must be at my best tomorrow so that I may charm the Prince of Wales and make my husband the envy of his peers for having such a wife. Be off to bed, now. It will be a busy day for all of us tomorrow."

Andre said good night to her and left the room. She did not completely close the door, but left it open just a crack to listen for a moment. She heard what she expected, the soft sounds of Marguerite Blakeney weeping.

5 ⎯⎯⎯⎯⎯⎯⎯⎯⎯⎯⎯⎯⎯

The Blakeney estate looked like a scene from an historical romance. All day, starting shortly after ten in the morning, guests had been arriving for the festivities. Most came in three main shifts. The earliest arrivals came for the shoot, attired in their finest sporting clothes and bringing with them their guns and servants, as well as a full change of clothing for the evening. Others came in time for high tea in the afternoon, following the shoot. The greatest number came for dinner, which was served promptly at seven.

The grooms were kept busy by the constant stream of coaches and carriages as the cream of London society arrived with their liveried footmen. A parade of richly enameled coaches with gilt trim and coats of arms kept the stablemaster and his charges working throughout the day to see to the comfort and feeding of the horses.

By midafternoon, the grounds of the estate were full of strolling couples, women in silk dresses and velvet robes, their hair elaborately arranged and topped with stylish hats with plumes, which they wore at rakish angles; men in suits of velvet and brocade and silk, richly embroidered and trimmed with lace and gold. Jewelry flashed in the sun, adorning throats and bosoms; in some secluded wooded spots, a few daring couples sported with no clothes at all, the women biting down on handkerchiefs to avoid crying out and drawing attention to their scandalous behavior. A large group stood on the upper terrace, looking down into the maze and laughing and shouting encouragement to those attempting to puzzle out the pathways through the hedges and those few who knew the secret of the urns kept it to themselves, enjoying the befuddlement of their unenlightened friends.

Lord Grenville was in attendance, as was William Pitt. Edmund Burke was one of the late arrivals, coming in time for dinner. His rival in Parliament, Charles James Fox, followed closely on his heels. The Prince of Wales was one of the earlier arrivals and, though he shot poorly that day, he enjoyed himself immensely, taking a liking to the fashionable Sir Percy Blakeney from the start. Sheridan, the playwright and politician, arrived shortly after teatime and began to drink at once. A number of the gentlemen started to take bets to see how long he would remain standing.

The Blakeney staff left nothing to be desired as they worked tirelessly all day. The cooks outdid themselves with basted chicken, roast pheasant, steak and kidney pies, boiled vegetables, small sandwiches, scones, biscuits and plum puddings, fruits and tarts, and gallons upon gallons of wine and stout. There was an orchestra of strings to accompany the dancing after dinner and those much too full for such activity retired to the sitting rooms, where the women and the men congregated separately on either side of the ballroom in their respective parlors, the women chatting, sipping cordials, and playing card games while the men enjoyed their pipes and port.

Beneath a haze of smoke, they puffed on their long clay churchwardens and short clay pocket pipes filled with shag and Latakia. Several of the wealthier guests proudly showed off their meerschaums, which were in great demand but could only be procured by those rich enough to hire skilled carvers to create them. Intricately carved from deposits of hydrous silicate of magnesia, a mineral substance formed by nature from the remains of prehistoric sea creatures, these exquisite pipes were treasured by their owners, who were fond of comparing their abilities to season them. Several of the gentlemen actually had their servants instructed in the proper art of smoking them, so that the pipes could be smoked constantly throughout the day until, after some two hundred bowlfuls or more, they had colored from an alabaster white to a light rosy pink, to a golden yellow and finally to a rich, dark brown. These pipes were as ostentatious as Sir Percy's guests and they

represented the wealth, stature, and fancies of the men who
smoked them. Some were artfully carved into the shapes of
stags being attacked by wolves, others bore the aspect of
hunters and their dogs, nude women and the heads of 17th-
century noblemen. Everywhere there was evidence of pam-
pered luxury and rich indulgence and, in such surroundings, it
was hard to believe that just across the Channel, there were
people starving in the streets of Paris.

Marguerite Blakeney was the instant center of attention, attired elegantly, yet simply in a dress of ivory-colored silk,
which set off her auburn hair and fair complexion to their best
advantage. Her easy manner, her sweet, musical voice, and
her delightful, carefree laugh immediately captivated all the
men, and her graceful charm and open friendliness held off
the envy of the women who had not been so richly blessed by
nature. Everyone admired Sir Percy Blakeney's clever, witty
wife and although they found Sir Percy to be a charming, out-
rageously stylish, and generally decent fellow, they wondered
at the pairing of this bright, elegant French actress and the
vague, inane, and dull-witted peacock who was all plumage
and no substance. The women smiled knowing smiles and said
that Marguerite had married Blakeney for his money, though
not one of them faulted her for making a good match. The
men, especially the younger ones, paid careful attention to the
exaggerated, *incroyable* fashion of his Parisian suit, his droll,
insouciant manner, and his fatuous laugh. In Blakeney, they
saw a proper model to emulate: a man of studied elegance,
good grace, and vapid wit; someone socially companionable,
yet nonthreatening; rich, yet unambitious; gregarious, yet unprepossessing; politic, yet apolitical. In short, a man perfectly
suited to climb to the highest rung of the social ladder and remain there, comfortably perched.

The highlight of the evening, however, occurred when Andrew Ffoulkes arrived, along with Tony Dewhurst, just as
dessert was being served, the timing of their arrival having
been agreed upon between the three of them and prearranged.
They brought with them, of course, the distinguished Duc de
Chalis.

There had been, since the beginning of the French Revolution, a steady stream of French emigrés arriving on the shores
of England. It began, for the most part, in 1790, in the month
of February, when the National Assembly introduced a new

military constitution allowing for conscription and abolishing the purchase of commissions. When, in 1791, the Legislative Assembly replaced the oath of allegiance to the king with a new military oath, the aim being to prevent an army of Royalists that would be in opposition to the Revolution, military officers, most of them noblemen, left France in droves. They were soon followed by civilian aristocrats, who saw the writing on the walls; it thereafter became quite commonplace to hear the king's English being mutilated in drawing rooms throughout all of London and its environs. However, in recent months, when the blood of the *ci-devant* oppressors was needed to fuel revolutionary fervor, the steady stream had become an almost nonexistent trickle and, as a result, the sudden appearance of the Duc de Chalis was an occasion for surprise and speculation.

A murmuring went through the crowd when de Chalis was announced. With all seated at the dining tables, Ffoulkes, Dewhurst and de Chalis at once became the focus of everyone's attention. Surprising as the French aristocrat's arrival was, even more surprising was his announcement that he had only narrowly escaped the guillotine, having received the death sentence from the Committee of Public Safety, and that he and his sons would have been headless corpses had they not been rescued by a daring Englishman.

"Who was this splendid fellow to whose courage we owe the pleasure of your company, good sir?" the Prince of Wales asked.

"I regret to say," said the elderly de Chalis, in perfect although accented English, "that I cannot tell you his name, Your Highness."

"What?" said the prince. "But see here, my dear fellow, we must know the name of this brave chap, so that we may single him out for the accolades which are justly his. This is no time for modesty. England needs her heroes. Tell the fellow to come forth!"

"I am afraid that I have been misunderstood, Your Highness," said the duke. "I did not mean that I *will not* tell you his name, but that I *cannot* tell you his name. It is unknown to me. What is more, I can no more describe him to you and this fine assemblage than I can tell you his name. I have learned that I have never seen his true face."

At this remark, another wave of murmuring swept through

the crowd, but it was brought to a quick halt by the Prince of Wales rapping his hand upon the table for silence.

"But how is this possible, *Monsieur le Duc*? How can this man have rescued you from certain death and you have never seen his face?"

"I have never seen his *true* face, Your Highness," replied de Chalis. "This Englishman is a consummate actor and a master of disguise. I know him only by a curious appellation imparted to me by certain individuals who are in league with him. This man prefers to do his work in secret and it seems that he has set himself the task of saving as many innocent lives from the guillotine as possible. Would that I knew his name and face so I could thank him, for I owe him everything, but all I know of this gallant gentleman is that he calls himself 'the Scarlet Pimpernel.' "

"Say what?" slurred Sheridan, leaning forward drunkenly and fixing his bleary eyes upon the duke. "The Scarlet Pimple, did you say?"

"Oh, *hush*, Richard!" said his dinner partner, an aspiring actress well out of her depth in this society, whose knees had been tightly clamped together throughout all of dinner in order to frustrate Sheridan's groping fingers. She gave him a shove with her elbow, not very hard, but hard enough, considering his state, to topple him from his chair and send him to the floor, where he remained.

A gentleman seated across from him turned to face a friend of his across the table and, indicating the seat vacated by the dramatist, quickly said, "That's five pounds you owe me."

"The Scarlet Pimpernel," said Dewhurst, at the same time motioning the servants to prepare a place for the old Frenchman at the table. "A small, star-shaped red flower, I believe."

"How very fascinating!" said Lord Grenville. "I say, Dewhurst, can you shed any light upon this situation?"

"Only a little, I'm afraid, milord. For the most part, I am as much in the dark about this singular gentleman as are the rest of you. As some of you may know, Percy and I are old acquaintances, having met abroad and spent much pleasurable time together on numerous occasions. Percy was the proud owner of an absolutely splendid yacht, a beauty of a schooner called the *Day Dream*. We had sojourned in the Bay of Biscay aboard that lovely craft and I had determined that I had to have her."

"The Pimpernel, Dewhurst!" said the Prince of Wales. "What of this Scarlet Pimpernel?"

"I'm getting to that, Your Highness," Dewhurst said, beginning to saunter round the table slowly, enjoying his role immensely. He came to the spot where Sheridan had fallen, stepped over him and paused a moment, then picked up the playwright's glass, which was still three-quarters full. "Faith and I believe ole Richard's finished with this glass. Well, waste not, want not." He took a sip, then glanced down at the floor. "I say, Burke, I've heard that Sheridan could really hold the floor in Parliament and now I see that he's adept at holding the floor here, as well."

This sally was greeted with uproarious laughter and Edmund Burke, especially, laughed heartily, pounding on the table and shouting, "Well said, well said!"

"Tony, stop with this nonsense and get on with it!" said William Pitt. "What does Percy's boat have to do with this mysterious Scarlet Pimpernel?"

"A great deal, Bill, a very great deal," said Dewhurst, "and I might add that it is *my* boat, now."

"What?" said Marguerite. "Percy, you sold the *Day Dream* to Tony Dewhurst?"

"Odd's life, m'dear," said Finn, "what do I need with such a boat in London? Sail her upon the Thames? Better employ a racing horse to pull a plough, I say."

"Yes, well, Percy sold the *Day Dream* to me," Dewhurst went on, "and I might add that he was very generous, doubtless anxious to stop my constant pestering of him on that account. Well, gentlemen and ladies, much as I am loath to admit it, I am not much of a sailor, I'm afraid. In fact, I'm not a sailor at all, being quite content to leave such matters in the very capable hands of the *Day Dream*'s Captain Briggs, who had agreed, with Percy's urging, to stay on with his entire crew. However, I suddenly found myself in the situation of a child whose eyes were bigger than his mouth, for when I sat down with Briggs and became acquainted with the amount needed for the upkeep of the *Day Dream*, I was somewhat taken aback. I mean, what do I know of such things as hauling, painting, scraping, caulking, and so on? Though I am not known for being frugal, I could see that I had acquired a most expensive toy. Therefore, when Briggs informed me that he had been approached by an agent acting for some gentleman with regard to hiring the *Day Dream* for the purpose of bringing some goods over from France, I was quite agreeable. After all, a toy that pays for its own upkeep is considerably more attractive than one which slowly bleeds its owner dry.'' He chuckled. "As Ffoulkes here, an experienced sailor, told me, a boat is nothing more than a hole in the water into which money is poured.''

There was some laughter at this, but clearly, the audience was growing impatient to hear about this Scarlet Pimpernel.

"And so I agreed to hire out the *Day Dream*, so long as I was not using her," said Dewhurst. "Well, imagine my surprise when I discovered that the goods brought over from France were the Duc de Chalis and his family! Briggs passed on a note to me, signed with this star-shaped flower, begging me, as a man of some position, to use my influence to help the Duc de Chalis and his sons begin anew in England and to pardon the slight deception in the name of freedom and humanity! What is more, I have learned that the moment that our new arrivals here set foot on English soil, a note, signed with that very star-shaped flower, had been delivered to Citizen Fouquier-Tinville, the public prosecutor, informing him that the guillotine had been cheated of three victims and that this was only the beginning!''

There was spontaneous applause at this and it took some time for the tumult to die down before Dewhurst could continue.

"Well, needless to say, my friends, not only was I astounded at the daring of this adventurer who is unknown to me, but I was humbled by his dedication to the principles that we all, as Englishmen, hold to be so dear. This Scarlet Pimpernel, as he calls himself, is a sterling example to us all. I know not who he is, nor do I know why he has chosen to cloak himself in secrecy, but I do know this: I am proud that, in some small measure, I was able to assist him. I have instructed Briggs that in the event he should be approached once more in a similar regard, he is to return in full the fee paid for the hiring of the *Day Dream* and make the boat available at any time for this Scarlet Pimpernel, to use as he sees fit, with my most sincere compliments, for further daring rescues! Ffoulkes, here, has consented to join me in doing everything in my power to make those rescued by this gallant at home in England and I urge all of you here this night to join me in a toast to this courageous man and to lend him your support! Gentlemen," he said, raising his glass high, "I give you the Scarlet Pimpernel!"

They all rose as one, with their glasses held aloft, and echoed the toast.

"The Scarlet Pimpernel!"

God damn, thought Finn. Too bad we can't recruit this character into the corps. He'd be a natural. They all drank the toast and sat back down to engage in animated discussion and interrogation of the Duc de Chalis. The remainder of the evening was taken up with speculation concerning the Scarlet Pimpernel. Dewhurst and de Chalis could not have played their roles any better. The unknown Englishman had instantly captured everyone's imagination.

After dinner, many of the guests went dancing in the ballroom, but a large group of gentlemen congregated in the parlor, there to smoke their pipes and sample the bottled fruit of Blakeney's cellar while they discussed what went on across the Channel and, in particular, the involvement of the unknown Englishman in the rescue of French aristocrats.

Edmund Burke took advantage of the situation to launch into a heady polemic concerning his opinions on the revolt in France. Finn lit up his pipe and sidled up to Dewhurst, speaking not quite quietly enough to avoid being overheard.

"What's he on about, I wonder?" he said, in a somewhat bored tone.

Sheridan, who had regained consciousness and, though unsteady on his feet, seemed intent on draining Blakeney's cellar dry, heard him and lurched over to them.

"He's on about the Revolution once again," he said unevenly. "I've heard this dreary song before in Parliament. Though he seems to have committed it to memory, it doesn't get much better with repeat performances."

Burke, meanwhile, was gaining steam in his diatribe against the leaders of the Republic.

"It is right that these men should hide their heads," he said, vehemently. "It is right that they should bear their part in the ruin which their counsel has brought on their sovereign and their country. They have seen the medicine of the state corrupted into its poison! They have seen the French rebel against a mild and lawful monarch! Their resistance was made to concession; their revolt from protection; their blow aimed at a hand holding out graces, favors, and immunities!''

Sheridan belched loudly and Burke shot him a venomous look.

"I say, Burke," said Finn, "that was a most torrential outburst. I am truly awed by the fervor of your oratory. Would that I could speak with such a passion. Is there, then, no hope for France at all?"

"None, if they continue on their present course," said Burke, grasping his lapels and puffing himself up. "People will not look forward to posterity who never look backward to their ancestors."

"True, true," said Finn, putting on a thoughtful look. "If we English look backward to *our* ancestors, we will find them running about with their arses hanging out and painted blue. Faith and we've come a long way since then, eh, what? What with such humble beginnings, think what posterity lies ahead for us!"

For a moment, there was total silence as everyone stared at him uncertainly. Burke looked totally bewildered, but a smile began to twitch at the corner of Sheridan's mouth and the playwright hid it with his hand.

"France, my dear Blakeney," Burke said, in an effort to get things back on track, "has bought poverty by crime. You've just returned from Paris; surely you must agree that France has not sacrificed her virtue to her interest, but rather she has abandoned her interest that she might prostitute her virtue."

"Odd's life, that may well be," said Finn. "I've had my estate in Rouen seized for the purposes of securing needed revenue for the new French government. A bad business for me, I'm afraid, though an advantageous one for them. It might well be in France's interest to prostitute her virtue if she makes such gains by it. I've known not a few demimondaines who have rebuilt their crumbling virtue in a like manner."

Sheridan started coughing, but Burke seemed totally at sea. He gazed at Finn in complete astonishment.

"As for this Pimpernel fellow whom everyone seems so concerned about," Finn continued blithely, "I cannot flaw him for his boldness or idealism, but given all the bloodletting being done across the water, rescuing one or two aristocrats would seem like pissing in the wind, no? Still, I do wish the fellow well and I only hope that the French navy does not learn of Dewhurst's part in all of this, else they might well try to sink his newly purchased boat. Though, in truth, I doubt that they have any craft that would be capable of catching her.''

"As for that," said Dewhurst, with a grin, "if the French did sink the *Day Dream*, it would relieve me of the expense of maintaining her! However, you're quite right, Percy, there is a certain amount of risk in lending aid to this Scarlet Pimpernel. Yet, any risk *I* may incur is nothing compared to the risks that he must take. I admit that there might be some risk for me, but what is life without an element of risk? Nothing but mere existence. If you ask me, gentlemen, this Pimpernel fellow is a true sportsman! I can think of nothing quite so game as playing leapfrog with the French and thumbing your nose at Danton, Robespierre, and the entire bunch of them!"

"There is much more than sport involved in this affair, young Dewhurst," Burke said, stiffly. "We cannot afford to merely thumb our noses at the French. This Revolution of theirs is a plague and the precautions of the most severe quarantine ought to be established against it!"

"Begad, that was well said," said Finn. "You know, Burke, someone told me tonight that when you rise to speak in Parliament, your fellow members are moved to go out to dinner. I can well see why, since such passionate invective must do a great deal to stimulate the juices! It is fortunate for us, gentlemen, that we've already eaten. As it is, such fine speech ought to do great wonders for our digestion."

There were chuckles at Finn's remarks, though they were quickly stifled. Burke had gone red in the face, but Finn had a look of such guileless stupidity upon his face that the politician could think of no way to reply. Out of the corner of his eye, Finn could see that Sheridan was biting on his finger in an effort to keep from laughing. Later on, the playwright drew him to one side, in a corner somewhat removed from all the general discussion.

"See here, Blakeney," Sheridan said, speaking thickly and swaying from side to side, "I have not yet quite decided what to make of you. You seem to be a male Mrs. Malaprop at times, and yet I see a bit of Swift in you, I think. You seem to be laughing up your sleeve."

Finn affected a look of puzzlement. "I'm not at all sure what you mean, old fellow. Truthfully, I'd never laugh at any guests of mine, though I must admit that your rendition of the dying swan at dinner was a bit amusing. I'm afraid that I don't get your meaning."

Sheridan stared at him for a moment. "I think you do, Blakeney. Yes, I think you do. I don't know if you pricked Burke on purpose or if it was just a happy circumstance of all your rambling babble, but you've roused my curiosity. Tell me, what is your *real* feeling concerning the revolt in France and this Scarlet Pimple, or whatever his name is?"

"My *real* feeling?" Finn said, raising his eyebrows. "Begad, my real feeling is that I'm glad to be out of it! The climate in Paris is decidedly unhealthy at this time of year. I'm happy that de Chalis has seen fit to seek a change of weather. Doubtless he will live longer. As for any others who choose to follow his example, I can only wish them bon voyage and hope that they encounter no difficulties in making their travel plans."

"Indeed," said Sheridan. "And what of this Pimpernel chap?"

"Well, I'm sure I don't know what to think of him," said Finn. "He seems like quite a bold and dashing fellow, destined to be all the rage of London. He's already won the hearts of Ffoulkes and Dewhurst and, I'll wager, of most of the women here tonight. What do *you* think of him, Sheridan?"

"I think he's a monumental fool who'll get his head chopped off," said Sheridan, adding a belch for punctuation. "But I must admit that I admire his pluck."

"Perhaps you'll write a play about him," Finn said.

"Not I," said Sheridan. "His tale is the stuff of romantic fiction for women to sigh over in their drawing rooms. Besides, he has only just begun his mad career and chances are it will be cut short by the public prosecutor's blade."

"That would be a pity," Finn said.

"Aye, it would. I wouldn't even have enough material for my first act."

By midnight, the guests had all departed. Marguerite went up to bed, exhausted. Ffoulkes and Dewhurst were the last to leave, along with old de Chalis, who quietly told Finn that if there was ever anything that he could do for him, he had but to ask. When they had gone, one of the servants came up to Finn and handed him an envelope.

"What's this?" said Finn.

"One of the guests told me to give this to you after everyone had gone, milord," the servant said.

Finn tensed. "Who was it?"

"I don't know, milord. A gentleman."

"What did he look like?"

The young man shrugged. "He looked like a gentleman, milord."

Finn frowned. "Never mind. That will do. Go on about your duties."

He opened up the note. It was short and to the point. It said, "*The maze, at one o'clock.*" It was unsigned, but Finn knew who it was from.

The house seemed strangely empty now that all the guests had left. As Finn walked back into the reception hall, the heels of his shoes made sharp echoing sounds that filled the spacious room, which only a short while ago resounded with laughter, boisterous conversation, and violin music. It was a lovely way to live, Finn thought. It might be very pleasant to spend the next several years as Sir Percy Blakeney, if it wasn't for the fact that his lifespan could be drastically curtailed by some error he had yet to make.

There was still some time before one o'clock. Finn quickly went up to his rooms and changed out of his elegant, cream-colored suit, dressing in black riding clothes and boots, the better to blend in with the darkness. Just to be on the safe side, he tucked a short dagger into his belt and took along a polished ebony sword cane with a heavy, solid silver head.

It was chilly and a mist had settled on the grounds. His boots made slight crunching sounds upon the gravel path as he walked around to the side of the house, his crackling steps a percussive counterpoint to the chirping of the crickets. He stepped off the path and onto the grass, heading for the elaborately arranged rows of perfectly trimmed hedges, eight feet high and four feet thick. There was no evidence of any other human presence about save for himself.

It occurred to him that the setting was perfectly suited for a trap. In the darkness, with the tall hedges all around him, it would be virtually impossible to see anything. Finn had good night vision, but the visibility was limited as a result of the darkness and the mist. The thought that somewhere nearby would be a man trained at least as well as he was made him move slowly and cautiously as he entered the maze. Lucas had shown him how the placement of the urns indicated which turn to take. The benches were positioned so that the urns could only be seen from the correct paths, the view of them being otherwise blocked by the benches. Obviously, Mongoose knew this trick as well, else why choose the maze for a meeting place?

Moving with stealth, Finn made his way to the grassy square at the center of the maze. He could make out the ghostly white benches placed around the perimeter of the square, but not much else. He wished he had been issued night glasses, but the fact that he lacked such equipment did not mean that Mongoose would be equally at a disadvantage. Still, there was nothing else to do but sit down upon a bench and wait until Mongoose made his move. Finn waited nervously in the darkness, listening to the chirping of the crickets. At a little after one o'clock, he heard a faint sound of movement close by and then a familiar voice called out, softly, "Delaney?"

"I'm right here," he said. "What's the matter, can't you see me?"

There was a chuckle that seemed to come from only a few yards away, but Finn could not accurately gauge the direction or the distance.

"Nice try, Delaney, but I happen to know that you weren't issued night glasses. The only thing they gave you was a hypo ring, which just goes to show you how paranoid they're getting."

"Where are you?"

"Nearby," Mongoose replied. He chuckled once more. "Where's Priest? I didn't see him at the party."

"He's around," Finn lied. "I didn't see you, either. But then, the way you keep changing your appearance, I wouldn't have recognized you anyway. What's your face look like these days? The last time I saw you, it had been rearranged a bit."

The brief silence told Finn that he had scored a hit with his reference to the torture that had disfigured Mongoose.

"Well, we both look a bit different these days, don't we?" Mongoose said. Finn realized that he was moving as he spoke. He seemed to be just outside the center of the maze now, in one of the paths between the hedgerows. Walking softly, Finn moved in the direction of his voice. "I see you've got de la Croix with you," Mongoose continued. "Oh, yes, that's right, it's Private Cross now, isn't it? Well, it appears to be quite a reunion, all of us back together once again."

"It must be kismet," Finn said. "After the way you bungled your last mission, I thought they'd never let you near a field assignment again. Yet here you are. What a surprise." Finn turned down another pathway, his eyes straining to penetrate the mist and darkness. "I heard you were busted down to desk jockey. Seems to me you were pretty lucky to get even that."

"I wasn't meant to be a glorified clerk, Delaney," Mongoose said, with an edge to his voice. "Having me sitting behind a console was a sinful waste of talent and ability."

"Your talent and ability almost got you killed last time," said Finn, moving closer. "If it hadn't been for us, Adrian Taylor would have vivisected you."

"Perhaps," said Mongoose. "Who's to say how it might have turned out without your interference? You may have saved my life, in which case I suppose I should be grateful, but you also ruined my career. I realize that the one shouldn't cancel out the other, but somehow it seems to. You'll pardon me if I don't seem properly appreciative."

"Why don't we cut out this kids' game, Mongoose?" Finn said. "Come out and show yourself."

"I'm afraid I'm not quite ready to do that just yet," Mongoose said. "You see, we really have no basis for trust in this relationship. I know you've sent Priest to see Fitzroy. I just came from there. They didn't see me, of course, but I saw them. The funny thing is, I really was your contact. We could have worked together, had you chosen to, but Fitzroy will obviously have me checked out. To tell the truth, I expected it. He's served his purpose, however. It really doesn't matter. The only thing you have accomplished is adding more spice to the game."

Slowly, noiselessly, Finn slid the sword blade out of the cane. Mongoose sounded very close now, just on the opposite side of the hedge, separated from him by about four feet of bush.

"It was really very boring in evaluations," Mongoose said.

"It was a dead end for me. There was no challenge. This way—"

Finn plunged the sword deeply through the hedge, following it with the length of his entire arm. He heard Mongoose gasp.

"Very good, Delaney! But not good enough."

Finn heard the sound of running footsteps. Cursing, he pulled the sword back out of the hedge and took off at a sprint, brushing his hand against the hedge as he ran to feel for the next gap in the bushes. He reached it, plunged through, made a quick right turn and ran down the path after Mongoose, his sword held out before him. Mongoose was running for the exit and there was only one way to get out of the maze, beyond which the grounds were open for several hundred yards.

Finn came to a bench, noticed the placement of the urn, and turned down the path to the left. A right turn, another left . . . and he came to a dead end, running right into a leafy wall blocking off the pathway. Startled, he was confused for a moment until he realized that Mongoose must have moved the urns as he entered the maze behind him. He ran back the way he came, this time taking the "wrong" turns. He came to a dead end again.

"*Son of a bitch!*" he swore. Mongoose had only moved some of the urns. But which ones had he moved? It took him almost a half an hour to find the exit. By that time, Mongoose was long gone. Finn stood at the entrance to the maze, breathing hard. Except for the sounds of the crickets and his own labored breathing, he couldn't hear a thing.

Thick fog obscured the grounds. He felt the tip of the blade. It was wet with blood.

6 ─────────────────────

At breakfast the following morning, one of the servants came in with a message from the head gardener, warning Sir Percy and Lady Marguerite against going walking in the maze that morning. It seemed that one of the guests had decided to play a prank the previous night and had moved a number of the urns. The gardener promised that he would have it all set straight by the afternoon.

"Wouldn't surprise me if it was that Sheridan chap," said Finn. "He seemed quite exuberant last night. Well, then, my dear," he said in a casual manner, "what did you think of the cream of London society?"

"I am more concerned as to what they thought of me," Marguerite replied, evasively. "I hope, for your sake, that I made a favorable impression last night."

"To be sure, you simply bowled them over," Finn said. "No doubt, you'll be receiving a great many invitations now and I'll be forced to follow you from ball to ball like an attendant."

"As it happens, I've already been invited to a tea at Lady Bollingbrook's," said Marguerite. "It's for ladies only, Percy, so you will be spared the agony of having to attend. That is, if you have no objection to my going?"

"Object? Begad, why should I? You must go, of course. Otherwise, Lady What's-her-name might take offense. When is this tea to take place?"

"This afternoon."

"Ah, well, you see? It works out perfectly. I have certain business matters that require my attention today and I was afraid that you would be left with nothing at all to do other than staying at Richmond and wallowing in boredom. Far better for you to go to this Lady Something-or-other's and cultivate some friendships."

"Then I shall go," said Marguerite, quietly. "I wouldn't want to interfere with any of your plans."

"Well now, if you're having tea in London, you can't possibly be in my way then, can you?" Finn said jauntily. "For that matter, my being absent will enable you to enjoy yourself without having to suffer my sad attempts at witty conversation. It works out well for all concerned."

"Yes, I suppose it does," said Marguerite, without looking at him.

The arrival of Lucas forestalled any further conversation, much to Finn's relief. Lucas said that he had brought an urgent message from Percy's solicitors in London and they withdrew, leaving Lady Blakeney to finish eating breakfast alone. Andre was summoned and the three friends went into one of the smaller parlors. They closed and locked the doors after themselves.

"I'm really beginning to feel terrible about the way I'm forced to treat that lady," Finn said.

Lucas glanced at him sharply. "You start caring about her, Finn, and it's going to get very rough on you," he said. "Remember, she sent a whole family to the guillotine. You're not getting involved with her, are you?"

Andre watched Finn closely, but said nothing.

"No, of course not," Finn said. "Only . . . well, forget it. What happened with Fitzroy?"

Lucas picked up a glass from a silver tray upon the table and poured himself some port from the decanter. He looked tired.

"I didn't get much rest," he said. "I signaled Fitzroy as soon as I got to Calais and he came out to meet me. He wanted to know why I didn't go through channels and use our contact over here." He smiled, wryly. "I told him. Fitzroy had never heard of Mongoose. Our contact in England is supposed to be an Observer named Captain Jack Carnehan. Carnehan's description matches that of the groom who gave me that note from Mongoose, the same groom whom no one else around here seems to have seen," he added.

"How did Major Fitzroy react?" said Andre.

"He didn't take it very well," said Lucas. "He had to check it out, of course. He clocked out ahead and made a routine inquiry and, not surprisingly, discovered that there is no officer in the Observer Corps named Jack Carnehan. At that point, he immediately contacted the TIA, thinking that they were involved in this mission and that he hadn't been informed. The new director, Allendale, assured him that such was not the case and insisted that we had made a mistake. When Fitzroy told him about the ersatz Capt. Carnehan, Allendale ran a check on Mongoose. The records had him listed as inactive, on medical leave. Fitzroy insisted that Allendale check in with Darrow, as well as agent Cobra. Cobra was unavailable for some reason, but Allendale set up a secure-line conference with Darrow, just to mollify Fitzroy. Darrow told him that Mongoose had been given medical leave following his last mission in the field, but that he had returned to active duty shortly thereafter, which so far coincides with what we already know. If Mongoose had been given medical leave again, said Darrow, it happened after his resignation and he wasn't aware of the circumstances.

"Allendale wanted to know why Mongoose had been removed from the field duty roster. Darrow was a bit stiff about that, but he did say that it was all a matter of record and he was surprised that Allendale had to ask. The reason he had to ask, as it turned out, is that Mongoose had the records altered. He managed to transfer himself out of evaluations and then place himself on medical leave, so that he would not be missed. Then—get this—he forged departure tags for himself under the name of Lieutenant Vasily Rurik. The *real* Lt. Rurik is on medical leave from the Observers, recovering from wounds sustained on duty during an arbitration action in the 20th century. Mongoose had access to his records when he was in evaluations. He assumed Rurik's identity, requisitioned a chronoplate for the purpose of Observer duty in the War of the First Coalition, clocked out, and promptly disappeared."

Finn nodded. "He bypassed the tracer functions on the plate, showed up here, and reported to Fitzroy as Carnehan. Fitzroy gave him a full briefing on the mission status, naturally. The guy's got nerve, I'll hand him that. He showed up last night."

"You *saw* him?" Lucas said.

"Not exactly. I had a note delivered to me, telling me to meet him in the maze at one o'clock."

"Why didn't you tell me?" Andre interrupted.

"Because you went up to attend Marguerite and that was where I wanted you. For all I knew, the note was just a ruse to get me out of the house. I wish I had told you, but it's too late to cry about that now. I never saw Mongoose. We spoke, but he kept out of sight. I managed to get close enough to stick him through the hedge with a sword cane, but I think I only grazed him. He ran and I tried to follow, but he'd switched all the urns around and by the time I found my way out of that blasted maze, he was long gone. I should have remembered the sequence of the turns," he said to Lucas.

"You should have told me," Andre said, angrily. "I could have waited for him outside the maze. You let him escape, just because you didn't trust me enough to—"

"I'm sure that isn't true," said Lucas. "Still, that wasn't very smart, Finn. Suppose we were wrong about him and he was on the level?"

Finn shook his head. "He told me that he wasn't. Besides, if he was on the level, why didn't he show himself? No, when he saw that I wasn't buying his story, he made it clear that he was acting on his own. He knew I sent you to Fitzroy. He said he saw you with him in Paris."

"What's he want?" said Lucas. "Did he say anything at all about why he did it?"

"From what little he did say," Finn replied, "it's my impression that this is some sort of last fling for him. He knew he had reached a dead end in evaluations and rather than go crazy sitting behind a desk all day, he decided to go crazy on the Minus Side." Finn sighed. "I don't know what the hell he wants. He's out to prove something, I don't know."

Lucas shook his head. "If he really thinks he can get away with what he's done, he's crazier than I thought. In any case, we've got specific orders as far as he's concerned. We're to keep our hands off him unless he does something that actively endangers the adjustment. Don't ask me how we're supposed to define that, I haven't the faintest idea. Allendale is sending a TIA team back to bring him in. He wants him alive, both to make an example of him and to find out how he managed to screw around with the records. Darrow's in for it, too, because he was soft on him and didn't bust him out of the agency.''

"So much for not having the spooks underfoot," said Delaney. "I knew this mission was too good to be true. It was too easy."

"So far, at least," said Lucas. "It's about to get a bit more difficult. Fitzroy's got orders for us. It's time for the Scarlet Pimpernel to make a trip to Paris. Think of something to tell Marguerite and get hold of Ffoulkes and Dewhurst. We have to leave this evening."

"Who's the target?" Finn said.

"The Marquis de Leforte," said Lucas. "Not a very nice man, by all accounts. Treated the peasants as if they were less than animals, so consequently they'd like very much to kill him now that he's vulnerable."

"How's Blakeney supposed to find him?" Andre said.

"That shouldn't be too difficult," said Lucas. "Leforte's in the Bastille. He's already been tried and condemned to death." He smiled, mirthlessly. "All we have to do is get him out."

"Get him out of the Bastille?" Finn said. *"How?"*

"That's what I asked Fitzroy," said Lucas. "His answer was, 'I'm sure you'll think of something. After all, Blakeney did.' ''

It was four o'clock in the morning and Finn and Lucas stood in the street, looking up at the north tower of the Bastille. Andre, under protest, had stayed behind with Marguerite. She hadn't liked it, but they had made her understand that her job was just as important as theirs; perhaps more so. Someone had to watch Marguerite while they were gone, to make certain that Mongoose didn't try anything with regard to her. They had no idea what he intended to do and they couldn't afford to take any chances.

They had a plan of the Bastile, thanks to Fitzroy, and they knew where the Marquis de Leforte was being held. He was imprisoned in the north tower, in cell number 106. But knowing where he was and getting him out were two very different things. One was a *fait accompli*, the other seemed impossible.

Dewhurst was waiting for them on board the *Day Dream*, which lay at anchor off Boulogne-sur-Mer. Ffoulkes was in that seaside town, about twenty miles from Calais, awaiting their arrival. Several newly recruited members of the League of the Scarlet Pimpernel were in a small apartment in Paris, awaiting instructions from their leader. Everything was in a state of readiness. Now all they needed was a plan.

"I'm open to suggestions," Finn said, wryly. "We've got exactly eight hours before Leforte's due to be executed. You got any ideas?"

"Yeah," said Lucas. "I say we go find Fitzroy and threaten to disembowel him unless he gets us some equipment. With the right stuff, we could walk right in there and take him out."

"A couple of AR-107's would be real nice," said Finn.

"I was thinking along somewhat less lethal lines," said Lucas. "Like, some nose filters and a few gas grenades, real basic stuff. Just put everyone in there to sleep, Leforte included, and walk in, open up his cell and carry the poor bastard out."

"Fitzroy won't play, huh?"

Lucas took a deep breath and let it out slowly. "No, he won't play. According to history, at least so far as TIA intelligence has determined, Blakeney got him out."

"I don't suppose Blakeney had any gas grenades," said Finn. "Did the TIA tell us how he did it?"

"Unfortunately, there's no record of that," said Lucas. "All they were able to learn, according to Fitzroy, is that Leforte was captured trying to sneak out of Paris dressed as an old woman, thrown in the Bastille, tried, condemned, but never executed. The Scarlet Pimpernel took credit for his escape, by sending one of those notes of his to the public prosecutor. It would've been nice if they could have clocked back to see how it was done, but Blakeney's already dead. However it was done, we're going to have to be the ones to do it."

"Sure would be nice if we could hop on a plate and jump ahead a few hours so we could see how we did it," Finn said. "But then, we'd have to do it first before we could see how it was done. Ain't temporal physics wonderful?"

"It's times like these that make me wish I'd kept my lab job," Lucas said.

"It's times like these that make me wish I'd stayed in the regular army," Finn said. "But then, if I had, I'd probably be dead by now. So much for the old 'what ifs.' We'd better come up with something fast, partner."

"I'm agreeable," said Lucas. "What did you have in mind?"

"Beating the living daylights out of Fitzroy, stealing his plate, knocking out the tracer circuits, and going to Barbados."

"We'll save that as a last resort, okay?" Lucas said. "Come on, we've been in tougher spots than this. Let's work it out."

"Okay. Let's take it one step at a time. What are the odds of our getting in there and taking Leforte out between now and sunrise?"

"Not very good," said Lucas. "These new citizens have become very conscious of their new positions. If anyone's got any business being in there, they're known to the guards. It's like an 'old boy' network. It's doubtful that we could bluff our way in and if we tried to force our way in without the right equipment, we'd have a whole garrison down on us before we got halfway up the tower."

"Okay, so forget storming the Bastille," said Finn. "That leaves us with the option of trying to take him when they bring him out."

"Which should be anytime between ten o'clock and noon tomorrow, when he's scheduled to be executed," Lucas said. "They'll bring him down into the courtyard in the prison, put him in a tumbrel, and take him out under guard along the most direct route to the Place de la Révolution. The entire route should be packed with spectators, since Leforte is so well loved. That means that the tumbrel won't be going very fast."

Finn nodded. "I'd guess a little faster than a walking pace, just to give everyone a chance to spit at the marquis. If we're going to put the snatch on him, it'll have to be then, somewhere between the Place de la Révolution and here."

Lucas pursed his lips thoughtfully. "The crowd's going to be the main problem," he said. "We won't be able to seize control of the cart and drive him away, because we'll never make it through the crowd. If we try to pull him out of the tumbrel, they'll tear us to pieces before we can go several yards."

"Scratch that idea," Finn said. "That leaves us the Place de la Révolution. The crowd's going to be thicker there than anywhere else along the route."

"That could work for us," said Lucas. "They'll be at a fever pitch by the time Leforte gets there. What we need is mass hysteria, confusion. Something to drive them crazy enough so that they'll be running in all directions. If we can create some kind of a diversion in the square, we might be able to grab Leforte and get lost in the crowd. All we need to do is to get him out of that square. Then we can take him to the safehouse, knock him out with that trick ring of yours, and have Fitzroy clock us to Boulogne-sur-Mer. But we'll need something to disguise Leforte until we can get him out of the square."

"No big deal," said Finn. "We can throw a shawl and a cloak over him. Now all we need to do is figure out some sort of a diversion. How about a fire?"

"It would be risky," Lucas said. "We don't want to get anyone killed inadvertently."

"We can take steps to minimize that possibility," said Finn. "Don't forget, we've got some extra manpower. We've got league members Barrett, Moore, Smythe-Peters and the Byrne brothers standing by. All we have to do is pick a likely building, get one of the boys to start a small fire that'll make a lot of smoke, then torch the place but good. We'll need a healthy blaze to steal the show. There's enough time to pick a site, get instructions to the boys, and start them off making Molotov cocktails. It should do the trick."

"I hope so," Lucas said. "Well, I can't think of a better idea at the moment, anyway. Come on, let's pick our spot."

At ten-thirty in the morning, Leforte's jailors opened up his cell and led the stunned marquis downstairs to the courtyard of the Bastille. The aristocrat had not slept at all that night. He spent what he believed to be his last night on earth praying. A man who had never paid more than lip service to religion, Leforte found faith in the last hours of his life. He had no hope, none whatsoever. He knew only too well how much the people hated him and how justified that hate was; he knew that he could expect no mercy. He had known it when they had arrested him, just as he thought that he was going to make good his escape. Ironically, on the day before he was scheduled to die, he had learned that the man who was responsible for his arrest would soon be following him up the steps leading to the guillotine. One of the guards had told him that Sergeant Bibot had also been thrown into a cell in the north tower, for allowing the Duc de Chalis to escape. The guard, a blood-thirsty old peasant, had found the irony amusing, but the fact that Bibot was to die brought little comfort to Leforte. Instead of dwelling on the thought that the man who had brought him to this fate would share it, Leforte thought about de Chalis, an old man who had won his freedom. It seemed monstrously unfair. De Chalis was in the twilight of his years; he could not have long to live. Leforte was thirty-seven and in the prime of life.

He had been very much afraid, but now the fear had spent itself. Leforte felt numb. He found that singularly puzzling. Over and over, he kept thinking to himself, "I'm going to die. Why don't I feel anything?"

They put him in the tumbrel, a crude, two-wheeled wooden cart, and a small escort of soldiers of the Republic formed up on either side. The driver, who reeked of garlic, looked at him only once, dispassionately spat upon his shirt, then turned his back on him and flapped the reins up and down several times to get the horses moving. The tumbrel moved forward with a jerk, going through the gate with Leforte as its sole piece of human cargo. The marquis took a deep and shuddering breath, resolving that he would not give the peasants the satisfaction of seeing him cower in fear. In point of fact, he was not afraid. He had accepted death with a deep despondency and he had run the gamut of all possible emotions. There was nothing left.

I will go to my death with dignity, he thought. To the very end, I will show this rabble that I am better than they are.

The street was lined with people. He was surprised to see how many of them had turned out to see him off. The noise was deafening. They laughed, they screamed, they jeered and rushed the tumbrel, trying to grab a piece of his clothing, to touch him, strike him, spit upon him, or throw garbage at him. They followed the tumbrel as it proceeded down the street toward the Place de la Révolution and the soldiers made only the most token efforts to hold them back. The cart turned down another street and an old woman tried to clamber up onto the tumbrel. Leforte stared through her as she screamed unintelligibly at him. One of the soldiers pulled her off the cart, then turned to look at Leforte with a mixture of disgust and irritation. A hole appeared in the middle of the soldier's forehead.

Leforte stared at it and frowned. The cart lurched forward and the soldier fell, being left behind as the procession continued. Puzzled, Leforte turned around to stare at the fallen soldier and then another soldier fell. This time, he heard the shot. Almost immediately, another shot rang out and the driver pitched forward off the tumbrel to fall in a lifeless heap upon the street. Another shot, another soldier fell.

The mob went wild.

"What the hell?" said Finn. "Someone's picking off the soldiers!"

"Did you tell them to—"

"I didn't tell them to shoot anybody!" Finn said. "They're not even supposed to be here! I sent word to them to wait in the square until Leforte arrived!"

All around them, the crowd was surging in all directions as people ran in panic from the shooting, shoving each other and trampling those unfortunate enough to have lost their balance in the melee and to have fallen. Only one soldier remained from the small squad assigned to escort the Marquis de Leforte, and he had no desire to join the others. He dropped his musket and ran for the shelter of a building across the street. The horses, wearing blinders and by now long used to such cacophany, remained standing where they were, but they sensed the fear around them and pawed at the cobblestones skittishly. Leforte stood in the tumbrel helplessly, his hands bound, not knowing what to do.

"Up there," said Lucas, pointing to a window on the second floor of a house across the street.

"Let's go," said Finn.

They pushed their way through the mob and rushed toward the house from which the shots were coming. By now, however, they were not the only ones who had marked the room on the second floor and they made it through the doorway of the house just ahead of several other men, one of whom was brandishing a pistol. The door to the room they sought was open and they all burst into the room to find not a gunman, but a small boy of about twelve or thirteen years with jet black hair and piercing dark eyes. He sat slumped against the wall beside a man's corpse and as they entered, he began to cry.

"My father!" he wailed. "That man killed my father!"

At the same moment, a cry went up outside and they heard the sound of horses hooves upon the cobblestones. One of the men who had rushed into the room behind them ran over to the window, with Lucas just behind him.

"It's Leforte!" the man shouted. "Leforte is escaping!"

As Lucas reached the window, he saw the tumbrel being driven down the street at a furious pace, the horses being whipped up by the same old woman who had only moments ago tried to climb up into the cart.

"Stop him!" cried the man, leaning far out of the window. "Stop him, he's getting away!"

The boy kept wailing about his dead father. The men who had rushed up into the room behind Finn and Lucas ran back outside, after the one armed with the pistol let off a wild shot in the direction of the escaping tumbrel. Finn and Lucas remained behind with the boy.

Lucas kneeled down beside him, putting one hand on the youngster's head. "What happened, son?" he said.

"My father," sobbed the boy, "that man came in here and killed my father!"

"*What* man?"

"He killed my father!" the boy wailed. "He killed him! Then he hit me and said that if I made any noise, he would kill me, too!"

Finn bent down over the father's body. "Shot through the head," he said. "From behind." He stood up. "Look here," he said, as Lucas tried to comfort the boy. He pointed to a pair of pistols lying on the floor beneath a table by the windowsill. "He had several pistols, already loaded. That's how he was able to shoot so quickly. There's only two here, I figure he had at least two or three others. He heard us coming up the stairs, grabbed up the pistols that he could carry, jumped through the window down into the street, and lost himself in the crowd while his confederate made off with the tumbrel."

"You don't think that one of—"

Finn held a finger to his lips. "Not in front of the boy," he said. Finn had noticed that the boy had stopped his wailing and was only sniffling now, watching them fearfully. "It's all right, son," said Finn. "Nobody's going to harm you now."

"Come on," said Lucas, helping the boy up. "Where is your mother, do you know?"

"No," the boy said, pulling away from him as Lucas tried to help him to his feet. "No, don't touch me!"

"It's all right," said Lucas, pulling him up by the arm as the boy struggled with him. "We won't hurt you, I promise you. Don't be afraid. There's nothing—"

Something fell to the floor with a thump and Lucas glanced down to see a pistol lying on the floor.

"What. . . ."

The boy jerked away and pulled another pistol from inside his tattered jacket, swinging at Lucas with it. Instinctively, Lucas blocked the blow, but the boy had twisted free from his grasp and he quickly made for the door. Finn leaped across the room and brought the boy down with a flying tackle.

"Merde!" screamed the boy. "Let me go, you big ox! Let me go or else I'll kill you! Let me go, I said!"

He squirmed in Finn's grasp like a little fish, kicking and clawing at Finn's face in an effort to get at his eyes.

"I've got him," Lucas said, grabbing the boy by the scruff of the neck and hauling him to his feet. "All right now, you little hellion, you've got some—*HUHHH*!"

He doubled over as the boy brought his knee up hard into his groin. The blow made Lucas release his hold upon the boy and he tried to run again, but Finn kicked his feet out from under him, sending him sprawling to the floor. Immediately, the boy was up again, but this time Finn brought him down with a right cross to the jaw and he fell to the floor again, unconscious.

"Little bastard," Delaney said. "You all right, Lucas?"

Still doubled over and clutching at himself, Priest looked up and nodded, his eyes wide with pain as he fought to get his breath back.

"How do you like that little son of a bitch?" said Finn. "There was never anybody else in here, he did it all himself!"

"I hope you didn't kill him," Lucas wheezed.

"If I did, it'd serve him right," Finn said. "Don't worry, I didn't hit him very hard. He should be coming around in a little while. We'd better get out of here, though. I think we'll take this little sniper with us."

He picked the boy up and threw him over his shoulder. "Come on," he said. "Straighten up and let's get out of here.

If anybody says anything, my 'son' here got knocked down in the crush outside. We'd better get word to the boys waiting in the square that the whole thing's off and have them get back to the boat."

"I'll take care of that," said Lucas, still feeling the effects of the knee to his essentials. "Where will you be?"

"At Fitzroy's safehouse. I want to ask this kid a few questions. I've got a sneaking suspicion that I know who that 'old woman' was."

"You shouldn't have brought him here," Fitzroy said.

"Relax, Major," Finn said. "He doesn't even know where the hell he is. Besides, I was in a hurry and there wasn't any time to make other arrangements."

"I sent you to rescue the Marquis de Leforte, and not only did you let him get away, but you beat up a little boy. I'm very disappointed in you two."

"If you'll recall," said Finn, "the whole idea was for Leforte to get away."

"As for your disappointment in us, Fitzroy," said Lucas, "you know what you can do with that. This wouldn't have happened if you had provided proper mission support. If you had issued us the right equipment, we could have—"

"Impossible," Fitzroy said.

"Look here, Major," Finn said, drawing himself up to his full height and glowering at the Observer, "in case you've forgotten, this isn't a standard adjustment anymore."

"If you're referring to Mongoose," said Fitzroy, "I already gave you your orders concerning him. He's to be left to the TIA team that will—"

"And where the hell were they just now?" Finn shouted.

"They should already be here," said Fitzroy. "They have nothing to do with this adjustment mission. Their target is Mongoose. Your orders are to—"

"I've had about enough of this," said Finn, grabbing Fitzroy by the throat and slamming him against the wall.

"Have you lost your mind?" Fitzroy croaked. *"I could have you court-martialed for this!"*

"So what? It wouldn't be the first time."

"He's coming around," said Lucas.

Delaney shoved Fitzroy into a corner and went over to the bed, where the boy was beginning to stir.

"All right, kid, wake up," said Finn, slapping the boy's face lightly.

"Get your filthy hands away, you dogfucker!" snarled the boy, sitting up quickly and slapping at Finn's hand.

Finn grabbed him by his thick black hair and jerked his head back so that it hit the wall behind the bed.

"Now listen here, you little shit," he said, "I don't give a damn how old you are. If you're old enough to kill grown men, you're old enough to be killed like a grown man, you understand me? Now you shut your mouth and do as you're told or I'll break every bone in your scrawny little body!"

The boy glared at Finn malevolently, but he kept his mouth shut.

"Good," said Finn. "I'm glad to see we understand each other. Now what's your name?"

"Jean," said the boy, sullenly.

"All right, Jean," said Finn. "You behave yourself and you might live to get out of this room. You helped an enemy of the Republic to escape. You know what the penalty for that is. France is—"

"You are not French," the boy said with a sneer. "You are English spies! I heard you talking."

"You speak English?" Lucas said.

"Only a little," said Jean. "I did not understand all that you said, but I know English when I hear it spoken!"

"You see?" said Fitzroy. "I told you you should not have brought him here. This place is useless now."

"I do not care whether you are French or English," said the boy. "It is all the same to me. Under the aristocrats, I starved. Comes the Revolution, still I starve. It is all the same to me."

"Then why did you kill those men to help Leforte escape?" said Finn.

"Because I was paid well to do it. He gave me fifty francs! For such a sum, I would kill Robespierre, himself."

"Bloodthirsty little savage, aren't you?" Finn said. "Who gave you the fifty francs?"

"I do not know his name," said Jean. "He called himself the Scarlet Pimpernel." Suddenly, the boy looked alarmed and he clapped his hand to his waist, his bravado gone for the moment.

"We didn't take your money," Finn said.

"It is for my brother and myself," said Jean, submissively.

"Please, monsieur, Pierre and I have not eaten for days."

"Where are your parents?" Lucas said.

"Dead."

"And your brother?"

"I will not tell you! You can kill me, but I will not tell you where Pierre is!"

"Relax," said Finn. "We're not interested in you or your brother. I want to know about the man who gave you that money."

"There is not much that I can tell you, monsieur."

"I'll be the judge of that," said Finn. "What did he look like?"

"About his size," said Jean, indicating Lucas with a jerk of his head. "Not thin, not heavy. Dark hair, dark eyes, a moustache like so," he said, indicating by pantomime a generous handlebar moustache. "Thick eyebrows meeting in the center of his forehead. He was dressed like a gentleman and he favored his left side, as though he were injured there."

"No beard?" said Lucas.

Jean shook his head.

"The kid's got sharp eyes," said Finn. "It was him, all right. The hair was probably a disguise, but that injured side is where I got him with the sword cane. Go on," he said to Jean.

"There is not much more to tell," said Jean. "I met him yesterday. I tried to pick his pocket and he caught me. He said that he would let me go and give me fifty francs as well if I was not afraid. He said that I could either lose my head for being a thief or do as he said and make some money." Jean shrugged. "The choice was simple. He took me up to that room where you found me. The man inside was asleep upon the bed. He struck this man, knocking him senseless, then bound and gagged him. He then took out some pistols and asked me if I knew how to shoot them. I told him that I did not. He showed me how and then I watched him load the pistols. He told me to wait in that room until the next day, when the Marquis de Leforte would be brought past the house on his way to the guillotine. He laid the pistols out and told me to shoot out the window and to aim high so that I would not hit the marquis. He said that the soldiers would come and that I was to hide beneath the bed, leaving the pistols out upon the floor. They would see the man tied up on the bed, think that the one who shot the pistols escaped, and not bother to look for a small boy. He said that if I did well, he would find me again and give me more money."

"But the man inside the room was dead," said Lucas.

"Yes, I killed him," said Jean.

"*You* killed him? Why?"

"It was a good plan, but I thought of a better one," said Jean. "If I shot high, then the soldiers would come into the room, looking for me. They would have untied that man and questioned him. They might have found me beneath the bed. I decided to try to kill the soldiers or as many of them as I could. I aimed very carefully," he said with pride. "I made it easier for him. This way, perhaps he will give me more money if I see him again. I killed the man inside the room because then I could say he was my father. A dead man cannot be questioned and no one would bother with a small boy, crying for his father."

Finn glanced at Lucas. "Can you *believe* this?" he said. "This kid is diabolical. He never shot a gun before and he picked off those soldiers like a pro."

"I should not have kept those pistols," Jean said, morosely. "You would not have caught me, then. That was my one mistake."

"Incredible," said Fitzroy. "Absolutely incredible. The boy's a born cold-blooded killer. Look at him! No trace of remorse!"

"And why should I care about them?" shouted Jean. "They are all the same! My father was run down in the street by an aristo in his coach! My mother died of hunger, giving my brother and me what little morsels she could find! Pierre and I roamed the streets like dogs, picking through the garbage. I am not sorry for what I have done and I never shall be!"

"Well, Delaney, you brought him here, now what are we supposed to do with him?" said Fitzroy.

"Hell, let him go," said Finn. "What else can we do?"

"You are Finn Delaney?" Jean said.

Finn glanced at the boy, then at Lucas. "Well, if we had any doubts about who hired this kid, that takes care of them. Yes, I'm Finn Delaney. He gave you a message for me, didn't he?"

"He said that if I met a man named Finn Delaney or one named Lucas Priest, I was to give him this," said Jean, producing a folded up piece of paper.

Finn unfolded the note and read it aloud. "The marquis will be delivered to the League of the Scarlet Pimpernel in Boulogne-sur-Mer. No one will be the wiser, except yourselves. That's one for me. The game continues. Tell Cobra he's out of his league."

"Cobra?" said Lucas.

Finn sighed. "Do you get the feeling that he's the only one who knows what the hell is going on around here?" He looked at Jean and jerked his head toward the door. "Get out of here."

Jean jumped up and ran for the door, moving as fast as he could before they changed their minds.

"That kid's going to grow up to be another Mongoose," Lucas said.

Finn snorted. "For all we know, he might've been his ancestor. Maybe we should have killed him."

"You can't be serious," said Fitzroy.

"That's right, I can't be," said Delaney. "This whole thing's a joke to somebody. If I could figure out the punchline, I might even laugh."

7

True to his word, Mongoose delivered the Marquis de Leforte to Andrew Ffoulkes in Boulogne-sur-Mer. Ffoulkes naturally thought that it was Blakeney who had done it and the other members of the league believed that the whole thing had been the result of a last-minute change in plans. They were only disappointed that they had not been involved. They had been looking forward to torching the Place de la Révolution.

The arrival of the Marquis de Leforte in London further spread the fame of the Scarlet Pimpernel and both Ffoulkes and Dewhurst found that they had more social invitations than they could handle as everyone wanted to know more about this man of mystery. It became the fashion among aristocratic French émigrés to wear a scarlet pimpernel in their lapels and this practice soon caught on throughout London society. Soon after Leforte's rescue, Ffoulkes reported to Lucas that Lord Hastings desired to join the league; the well-turned-out scion of one of England's foremost families was summarily recruited. At a dinner held at the Blakeney estate in honor of the Marquis de Leforte the week following his arrival, Finn was approached by a very handsomely dressed gentleman who looked vaguely familiar to him.

"Evening, Blakeney," said the man, a tall and broad-shouldered dandy with flaxen blond hair and bright blue eyes. "I'd like to have a word or two with you, if you don't mind?"

He took Delaney by the arm and gently steered him toward

a small and unoccupied sitting room.

"How's it going, Finn?" he said, softly. "Long time, no see."

Delaney tensed and stared at him intently. It was a moment before he recognized the TIA agent. "Cobra!"

"It's nice to be remembered," said the agent. "It's been a while, hasn't it? Fitzroy gave me that message from Mongoose. Same old Mongoose, eh? I thought I'd touch base with you and compare notes."

"How did Mongoose know they'd send you?" said Delaney.

"I don't think he knew, I think he guessed. Still, it was an educated guess. The odds were pretty good that they'd assign me to the case. I was the logical candidate. The two of us have worked together often in the past and, after him, I was the senior field operative. I was pulled off another mission for this one. I can't say I mind it very much. This certainly beats slogging through the New England swamps with Benedict Arnold."

"Don't make the mistake of thinking that this mission will be much easier," said Finn. "It's rapidly turning into a real nightmare."

"Don't get me wrong," said Cobra, "I'm not underestimating what we've got here, but it may not be quite as serious as you think. At least, not yet."

"No? What makes you think so?"

"Well, Mongoose delivered the Marquis de Leforte to the League of the Scarlet Pimpernel, didn't he? I think that's an excellent indication that he's not out to sabotage your adjustment."

"You neglected to mention that he got a bunch of people killed in the process," Finn said.

"Ah, yes, the boy. We're looking for him now. It seems that Mongoose was not really responsible for that. Nevertheless, evaluations is checking through on the effects of those deaths. Chances are that they won't constitute a serious disruption. People are dying left and right in Paris, a couple more deaths won't make much difference, especially since no one of historical significance was killed. We're very interested in that boy, though."

"I thought that your job was to find Mongoose."

"It is and I'm anxious to do that as soon as possible. That's why I came to see you."

"What makes you so sure he's not out to sabotage the adjustment?" Finn said. "You know something I don't?"

Cobra smiled. "I know Mongoose. In a way, I even understand him, though that's no mean feat. He wants to make you and Priest look bad, as well as Cross. The three of you are the ones who caught him with his pants down. This is just his way of getting even."

"For saving his life?"

"Sounds crazy, doesn't it? But you don't know him like I do. Mongoose *is* a little crazy. Maybe recent events have made him more so. It certainly appears that way. He has a death-wish. We've all got that to one extent or another—you, me, Priest—otherwise we wouldn't be here. Mongoose is a bit more extreme that way. It's part of what makes him so effective in the field. Death doesn't bother him, he flirts with it. He's always taken incredible chances and up until the Time-keeper affair, his risks have always paid off. I've seen him set himself up like you would not believe."

"Oh, I think I'd believe it," Finn said.

"Granted, he finally went too far," said Cobra. "He would have been killed if you hadn't intervened. I know you'd think that he'd be grateful, but his mind just doesn't work that way. What you did amounts to *coitus interruptus*, in a way. Now he's out to show us all that he's still got it. He stole a march on you and that's only the beginning. He's going to try to steal your thunder and lead me a merry chase until this thing is over with."

"And then what?"

"Your guess is as good as mine," said Cobra. "The biggest mistake they made was that they fixed his face and body, but they forgot to check his mind. I'm not saying that he's gone off the deep end, but there's no question that he's allowing his neurosis to control him. He's rational, but his rationality is skewed. Fitzroy maintains that if we don't catch him soon, there's no telling what he might do. He might even decide to join the underground or to clock forward to Plus Time and continue playing tag with us there. There is, of course, another possibility and that is that he might be reinstated."

"You're joking."

"Why should I be joking? Personally, I'd like to see it happen. We can't afford to waste talent like his. With reeducation, I'm sure Darrow would have reinstated him eventually."

"That's not what I heard," Finn said.

"Well, perhaps not. Mongoose made Darrow look bad. Still, he can be helped and the director doesn't always have the final word in these things."

"No? Who does?"

"I'm afraid I can't say," the agent said. "You see, the agency is not set up the same way as the Temporal Corps or the Observers. We can't work that way. The director always has a certain amount of authority, but there's a limit to what even the director is given access to. It wouldn't do to have one man in a position to know everything that goes on in the organization. That would be very bad for security. Also, it helps to have someone, like Darrow, to take the fall if necessary."

"You're telling me that Darrow resigned to cover for someone else?" said Finn.

"Is that what I said? Perhaps you misunderstood me. Anyway, now that we've been placed under the direct control of the Observer Corps, there's a new director and a certain amount of reorganizational instability—"

"You mean a power struggle."

"—and, as a result, my team of agents and myself have been placed under the command of the Observer on this mission. That means I'll be taking orders from Fitzroy, at least for the time being. And his orders are to direct me in apprehending Mongoose and making certain that he doesn't jeopardize this mission; but as I said, I don't believe he'll do that. At least, not intentionally."

"No, of course not," Finn said, dryly. "Whatever could have made me think such a thing?"

"Relax, Finn, will you? I'm on your side, believe me. The way things stand right now, I'm in a position to cooperate with you and I'd really like to do that. However, in order for us to be able to work together, there are certain things you're going to have to understand. It's what I've been trying to explain to you. You were a big help to me on that last mission and I'm trying to return the favor. Fitzroy doesn't like you very much. As far as he's concerned, you're a maverick and you're insubordinate. He doesn't want me to confer with you."

"So how come you're disobeying orders?"

"Because I want to help you. And because I need your help. You know that reorganizational instability I mentioned? It could go either way. If it goes one way, certain conditions will prevail that will result in my having to continue working under Fitzroy. If it goes the other way, well, let's just say that the agency will then go back to doing business as usual. You can draw your inferences from that. I'll tell you what that means to you and me, in real terms."

"Please do," said Finn, "I'm beginning to get lost in these semantics."

"Then I'll try to make myself as clear as possible. If the present conditions change, then . . . the 'old leadership' will return to power. I'll be able to act independently of Fitzroy and bring Mongoose in for interrogation and reeducation. He can be helped and made useful and productive once again. I'd very much like to see that happen."

"What's the alternative?" said Finn.

"The alternative is that the 'new leadership' will emerge preeminent, with a vested interest in seeing that no further reorganizational instability occurs, you get my meaning?"

"I think so," said Finn, "but how does that change anything with regard to—"

"I'll still have to apprehend Mongoose and deliver him for reeducation," Cobra said, "but in that case, I'd be delivering him to *different people*. Remember that he used to be the senior field operative."

"And as the senior field operative, he would know who—"

"Exactly."

"You're saying that they'd kill him to keep him from talking during reeducation? To keep the new director from finding out who *really* used to give the orders?"

Cobra nodded. "I have no idea whom they'd send to do the job. I'm a company man, Finn. I follow company leadership."

"But there are others who wouldn't," Finn said, "who would maintain loyalty to the old leadership, as you put it."

"That's right. I was contacted by them just before I clocked out on this mission and told the score. I told them what I told you, that I follow company leadership. I don't think I could have made myself any plainer. My job is to take Mongoose back and I intend to do it."

"But if the covert boys lose their bid for power, Mongoose will have to be eliminated. If you've made it clear that you're following the rulebook, you'll have to be eliminated, too."

"That's right," said Cobra. "There's every reason to believe that at least one member of my team here is awaiting orders to that effect."

"Jesus," Finn said, "you've got a problem. What are your people into that they're running so scared?"

"I honestly don't know," said Cobra. "If it becomes my job to find out, then I will, otherwise I'd just as soon remain ignorant. It's safer that way."

"What the hell do you expect me to do?"

"My problem is my problem," said the agent. "With a little luck and some cooperation on your part, it won't become your problem, as well. I don't want to push Mongoose into doing anything foolish. If I can find him and talk to him, I can make him understand what the situation is. Perhaps I can even convince him to lay low and refrain from any further interference in your adjustment until it's over, I don't know. What I'm asking you to do is back off."

"What do you mean, 'back off'?" said Finn.

"Just what I said. Give him room. Don't try to go after him on your own. I know how you feel about him, but I'm asking you to leave him alone, so long as he doesn't actively endanger the adjustment."

"How am I supposed to determine that?" said Finn.

"I'm asking you to trust my judgment. I need to stall for time, at least until it becomes clear which way the power play will go. When the situation gets finally resolved, I'll know. I don't want to have to go against my own people if I can help it. By the time it gets resolved, this adjustment might be over and then you'll be out of it. If I take Mongoose before it all gets settled, they'll try to hit both him and me, just to be on the safe side."

"And you said that this might not be as serious as I think?" Finn said. "This isn't only serious, it's turning into a full-fledged disaster!"

"It doesn't *have* to," Cobra said. "All I'm asking you to do is to continue playing your part and to leave Mongoose alone.

Let me handle it. It doesn't have to involve you."

"Brother, I can't get any more involved! Do you realize what you're asking us to do?"

"I know," said Cobra. "I know how it sits with you and I know that it's not going to be easy, but I've got to make you understand that the alternatives are far less attractive."

"Is that a threat?"

"I sincerely don't want it to be," said Cobra.

"Suppose I refuse?"

"It would not be in your interest. Your job is to insure temporal continuity. Mongoose has thus far shown no inclination to interfere with that aspect of your job. He's not out to create any disruptions, only to prove himself superior to you. You have my personal guarantee that I will back you up in every way possible in order to help you complete your mission. But I know that you're itching to get your hands on Mongoose, to settle both this score and an old one. I'm asking you to forget about it."

"If I don't?"

"Then I'll be forced to run interference for him to make sure that you don't get him," Cobra said. "I don't want to have to do that, Finn, believe me. Mongoose is not your job, he's my job. Your job is to play Percy Blakeney. All I'm asking you to do is to do your job and to let me do mine, in my own way, in my own time."

"I know you didn't have to tell me any of this," said Finn. "I appreciate your candor."

"Figure I owed it to you."

"What makes you think I won't go to Fitzroy with what you just told me?" Finn said.

"You could," said Cobra. "I wouldn't try to stop you. But if this conversation goes beyond the two of us, especially to Fitzroy, you'll be signing his death warrant and mine, as well; possibly, even yours."

"Yes, I can see that."

"So what's it going to be, Finn? Do we work together or at cross purposes?"

"You're backing me into a corner, Cobra."

"I know. I'm sorry. I have no choice."

"I'll let you know. How do I get in touch with you?"

"You don't. I'll get in touch with you. You're going to confer with Priest and Cross?"

Finn nodded.

"Yes, I suppose you'd have to," Cobra said. "I've gone out of my way to be straight with you. Don't let me down."

"It'll be kept between the four of us, you have my word on it," said Finn.

"Thanks."

"Just one more question," Finn said. "In case we don't back off, as you put it, how far are you prepared to go to protect Mongoose?"

Cobra stared at Finn steadily. "How far are you prepared to go to get him?"

Finn nodded and licked his lips. "Yeah," he said. "Wish I could say that it's been nice."

Cobra regarded him silently for a moment, then turned and walked away. He paused at the door.

"I said I owed you for the last time, Finn. Consider the slate wiped clean."

As Finn came out of the sitting room, there was no sign of Cobra. However, Marguerite saw Finn and approached.

"Percy, who was that man you were just with? I don't think I recall seeing him before."

"Oh, just someone I once knew, my dear," said Finn.

"What was his name?"

"Damned if I know. We met somewhere, but for the life of me, I simply can't remember where or when. I'm certain it will come to me."

"You don't remember him at all?"

Finn shrugged. "Odd's life, my dear, I can't be expected to recall the name of everyone I meet, now can I? Why worry about such trivial matters? If he was important, doubtless he would have made a more lasting impression."

"What a fleeting memory you have, my husband. I wonder that you recall *my* name!"

"Why, what a thing to say! What are you suggesting?"

"Only that I wonder how lasting an impression I made upon you," she said. "Sometimes it seems that you've forgotten me completely. It seems that—"

"Why, there's Lord Hastings!" Finn said, quickly. "I've been looking for him all this evening. You'll pardon me, my dear, but I simply *must* have a word with him concerning business matters. We can discuss this later, surely."

His stomach tied in knots, Finn fled Marguerite's presence and made his way across the crowded room towards Hastings. He felt her eyes on him as he rushed away, but he did not look back. He was afraid to.

He managed to avoid her for the remainder of the evening, always finding some excuse not to be alone with her and making certain that there was always a small group of what he had privately started calling "the Blakeneyites" around him. These were socially ambitious young men who had fastened onto him as a role model, copying his style of dress, aping his mannerisms, and laughing his nasal, inane laugh. He despised them, but as Blakeney, he encouraged them, stroking their tender egos and treating them like favorite sons. They served a threefold purpose. They helped to lend Blakeney an air of vapid stupidity as they all stood around together, striking casual poses and acting like mindless peacocks. They served as a barrier between him and Marguerite who, contrary to all expectations, was not growing bored and disenchanted with her husband, but was instead growing more and more determined to rekindle his interest in her. Already astonishingly beautiful, Marguerite took great pains to become even more so for her husband. She kept experimenting with perfumes, looking for a fragrance that would please him and, even when there were no guests about, she took great care to dress herself in an exquisite fashion and to appear as seductive as possible. At parties such as this, the Blakeneyites fawned over her as well, and kept her occupied. Finally, they helped to deter the advances of other women toward Sir Percy Blakeney. Why these women found the insipid character he had created attractive was a mystery to Finn, who had never understood most women anyway, except a certain type, like Andre, who were refreshingly direct and devoid of any affectations. Why Marguerite had not grown totally disgusted with him was a mystery, as well. The mission, which he had thought would be a fairly easy one, had developed unique and seemingly insurmountable difficulties. He was growing sick and tired of the whole charade.

It was with a huge feeling of relief that he went up to his rooms that night. In the morning, he would be leaving once again for France. The Scarlet Pimpernel had to perform another daring rescue. The Marquis de Sévigné had been judged in absentia by the Committee of Public Safety and condemned to death. Unable to get out of Paris, the aristocrat had been hidden by Marguerite's brother, Armand St. Just. Finn had passed the word to Ffoulkes and Dewhurst during the party.

It would be far less of a strain than the evening he had just endured. A pleasant sail across the English Channel on the *Day Dream* would be just the thing to clear his head and he could then discuss with Lucas what Cobra had told him. Hastings, Rodney Moore, and the Byrne brothers, Alastair and Tommy, would book passage across the Channel several hours behind him, giving Finn and Lucas all the time they needed to check in with Fitzroy and to decide upon a plan of action. All he needed now was sleep, and just one more drink.

He had brought a bottle of brandy up with him and he sat down on the bed, dressed only in his britches and unfastened shirt, and drank straight from the bottle. He had polished off one-third of the bottle when the door to his bedroom opened and Andre came in.

"It's a waste of good brandy to gulp it down like water," she said.

"Water? What's that?"

"Something happened tonight, didn't it?" she said. "Something shook you up. I could tell, Marguerite could tell, and I suppose that Lucas could tell, though he's probably waiting to ask you about it tomorrow. I don't have that luxury, since I'm being left behind again."

"I already explained that to you, Andre," Finn said, wearily. "I need you here, with Marguerite."

"No, you don't," she said. "Marguerite has a houseful of servants to look after her. Nor do I believe that Mongoose plans anything involving her. You're just protecting me."

"Look, I thought we went all through this," Finn said. "Your being a woman has nothing to do with it. It's—"

"I know."

"You know? Then what is—"

"You're going to tell me that it's because this is my first mission, right? Forrester said that this would be an easy one, but it hasn't turned out that way and you're only being protective because I'm inexperienced and you're afraid I'll make mistakes."

"All right, that's true. If you know—"

"If you really think that's true, Finn, then you're lying to yourself. I may be inexperienced insofar as temporal adjustments are concerned, but you wouldn't have accomplished the one in the seventeenth century without me. I'm an experienced soldier and if I was prone to making mistakes, I would have died back in medieval England. If you want to talk about mistakes, let's talk about yours.''

"Mine!"

"That's right," she said. "Let's talk about the mistake you made in letting Mongoose get away that night in the maze. Let's talk about the mistake you made in allowing him to get to Leforte before you did. I could not have done any worse. And while we're at it, let's talk about the mistake you made in falling in love with Marguerite Blakeney."

Finn stared at her, then looked down at the floor. "How did you know?"

"I know because I've been watching you. Also because up until this moment, my sole responsibility on this mission has been to stay with her, to keep her occupied and away from you as much as possible. Not only is that unfair, it's stupid. She's an intelligent woman, Finn, though it wouldn't take very much intelligence for her to see right through that ploy, as she did almost from the very start. I may be a woman, Finn, but I'm a soldier. My sex does not automatically qualify me to be an older sister or to heal a broken heart. I'm not very good at it. I haven't complained about it up till now because I *am* a soldier and you are my superior in rank, but it's reached the point where my company is doing her more harm than good."

"What do you mean?" said Finn.

"I told you, Finn, Marguerite's no fool. She knows I'm there to be a buffer between the two of you. She might not have liked it very much, but it might have been easier for her to live with that if she knew that you didn't care for her. The only problem is, she knows that you love her."

"How could she know that?"

"She'd have to be blind not to see it. Lucas knows that you're attracted to her, but I don't think he's realized yet that there's a great deal more to it than that. She knows you love her and she thinks you can't forgive her because of the St. Cyr affair. She's been on the verge of talking to me about it several times, but she can't bring herself to discuss it. It's obviously extremely painful for her. Also, she's very proud. She's determined to win you back without having to humiliate herself by begging your forgiveness."

"Before we go any further," Finn said, "let's just keep our

roles straight. It isn't me she wants, it's Blakeney. And—"

"No, it isn't Blakeney, Finn," said Andre. "It's you. Marguerite loves you."

"You're talking nonsense."

"Am I? Let me tell you about Marguerite and Percy Blakeney, Finn, I've become an expert on the subject. She talks to me because she has no one else to talk to. Marguerite was never in love with Percy Blakeney. She was in love with the idea of being loved by a man like Blakeney, a simple man, as she puts it. She had convinced herself that there was something touchingly pure and romantic in being loved by a simple man. When I said that she wasn't a fool, I didn't mean to imply that she was not naive.

"Blakeney was evidently pathetically clumsy in his courtship of her. In her own words, he followed her around like a little puppy. She found that rather sweet. Compared to the people she had associated with, he was a dullard. They were all much smarter than he was, far wittier and much more skilled in intellectual debate. To say that he floundered in their presence would be an understatement, but he kept trying because he wanted to impress her. I'm far more experienced in warfare than in love, but spending so much time with Marguerite has been an education. I believe that Blakeney aroused her maternal instincts and she confused them with affection. All that changed, of course, when Blakeney became cold to her as a result of her part in St. Cyr's execution.

"Do you recall that bet you and Lucas lost just before we clocked out on this mission?"

Finn blinked. "What the hell has *that* got to do with anything?"

"Not a great deal, except that it enabled me to understand a few things better," Andre said. "I imagine that you and Lucas thought that I had spent the whole night rutting with that male whore and it amused me to allow you to believe that. In fact, I was far too drunk to have much interest in sex, though I did ask him to illustrate some things in a purely clinical fashion. We talked for most of the night. Thanks to the implant programming, I'm a great deal better educated than I ever dreamed I would be, but as I've already told you, my education was incomplete in some respects. He was an excellent teacher, though not in the way that you must think. He was very good at explaining the various physical and emotional aspects of love, something I knew next to nothing about. What I found most fascinating was something he called 'chemistry.' I understand that it's a very old expression used to describe—''

"I know what chemistry is," Finn said, irritably.

"Well, I didn't," Andre said. "When he explained it to me, I found it a bit difficult to accept. Maybe it was because I had too much to drink or because nothing like that had ever happened to me, but the idea of two people having such a strong emotional response to one another with no real knowledge of each other seemed somehow improbable to me. Yet, I strongly suspect that that was what must have happened between you and Marguerite."

She paused, watching him.

"Your silence tells me that I've guessed correctly. In any other circumstance, I'm sure it would be wonderful for both of you. However, in this case, the problem is that you know and understand what happened, while Marguerite is hopelessly confused. She thought that her husband had grown bored with her at first, then she beleived that Blakeney came to hate her because of St. Cyr. Now, she knows that her husband loves her, lusts for her. What's more, she suddenly finds herself loving and lusting for her husband, a man who had never affected her that way before. She's also noticed that, in many ways, he's changed. His taste in food is different. Suddenly he can hold his liquor better than ever before. Someone at the first party that we had here reported your verbal fencing match with Pitt to her almost word for word and she was both delighted and astonished at your newfound ability. Finn, do you know what she asked one of the servants yesterday? She was afraid to ask me because she thought it might get back to you, so she went to the gamekeeper, who's served the family for years. I know about it because I've been following orders and keeping an eye on her. I eavesdropped. She asked the old man about your relatives."

"My *relatives*?"

Andre nodded. "She said she knew that you were an only child, but she was curious if you had any cousins, perhaps, who looked a great deal like you." She paused. "Of course, Algernon Blakeney didn't have a brother or a sister, so Percy obviously couldn't have any cousins who were his identical twins, could he?''

She approached Finn and took the bottle from his hand. ''I can't really help you anymore with Marguerite,'' she said. ''She keeps asking questions and I'm running out of answers. I don't know how you're going to handle this, Finn, but you're going to have to do it. I can't do it for you. She's just on the verge of believing the impossible, that her husband is an impostor. As Forrester might have said, she feels it in her gut. What are you going to do when it works its way up to her brain?''

Taking the bottle with her, she left the room and softly closed the door.

8 _____

They sat together amidships on board the *Day Dream* as Captain Briggs piloted the boat across the Channel. They had sailed on the morning tide. It was a clear day and the wind was brisk and cold, sending sheets of sea spray across the deck, the droplets pattering down like grapeshot. Finn held his short clay so that the bowl of the pipe was shielded by his hand from both the wind and spray as he stretched his legs out before him. The crew did not intrude on his and Lucas's privacy and Tony Dewhurst and Andrew Ffoulkes were both below in their cabins, having no desire to remain on deck in such damp and windy conditions. For Finn and Lucas, it was an ideal opportunity to talk. En route to Dover, Finn had told Lucas all about his meeting with TIA agent Cobra and his talk with Andre the night before.

"So she suspects that something's wrong," said Lucas. "That could be a real problem. I knew that you felt something for her, but I thought that maybe it was only sympathy or that she turned you on or perhaps a little of both, but this. . . . You had to go and lose your head over a pretty face. Worse, you let her know it. Hell, Finn, you're supposed to be a pro. Andre's a rookie and she's handled herself better on this mission than you have."

"You just don't understand," said Finn.

"No, I guess I don't."

"She's not just another pretty face, Lucas. I'm telling you,

117

this is the real thing. I know it probably sounds corny, but Andre called it, there was something happening between us from the very start. I've just been refusing to admit it to myself. Hell, I'm not some lovestruck kid, I'm old enough to be your grandfather and then some, but I'm telling you, I've never felt this strongly about anyone before. It's a revelation."

"It's pathetic, is what it is," said Lucas, dryly. "The problem is, what are you going to do about it? What *can* you do?"

"I've been thinking about that," Finn said. "Blakeney's dead. Even when this adjustment is over, when the Scarlet Pimpernel retires, *someone* is going to have to continue being Percy Blakeney. Forrester said that it might be indefinite, but since I'm already on the spot, why not make it permanent?"

"Are you serious?"

"Yes. Why not?"

"Christ, Finn, I can give you several obvious reasons why not," said Lucas. "For one thing, you're in the First Division. Adjustment specialists are just too valuable to waste on temporal relocation. You ought to know that. Besides—"

"They can't turn me down if I request a transfer," Finn said. "With my mission record, I've got that option."

"Technically, yes, you do," said Lucas, "but you're not thinking, Finn. You must really have it bad, because I can't believe you'd be so stupid. To begin with, if Fitzroy found out about this, he'd probably put you in for reeducation when this was over, after which you wouldn't even remember Marguerite, much less the fact that you wanted a transfer, which they wouldn't give you anyway, at least not to the relocation units. In fact, that might not be a bad idea. It would certainly solve your problem."

"It wouldn't help Marguerite very much," said Finn.

"Oh, I'm glad to see you've finally thought of how this would affect her," Lucas said. "Have you thought of what would happen when you clock back to Plus Time and someone from the relocation units gets sent back to substitute for Percy Blakeney, someone she'd have to live with for the rest of her life? If the two of you got together, would somebody else be the same? Even if you *were* allowed to remain here with her, there's one basic difference between you and someone from the relocation units. You've had antiagathic treatments and you're far too old to have them reversed. She'd age at the normal rate and you wouldn't. Leaving aside the fact that it would be a little difficult to explain to all your friends, how do you think she'd feel, watching herself grow old while you remained the same? How would *you* feel?"

Finn nodded. He looked crestfallen. "You're absolutely right. I'm being a complete idiot. I don't know what the hell's wrong with me."

Lucas looked at him and smiled, sympathetically. "You're in love," he said. "It's made idiots of better men than you before. I'm sorry, old buddy, I shouldn't have been so hard on you, but you can't say I didn't warn you. I told you it would be really rough on you if you started caring about her, though this wasn't exactly what I had in mind. You know, it's funny, but in basic training they run down just about every possible hazard you can encounter on the Minus Side, yet I don't recall anyone ever mentioning the hazard of falling in love with someone who belongs to another time. You'd think they would include that."

"Maybe they don't because there's not much you can do about it," Finn said.

"Well, there's certainly nothing we can do about it now," said Lucas. "Besides, we still have another problem on our hands. What are you going to tell Cobra?"

The corners of Finn's mouth turned down in a grim frown. "I don't know. I was going to ask you for suggestions. I know what I *want* to tell him, but it's not for me to decide alone. Besides, you're the senior officer on this team."

Lucas raised his eyebrows. "No kidding? God damn, someone record this for posterity, this is a first. Finn Delaney defers to the chain of command!"

"Go to hell."

"After you, old friend, you're not sticking me with this one. I'm not going to make any command decisions. I left my oak leaves back in Plus Time."

"All right, then, at least give me some feedback. What do you think our choices are?"

"The way Cobra laid it out for you," said Lucas, "it doesn't sound like we've got much in the way of choices. We either play it his way or we don't. If we do what he wants us to do, it's hard to say whether we'd be disobeying orders or not. Technically, there's nothing in our orders that says we have to go after Mongoose. In fact, Fitzroy was pretty specific on that point. Mongoose is Cobra's responsibility. However, there's nothing in our orders that says we have to back off and let Mongoose get away if we get a chance to stop him. If we do that, depending on who writes the report and how it's interpreted, we might be brought up on charges. Fitzroy's going to be submitting the report and he doesn't like us, anyway. Now we could go to Fitzroy and report what Cobra told you. If we do, we'll be forcing someone's hand and Mongoose, Cobra, or Fitzroy might get killed. Or all three of them might get killed. Or *we* might get killed. Or someone blows the adjustment; God knows, it could go wrong sixteen different ways.''

"If we *don't* tell Fitzroy and he finds out about it," Finn said, "we'll probably be court-martialed.''

"There's that," said Lucas. "There's also the fact that Mongoose's interference has already resulted in several deaths, courtesy of our overly zealous young friend, Jean. Given that those soldiers were killed by someone in their own time, Cobra might be correct in his assessment that temporal inertia will compensate for it. On the other hand, maybe it won't and we'll have another minor disruption on our hands. Plus there's the possibility that Mongoose might inadvertently cause a more serious disruption. That's assuming that Cobra's right again and that Mongoose has no interest in interfering with the adjustment. He could be wrong.''

"God, I hate those damn spooks," Finn said.

"Well, it took a while, but I think I've finally come around to your point of view," said Lucas. "I'd like to send the whole bunch of them into reeducation and then put them all to work in waste disposal about a million miles from Earth, preferably even farther.''

"It's a nice thought, but it doesn't solve our problem," Finn said.

"I've just been thinking that it would have made our job a whole lot easier if you had been a bit more on target with your sword cane that night.''

"I was wondering if you'd get around to that," said Finn.

Lucas sighed. "I'm actually surprised to hear myself say it, but killing him would wrap things up rather neatly, wouldn't it?''

"I hate to be the one to bring this up," Finn said, "but actually, it wouldn't. The new director of the agency wants him alive so he can pump him dry. If we killed Mongoose, we'd be directly disobeying orders, we'd have both the TIA and the Observer Corps coming down on us and, last but not least, we'd be guilty of murder.''

"I don't think they could make a case for murder," Lucas said, thoughtfully.

"They could if they wanted to," said Finn. "Manslaughter, at the very least. We'd be in it pretty deep."

"That didn't stop you when you tried to stick him in the maze," said Lucas.

"Things weren't quite so complicated then," said Finn. "Besides, I had no intention of getting caught."

"What were you planning to do with the body?"

"I hadn't thought it through that far," said Finn, "but there are several nice lakes on the estate. If I weighted him down, he'd sink very nicely and by the time he came up, if he ever did come up, we'd be long gone and no one would ever be able to recognize who it was."

"He'd have implants," Lucas said. "There'd be the problem of the termination signal."

Finn gazed down at his hand, contemplating his hypo ring. He exposed the needle and stared at it a moment. "Fitzroy was kind enough to issue me some sedatives," he said. "It would mean that we'd have to take him alive, but then we could put him to sleep and do a little sloppy surgery."

Lucas exhaled heavily. "I can't believe we're talking like this," he said.

Finn shrugged. "It's only talk. So far."

Lucas nodded. "Yeah. So far."

The three of them sat in a corner at a small and rickety table in a dark and unprepossessing inn called the Chat Gris, on the outskirts of Calais near Cap Gris Nez. The innkeeper, a surly, grizzled Frenchman named Brogard, did little to disguise his dislike for the Englishmen or his citizen's contempt for their aristocratic status. However, they were paying customers and the times in France were such that Brogard could ill afford to turn anyone away, much less rich patrons with healthy appetites who had also taken rooms in his establishment. He served them in a prompt, if perfunctory, manner and he kept his contact with them to a minimum, which suited Lucas, Finn, and Andrew Ffoulkes just fine.

"I have found the perfect place," said Ffoulkes in a low

voice, so as not to be overheard, although Brogard had removed himself to the far corner of the room and was obviously totally uninterested in anything that Englishmen had to say. "It's a tiny cottage belonging to a Père Blanchard," Ffoulkes said, "an old man of Royalist sympathies who was more than happy to allow us the use of his small hut with no questions asked, providing he received a very reasonable stipend to ease his final days. I think he suspects that I am a smuggler, though I'm certain he doesn't have a clue as to the sort of goods I'm dealing in." He grinned.

"Where is this cottage?" Lucas said.

"You take the St. Martin's road out of town, in the direction of the cliffs," said Ffoulkes. "At the crest of the road, there is a very narrow footpath, but you must watch for it or else you shall miss it. The footpath leads down to the cliffs, where you will find the cottage, securely nestled on the hillside and well hidden from the road and any prying eyes who would not know to look for it. Blanchard is old, as I have said, and a bit of a recluse. He has an arrangement with a local Jew named Reuben Goldstein to bring him supplies from town occasionally. Outside of that, he has no contact with anyone. It seemed ideal."

"Yes, it does seem ideal," Finn said. "You've done well, Andrew. It sounds like exactly what we need."

Ffoulkes smiled, obviously pleased. "What have you learned of the Marquis de Sévigné?"

Finn gave him the information Fitzroy had provided. "He is at present hiding in the apartments of Armand St. Just."

"An inspired hiding place!" said Ffoulkes. "Who would think of seeking a wanted aristocrat in the home of one of the members of the Committee of Public Safety?"

"Nevertheless, he must be moved quite soon," said Finn. "St. Just must be very careful. We have to keep any contact with him to a minimum, for his own protection. So long as the marquis is there, St. Just is in great danger."

Ffoulkes nodded, grimly. "Indeed. He must be moved at once. Where will he be taken? To our hideout near the West Barricade?"

"That's right," said Lucas. "He will be taken there tomorrow night, but we cannot risk keeping him there for very long. We must move swiftly."

"Tomorrow night," said Finn. "Shortly before daybreak."

"You plan to take him out when the gates are closed?" said Ffoulkes. "How will you get past the guards?"

"Leave that to me," said Finn. "Recent escapes have been conducted in broad daylight. They will be much more vigilant now during the normal hours of traffic in and out of Paris. We must alter our tactics and keep them off balance."

"Very well," said Ffoulkes. "What's to be my part?"

"Two of our men, Wilberforce and Barrett, have already left for Paris," Lucas said. "They will be at the apartment to meet the marquis when he arrives. They will then await further instructions."

"For the time being, remain here," said Finn. "Don't go out after Thursday. Expect to hear from us anytime after then. Send Rodney Moore and the Byrne brothers to Père Blanchard's hut. The marquis will be brought there. Make sure that Blanchard realizes that he will be implicated if he betrays us. Lucas and I shall meet you here. When we arrive and you know that it is safe, you will go to Père Blanchard's hut and signal the *Day Dream*, which will be lying off Cap Gris Nez. Tony will send a boat for you. Lucas and I shall arrange for separate passage back to Dover. The others return on board the *Day Dream*. Wilberforce and Barrett will be on their own and they understand the risks. Any questions?"

"You are leaving for Paris immediately, then?"

Finn nodded.

"That still does not leave you much time."

"Time enough," said Finn. "The important thing to remember is not to make our friend Brogard suspicious. Don't forget, we're dissolute young Englishmen with time and money on our hands, out to replenish our cellars with French grape. Ask a lot of questions around town to that effect between now and Thursday. Who is selling? What are they selling? Who is liable to offer the best price? And if you should run into any good bargains, feel free to buy me several cases."

Ffoulkes laughed and they parted company. As they posted to Paris in great haste, Finn's depression over Marguerite vanished completely, giving way to professional concern.

"What do you want to bet that Mongoose tries it again this time?" said Finn.

"If he does, it'll mean one of two things," said Lucas.

"Since he can't fool Fitzroy into keeping him briefed any-more, he'll have to have some sort of pipeline into the TIA team for information."

"Possible, I suppose, but highly unlikely," Finn said.

"I agree. The other alternative is that he's been watching us very, very closely because there's just no other way he'd know what we were planning."

"That's what I was thinking," Finn said. "It's occurred to me that he might have infiltrated us. For all we know, he could be one of the boys in the league, since we have no idea what he looks like now. Come to think of it, we never knew what he really looked like, did we? He's changed his appearance so many damn times, I wonder if *he* knows what he really looks like anymore. I've cut down the odds as much as I could when I planned this operation. No one knew in advance what they'd have to do."

"That still leaves room for error," Lucas said.

"Yes, and doubt. Still, it's about as tight as it could be, I think. We know for sure that Ffoulkes is okay because he took delivery of Leforte from Mongoose and Dewhurst was with him the night I met Mongoose in the maze, which also elimi-nates Dewhurst. Besides, Briggs was with Dewhurst when Le-forte was snatched. That still leaves the others. Wilberforce and Barrett have orders not to leave each other's sight. Rod-ney Moore is with the Byrne brothers, so no one will be alone. At least, no one *should* be alone except for Andy Ffoulkes. Have I left anything out?"

"No, that covers it. If anyone is where they shouldn't be, we've got ourselves a suspect. If they all alibi each other, then that scratches all of them and we can concentrate on the ones who remained behind on this trip. It's slow, but it's steady. It might work."

"It had better work," said Finn. "Well, you going to take the first shift or shall I?"

"You go ahead and sleep," said Lucas. "I'll wake you at the first change of horses."

They reached Paris without incident the next night and Finn paid the driver a handsome bonus, as promised, for keeping up a breakneck pace all the way. The exhausted driver took the money as though it were contaminated, coming from English hands, but it was quite a large sum and he did not complain.

The first thing they did upon entering the city was to check in at the safehouse with Fitzroy, who had established new quarters for himself near the Place de la Révolution. Even though they had traveled with all possible speed, they were running short of time, according to their schedule. Fitzroy confirmed that Alan Wilberforce and John Barrett had taken up their station in the tiny apartment near the West Barricade.

"The marquis should be there right now," Fitzroy said. "You still have some time, but you cut it pretty close."

"That was the plan," said Finn. "I want no problems or mistakes this time."

"I see," Fitzroy said. "I trust that there will be none. I've obtained the disguise you asked for. We still have a little time left. While you're getting prepared, we can go over the plan."

The streets were nearly empty as they neared their destination. It was very late and only a few people were about. Finn and Lucas had both changed their clothing. They appeared to be ordinary citizens and Finn had added a dark wig, whiskers, and a moustache, along with some additional facial makeup, so that he could meet with Wilberforce and Barrett and not be recognized as Percy Blakeney.

"If Wilberforce and Barrett do their part right, it should all go smoothly," Lucas said. "Unless one of them is Mongoose."

"We'll know soon enough," said Finn. "Just don't turn your back on either of them. One more time. You three start shooting your pistols at . . . ?"

"Three on the dot," said Lucas.

"Good. I'll wait until I hear the ruckus, then I'll make my move with the marquis. As soon as the guards get drawn away, I'm going for the gate. They'll probably leave a couple of men on the gate unless we get real lucky, but they'll be tired after a full shift and shouldn't pose a problem. I just hope to hell the horses are where Fitzroy said they would be."

"We've gone over it with him twice," said Lucas. "They'll be there. I just hope the marquis doesn't panic on us."

"If he does, I'll put him to sleep for a little while," said Finn. "I'll get him to Cap Gris Nez if I have to carry him."

They turned down a narrow side street and walked halfway down the block until they came to the house where Wilberforce and Barrett were waiting with the marquis. The room was on the second floor. The windows were covered, as per instructions.

"Wait down here," said Finn. "I'll send the boys down to you. I'll give you a five-minute head start, then I'll follow with the marquis."

Finn entered the building and slowly climbed the steps to the second floor, being careful not to make any noise. He came to the door of the apartment where the marquis was being hidden and softly knocked three times. The door opened just a crack.

"I come from the Pimpernel," Finn whispered.

He was admitted and he entered quickly. Just as quickly, Barrett shut the door behind him, lowering the hammer slowly on the pistol he held in his right hand.

"What is it?" Barrett said in a low, urgent voice. "Has anything gone wrong?"

Finn tensed. There was no one in the room except himself, the tall and slender Barrett, and the shorter, more heavily built Wilberforce. Both men were staring at him anxiously. There was no sign of the marquis.

"What do you mean?" said Finn, disguising his voice. "Where is the marquis?"

Barrett looked alarmed and he exchanged a quick glance with Wilberforce. "Why, he has gone with the boy, as the Pimpernel instructed," he said.

"The boy! *What* boy?"

"The little street urchin," said Wilberforce, looking concerned. "Jean, I think his name was. He brought the woman's clothing for the marquis and they went out together, posing as mother and son."

"What's the matter?" Barrett said. "Something's gone wrong, hasn't it?"

"No, no," Finn said, recovering quickly, "nothing has gone wrong. I just didn't know that the Pimpernel would use the boy, that's all."

They looked relieved. "Well, Alan and I were both a bit surprised that the Pimpernel would use a child," said Barrett, "but he did seem like a capable young chap and I must admit, it was a stroke of genius, using a little boy. Who would suspect a mother and her son?"

"Who, indeed?" said Finn. "I hadn't known the plan. I was only told the part I was to play."

"The Pimpernel likes doing things that way," said Barrett. "Less chance for the plan being discovered, what? Young Jean said we would be contacted regarding any change in plan or instructions for our departure. I expect that's your job, eh?"

"Right, that's what I came for," Finn said. "You are to stay the night. Make your way out of the city tomorrow afternoon. You are English gentlemen who had heard about the goings-on here and came to see how the Revolution had changed things for yourselves. You've had a perfectly marvelous time and now you're on your way home to tell your friends all about it. If you're asked about the Scarlet Pimpernel, you are to overwhelm them with questions in return. Everyone in London wants to know about the Pimpernel and who would know better than the soldiers at the gates? They should grow quite disgusted with you and pass you through without further inquiry."

The two men grinned at each other.

"I say this calls for a celebration," Barrett said. "We've got several bottles of claret waiting to be uncorked, old chap. Will you join us?"

"Wish I could, but I must be on about my business," Finn said. "You've done well. Good night and good fortune to you."

He left them and hurried back downstairs to Lucas.

"What's happened?" Lucas said, grabbing his arm.

"That son of a bitch has done it again!" said Finn. "He beat us to it and took the marquis out from right under our noses!"

"Took him? *How?*"

"You're not going to believe this," Finn said. "It was that kid, that miserable little pickpocket—"

"*You mean Jean? The same boy that we—*"

"That's him. He walked right up to the door, said the Pimpernel had sent him, and they turned the marquis over to him. We couldn't have missed him by more than twenty minutes!"

"Fitzroy is going to have a stroke," said Lucas. "What do we do now?"

"What else *can* we do? Get back to the coast. But first we're going to have to go to Fitzroy and tell him what happened.''

"I'm not looking forward to this," Lucas said, as they started walking back.

"Neither am I," said Finn, "but at least we've got something to tell him beyond the fact that we blew it. There can't be any doubt about it now. Mongoose is one of the members of the league. If we get back to Cap Gris Nez and find out that somebody wasn't where he should have been, that's our man."

"Otherwise, it's one of the men who remained behind in England," Lucas said. "But then, Hastings, Browning and the others wouldn't have known the plan."

"True, but they'd know about the hideout," Finn said. "They'd also know to follow whomever we sent on ahead to Paris. There's no other way he could have done it. One of them is Mongoose."

"Really?" said Fitzroy. "That's very interesting."

"That's all you have to say?" said Finn.

"No, not quite all," Fitzroy said. "I could say that I'm frankly surprised that it took the two of you so long to come to that conclusion. Cobra suspected it right from the start when he arrived. I could say that if you had been more thorough in preparing your men for this rescue attempt, instead of keeping them in the dark about what they were to do until the very last minute, this might not have happened. In fact, I could say a great deal more, but I'm not going to bother. Instead, I am going to assume full authority over this adjustment immediately. I have had about enough of your sorry inefficiency."

"Now just a minute," Lucas said, restraining Finn with a hand on his arm. "I didn't hear you objecting to the plan when we went over it with you. As for taking charge of this adjustment, aren't you overstepping your authority just a little? You're within bounds to pass on directives from Plus Time, but Observers aren't—"

' "I know very well what the function of an Observer is, Major Priest, I don't need you to tell me! Yes, you're quite correct, I am departing from normal procedure, but the two of you have left me no other choice. You've been outwitted twice, both times by a boy who can't be more than twelve years old!"

"You know very well that Mongoose had that kid—" Finn began, but Fitzroy interrupted him.

"I am inclined to agree with agent Cobra that Mongoose does not present an overt threat to this operation. It's clear to me that he desires nothing more than to embarrass the two of you, and he seems to be succeeding admirably. He's doing your job for you and doing it quite well, I might add. As long as it gets done, I don't really care who does it, so long as the Scarlet Pimpernel receives the credit."

"So what do you expect us to do?" Finn said, angrily. "You want us to sit on our hands while Mongoose does all the work?"

"That's a very tempting proposition," said Fitzroy. "However, I will tell you precisely what I expect you to do. I expect you to continue playing your parts and to refrain from any sort of independent action. *I* will devise the plans for all future rescues and I will expect you to follow them to the letter, to the last detail. I will have my support staff working, with agent Cobra's team standing by to observe each aspect of each operation, ready to act when Mongoose makes his move. The moment that the object of the rescue is safely out of danger, the agents will move in and apprehend their man. Between my own efforts in this regard and agent Cobra's investigation, Mongoose *will* be taken. I will do my very best to keep your part in this as uncomplicated as possible in order to avoid confusing you. I still need a Percy Blakeney. Unfortunately, Delaney, you're all I have to fill that role, so you will simply have to do, at least for the time being. Now I suggest the two of you make your way back to Cap Gris Nez, where Mongoose will undoubtedly deliver the Marquis de Sévigné to the League of the Scarlet Pimpernel. With any luck, perhaps the TIA agents will apprehend him there and you'll be spared any further embarrassment. Goodnight, gentlemen."

Finn was on the verge of making a temperamental reply, but Lucas took him by the arm and firmly pulled him toward the door. Fitzroy watched them with disdain as they left, then shook his head and chuckled.

"All right, Jean," he said in French, "come on out."

The closet door opened and the boy stepped out.

"How did you leave the marquis?"

"Asleep, downstairs," the boy replied. "I pricked him with the ring, just as you said." He glanced at the ring he wore on his left hand, identical to the one Finn had been given. "How does it work?"

"Don't concern yourself, Jean, you would not understand. You've done very well. Here." He gave the boy a purse. "This is for you and your brother. Take care that no one steals it from you. I'll have more work for you very soon."

"Thank you, monsieur."

"That will be all. Run along now. Take care that no one sees you leave."

9 ‾‾‾‾‾‾‾‾‾‾‾‾‾‾‾‾‾‾‾‾‾‾‾

Following the arrival of the Marquis de Sévigné in England, the Scarlet Pimpernel became a national obsession. A horse named Scarlet Pimpernel won at Ascot. A milliner in Knightsbridge offered for sale hats "à la Scarlet Pimpernel" and was soon swamped with orders. Several tailors began to specialize in suits and dresses "à la Scarlet Pimpernel" which, in spite of their designation, were available in a wide choice of colors. Scarlet Pimpernels were worn in lapels across the country, pinned to hats, worn as corsages, painted upon snuffboxes, made from silk and attached to horses' bridles, used as a garnish for a wide variety of dishes, and embroidered upon velvet slippers, dressing gowns, jackets and handkerchiefs. It seemed that the Scarlet Pimpernel was foremost in the mind of every Englishman, especially the ersatz Sir Percy Blakeney.

Mongoose had delivered the marquis to Père Blanchard's hut, dropping the aristocrat off at the crest of the St. Martin's road and directing him to follow the footpath down to the cottage. The nobleman arrived only slightly the worse for wear, suffering from dizziness and disorientation like the others before him. He had attributed the effects to the "sleeping draught" he had been given, ostensibly to prevent him from knowing how he was spirited out of Paris. However, Finn and Lucas both knew that what he had felt were not the aftereffects of a drug, but of travel from one place to another via chronoplate.

Finn had been encouraged upon learning that the marquis had been taken to the cottage, for the hut had not existed as a hiding place for them until Andrew Ffoulkes had arranged for it shortly after their arrival in France. Obviously, it meant that Mongoose knew their plans and therefore had to have assumed the guise of one of the members of the league. Yet, he had thwarted their efforts to expose him by decoying some of the men away from where they should have been. Just before they were to leave Paris, Wilberforce and Barrett had received a note signed with the red flower, instructing them to leave the city separately for the sake of greater security and telling them to rendezvous at Blanchard's cottage off the St. Martin's road. Finn recalled that they had gone out to purchase wine while they waited for the arrival of the marquis, which meant that one of them could easily have arranged for Jean to pick up the aristocrat and then deliver him to Père Blanchard's hut, since the other would be traveling alone. Rodney Moore and the Byrne brothers had been separated, as well. Ffoulkes had received a note similar to the one Barrett and Wilberforce were sent. He had found it up in his room shortly after Finn and Lucas left for Paris. It had instructed him of a change in plans, the reason being that the French had "spies everywhere" and it was best to keep altering the plans at the last minute in order to avoid exposing themselves. Ffoulkes had accepted the note without question and had followed the instructions to the letter. He had directed the Byrne brothers to remain at the cottage and he had sent Rodney Moore to watch the St. Martin's road, where he was to wait for an old woman driving a farm wagon to pass by and then watch to see if anyone followed. The "old woman" would obviously be the Pimpernel in disguise.

"He could be Moore or Barrett or Wilberforce," said Finn. "For that matter, it's possible that he could be one of the others who stayed behind in London. There's nothing that could have prevented him from picking the group up in Calais and following Ffoulkes or one of the others to the hut. Then he could have tailed Wilberforce and Barrett. There's any number of ways in which he could have managed it."

"At least we know to scratch the Byrne brothers," Lucas said. "They were together all the time."

"It's really starting to get to me," said Finn. "I feel like a fraud."

"You *are* a fraud," said Lucas, grinning.

"That isn't what I mean. The thing is, I am—that is, Blakeney is supposed to be the Pimpernel, but I haven't—that is, *he* hasn't rescued anybody!"

"So?"

"So Blakeney's only saving grace was that he only appeared to be an idiot, while being the Pimpernel in reality. I only appear to be the Pimpernel, while being an idiot in reality."

"What the hell are you talking about?" said Lucas.

Finn sighed. "I don't know. This whole thing is ridiculous. Look at us, sitting here like a couple of old men on a park bench. All we need are some bread crumbs and a flock of pigeons. We were talking about killing Mongoose because he's wreaking havoc with this mission, but what has he really done that's so damn terrible? He's been doing all our work for us and taking most of the risks. I've got a feeling that we should be thanking him!"

"That's exactly what he wants," said Cobra.

They both started and turned to see the agent standing right behind them, leaning against a tree. They hadn't even heard him approach. He was still dressed the way he had been at the party, in his dandy's suit, cut in the *incroyable* style which Percy Blakeney had made so popular in London.

"Jesus!" Finn said. "Don't *do* that!"

"You boys are really slipping," Cobra said. "Mongoose must be getting to you."

"How long have you been standing there?" said Lucas.

"Long enough." He held out an elegant silver case. "Cigarettes?"

"I could use one," Finn said. "Thanks."

He lit their cigarettes for them and took one himself. "Can't stand those damn clay pipes, myself," he said. "It's like smoking chalk. Anyway, killing Mongoose would be a big mistake. For one thing, if you were lucky enough to beat me to him, I'd be right there to stop you. The only way that you could eliminate him would be to eliminate me, first. Not impossible, I'll grant you, but it would just buy you a great deal of trouble and it seems you've already got more than you can handle."

"You don't say," said Finn, wryly.

"I've been watching you two rather closely," said the agent. "Who do you think drove the coach that took you to Paris?"

"That was you?" said Finn.

"None other. Mongoose isn't the only expert at disguise, you know. I should add that I appreciated the generous tip. That was a tiring journey."

"If you're so on top of things," said Lucas, "where were you when the marquis was taken?"

"Following you," said Cobra. "At this point, I'm a little more concerned about what you two might do than I am about Mongoose. His death might solve your problem, but it would not solve mine. I asked you to cooperate with me on this. I need you working with me, not against me. You've got nothing to lose by following my instructions."

"I wish it were that simple," Lucas said. "It might appear that all that Mongoose has done so far has been to make us look like fools, which might very well be his sole intent, but you're forgetting that he's breaking all the rules, even going so far as to involve someone from this time period in this disruption."

"You mean the boy."

"Yes, damn it, I mean the boy! Due to his interference, that boy has already killed several people. Mongoose has to realize that he's already altered the course of that boy's entire life, yet he continues to use him to further his own ends. That's a disruption in itself and there's no telling what effect it will have. The point is that Mongoose obviously doesn't care."

"You're quite right about that," Cobra said. "Involving the boy was dangerous. The boy can't be overlooked and I intend to take care of it."

"Have you found him yet?" said Finn.

"No, but then I've been extremely careful not to look for him."

Finn rubbed his forehead wearily. "This is beginning to give me migraines. You mind telling me why not?"

"Not at all. If my people find the boy, they might very well find Mongoose. I'm not yet ready for Mongoose to be found."

"Has it occurred to you that by procrastinating on this case because of the agency's internecine power struggle, *you* have become a threat to this adjustment?" Lucas said.

"Yes, that has occurred to me. I'm taking a calculated risk."

"I've got news for you, friend," said Finn. "That decision isn't yours to make."

"No one else is in a position to make it," Cobra said. "Try

to see my side of it. With Mongoose dead, admittedly, most of your problems would be solved. However, he's no good to anybody dead. Leaving aside the fact that he used to be a damn good operative and could be again, he's exposed a massive flaw in the databank security system by cracking it. Alive, he can tell us how he did that. It doesn't really matter who winds up being in control of the agency, that would benefit everyone. With Mongoose dead, we might never find out how he keyed into the system, which means that there's a chance that somebody else might figure out how to do exactly the same thing. We might not be so lucky next time. Mongoose purposely left us a lot of clues. Someone else may not be so considerate. You really want to try going out on a mission when the records used to brief you have been tampered with?''

Neither Finn nor Lucas spoke.

"You see? You really have no choice. Mongoose must be taken alive. Fitzroy understands that.''

"He just doesn't understand that you're stalling, waiting for the proper time to act,'' said Finn.

"That's for his own protection,'' said the agent. "And I remind you that I didn't have to tell you that. I'm going out of my way to play it straight with you two.''

"So long as we're all being so frank and open with each other in this new era of intra-agency cooperation,'' Lucas said sarcastically, "I'd like to ask you what you think will happen if the old guard in the agency lose out in their bid for control.''

"Well, that all depends,'' said Cobra. "Under the new administration, the autonomy of the agency has been severely curtailed. I'm not particularly qualified to assess the situation, but I can offer some educated guesses. Essentially, what the new director and his people have to do in order to bring matters fully under their control is to find a highly elite group of, well, moles within the agency. That's not an easy task. When the new director assumed his office, one of his first acts was to order a compilation of a complete roster of all TIA personnel and their field people.''

"Field people?'' Lucas said.

"Indigenous personnel in the employ of field office section heads.''

"Hold it,'' Finn said. "Do I understand you correctly? Are you telling us that TIA agents in the field *employ* people within those time periods?''

"Certainly.''

Finn was aghast. *"Are you people out of your fucking minds?* That's in direct violation of—"

"I know, I know," said Cobra, patiently. "However, consider the job the section heads have to do. Their problems are almost insurmountable. Can you imagine the amount of personnel that would be required in order to allow them to gather all the necessary intelligence to profile the historical scenarios to which they are assigned? It would be a highly unstable situation if we brought that many people in. Besides, all anybody's really interested in are the results. Without them, you people would not be able to function. So, there's always been a sort of unofficial policy of looking the other way when indigenous personnel have been brought in. The section heads have always been very careful about using them. But now that the new administration has requested a complete personnel roster, it's all become official. Of course, any such roster would be impossible to compile. No section head would be willing to reveal who his field people are and how many of them he uses. It would compromise the whole setup. That's what really brought this whole thing out into the open."

"So you've got the new administration and regular agency personnel on the one side," Lucas said, "and the section heads, field agents such as yourself, and covert operations on the other. Who has final authority, practically speaking?"

"Practically speaking, both sides have final authority," Cobra said. "That's why we have our little problem. So long as the new administration doesn't know who directs covert operations, the handful of people who *do* know continue to take their orders from the 'old guard,' as you put it. Mongoose is only one of several people whom I imagine have access to that information, which is why the director wants him so badly. The point is, he might not need him. Right now, he's ordered a scanning procedure for all agency personnel. Sooner or later, he's bound to interrogate somebody who has the right answers. Whoever directs covert operations is probably pulling all the strings available in order to block the scanning operation."

"How would they do that?" said Lucas.

"I imagine they'd have to coerce an influential member of the Referee Corps."

"Could they *do* that?" Lucas said.

"It's been done before."

"That's wonderful," said Finn. "Next time someone tells me that my paranoia is unjustified, I'll laugh in their face."

"I don't understand how they can justify their actions considering what's at stake," said Lucas. "The only thing that has prevented a temporal split so far is the inertia of the timestream and a hell of a lot of luck. The whole mechanism for insuring temporal continuity is held together with nothing more than spit and they're playing these kind of games."

"Only because they have to," Cobra said. "I'm not saying that egos and the desire for power don't enter into it, but both sides feel that the other is acting to the detriment of temporal continuity. The 'old guard' feels that their system of intelligence-gathering and directing operations is the only thing maintaining temporal continuity. My guess is that that's why the agency tried to take over control of temporal adjustments from the First Division. On the other hand, a valid argument can be made for the position that the TIA has become like an octopus with more tentacles than it can control or knows it has."

"And where do you stand?" Lucas said.

"I'm a fatalist, Priest," said Cobra. "I was out on a mission when the breakdown in the chain of command occurred, otherwise Mongoose's job as head of field operations would have gone to me. If that had happened, I probably would have been the first one interrogated and none of this would have happened. On the other hand, my being out on a mission at precisely that time may not have been circumstantial, if you get my meaning."

"So you're saying you're going with whichever way the wind blows," Finn said.

"I'm following the orders of my superiors," said Cobra. "I'm not asking you to do anything other than what you've been ordered to do. I realize that you have a lot of leeway in interpreting those orders. I'm only asking you to exercise that option." He paused to field-strip his cigarette. "Frankly, I think that all any of us can do is go through the motions. I'm convinced that a temporal split is inevitable. There's simply been too much temporal pollution. We can't control it any more. It's like riding a runaway horse. You can't stop it, all you can do is try to stay in the saddle."

"There's just one problem with that kind of thinking," Lucas said. "It presupposes that there's already been so much interference with historical events that a breakdown in the timestream is unavoidable. If that's the case, we might as well give up and go home. The point, to follow your analogy, is not to concentrate on staying in the saddle, but to keep the horse from taking the bit between its teeth and running away with you in the first place. How the hell do you expect to function if you believe that the outcome has already been decided?''

"You continue to function because there's nothing else to do," said Cobra. "You think about it too much and you won't be able to function at all. For instance, have you considered the possibility that there might already have been a timestream split at some point in the past and that we're part of it?''

"Then why aren't there two of each of us around?" said Finn.

Cobra smiled. "You never know," he said. "When you get back, maybe there will be.''

"Maybe," said Lucas. "That might very well depend on what we do about Mongoose.''

"I'll make a deal with you," Cobra said. "You open to a proposition?''

"We'll listen," Finn said.

"I can't trust my own people," Cobra said, "but I can trust the two of you. If the new director is made to back off and covert operations continues being autonomous, the investigation will be called off and my problem will be solved. If it goes the other way, I'm still duty-bound to deliver Mongoose, but there might be people in my team with orders to eliminate him if that happens. In that event, I'll need help.''

"What's your proposal?" Finn said.

"I think that I can see a way out of our present predicament," said Cobra. "You want Mongoose stopped, neutralized before he does something to screw up your mission. I want him alive and I don't want to interfere with you doing your job as you see it. I think that I may have a line on Mongoose, but my hands are tied right now. As a result, I can't help you. However, I can misdirect my own people. I'll be taking a chance, but I think I can pull it off. I also think that I can apprehend Mongoose within a matter of days. I propose to do just that, as soon as possible, and then hand him over to you.''

"There's only one problem with that idea," Lucas said. "We can't protect him for you and continue with this adjustment at the same time. The Scarlet Pimpernel still has work to do. We won't be able to guarantee his safety."

"You can if I give you a chronoplate," said Cobra. "I'll stay here with Finn and help him to continue doing the Pimpernel's work. You and Andre can take the chronoplate and, with Mongoose in your custody, you can get lost."

"You're asking us to desert," said Lucas.

"No, just to go A.W.O.L. for a while."

"Really?" Finn said. "Who gets to explain their sudden disappearance to Fitzroy?"

"Leave that to me," said Cobra.

"Forget it, we're leaving nothing to you," said Finn. "We came here to do a job and all you've done since you arrived is complicate things. This would have been a simple adjustment mission, inasmuch as any mission can be simple, if it wasn't for the TIA. All you guys were ever meant to do was gather historical intelligence to compensate for inaccuracies and omissions in the books and that's *it*, period. Somewhere along the line, you decided to become historical policemen. I find the idea that your people might have a Referee or two in their pocket frankly frightening. Next thing you know, the agency is going to start getting involved in arbitration conflicts. Maybe you people should change your initials to CIA or KGB. They did much the same sort of thing before one became a multinational corporation and the other became a monarchy."

"I can well understand your frustration, Finn, but I don't set agency policy, you know."

"You just got through telling us that you're the only one in a position to do just that on this adjustment," Finn said. "Do you know what you're doing or are you just making all this up as you go along?"

"I take it you're refusing to cooperate, then?" said Cobra.

"You take it wrong, Agent Cobra," said Delaney. "*You're* the one who's refusing to cooperate. If I wasn't convinced that there might actually be a real threat to Fitzroy's life, I'd tell him exactly what you're doing. I'll give you one thing, you've demonstrated that Mongoose must be taken alive, if for no other reason than that the new Observer-backed administration of your agency needs to learn who's really been calling the shots all this time."

"I see no conflict there," said Cobra.

"Well then, *I'll* make a deal with *you*," said Finn, "and we can stop all this nonsense. Lucas and I will agree to back off and leave Mongoose to you provided that you stop wasting your time shadowing us, get onto Mongoose, and either arrest him or make certain that he doesn't sabotage this mission. Tell us who your suspect is. We won't move against him without any proof, but at least we can watch him and work around him."

"Or else?" said Cobra.

"Or else we grab him ourselves the moment we have an opportunity and turn him over to Fitzroy, who'll clock him out before your people have a chance to do much more than widen their eyes in surprise. And that's *my* proposition."

Cobra smiled. "That makes a good deal of sense," he said. "There's really only one slight problem with that idea."

"I somehow had a feeling that there might be," Finn said.

"I doubt that you know what it is, though," Cobra said, grinning. "All right, Finn, I'll play my ace. I'll play it because I think you'll have no choice but to fold. I'll even accept your proposition, conditionally."

"What's the condition?" Lucas said.

"That you follow my direction from this point on, regardless of what Fitzroy says."

"Brother, it had better be one hell of an ace you're going to play," said Finn. "If you think you can undermine Fitzroy—"

"My suspect *is* Fitzroy," said Cobra.

Andrew Ffoulkes and Tony Dewhurst didn't recognize the young man who had arrived in Dover with Lucas and Percy Blakeney. Dewhurst thought that the young man looked somehow familiar, but he could not place where he had seen him. What puzzled both of them was the fact that this dark-haired, bearded young man whom neither of them knew was suddenly a member of their league, the only one besides themselves, Lucas, and Andre who was allowed to know that Percy Blakeney was the Pimpernel.

"Curious chap, that," Ffoulkes said to Blakeney as they sat together in The Fisherman's Rest. "Keeps to himself, all right. He hasn't said two words to us."

Finn nodded. "Rico is not the friendly sort, I'll warrant. Gets along with damn few people."

"He's an Italian, then?" said Dewhurst.

"Neapolitano," Finn said. "Doesn't speak English very well, but he's fluent in French."

"Damn it, Percy," Ffoulkes said, "who in God's name *is* he? I thought we had agreed that we would pass on all members of the league together!"

"Steady, Andrew," Dewhurst said. "Percy knows what he's about."

"No, no, it's all right," Finn said, placatingly. "It's true, we did agree upon that and I apologize for not consulting with you. However, Rico is a rather special case. He is an old friend of mine. I wrote to him some time ago, asking him to come and join us."

"Didn't I meet him once in Naples, aboard the *Day Dream*?" Dewhurst said, frowning.

Finn raised his eyebrows. "Why, I think you might have, Tony. Yes, I do seem to recall your meeting briefly."

Dewhurst nodded. "I was certain that he looked familiar. That must be it, then. Why all the mystery?"

Finn smiled. "No mystery, really. I simply wasn't sure if he could come. I meant to discuss it with you, I suppose, but what with one thing and another, it must have slipped my mind."

Dewhurst and Ffoulkes both looked at Rico, who was sitting at a corner table by himself, smoking a pipe.

"What's so special about him, then?" said Ffoulkes.

"He's to be our main agent in Paris," said Finn. "Knows the city well, spent a good part of his childhood there. I wanted to have someone who was not known to be associated with us to keep in close contact with St. Just. In fact, the less we're seen together with him, the better. That's why I've arranged for separate passage for him to Calais."

"None of the others knows him, then?" said Dewhurst.

"No, that's how I wanted it," said Finn. "The French government is furious with us, you know. They've set their spies to watching everyone. I expect they'll be nosing about in London soon, if they're not there already. We must take all steps possible to protect ourselves and St. Just, in particular, especially since Marguerite wants me to bring him over for a visit. He'll be seen with all of us at Richmond and I can't chance his being seen with any of our group when he returns to Paris."

"You really believe that the Frenchies will set their dogs on us in *London*?" Ffoulkes said.

"I have no doubt of it," said Finn. "Pitt says that they'll be sending an accredited representative to England. You can be sure that he will be a spy."

"Well, we'll be sure to tweak his nose for him," said Ffoulkes, grinning widely.

"You will do no such thing," Finn said. "When this representative arrives, I expect you to treat him with all due respect, regardless of your feelings. Don't make the mistake of thinking you'll be safe in England. Don't underestimate the French. A good card player never gives away his hand, Andrew. The French won't send a fool." He got up from the table. "I'll be upstairs. Let me know when Briggs arrives."

He went up the stairs and, a moment later, Rico followed after him.

"Grim-looking fellow," Dewhurst said.

"When was it that you met him?" Ffoulkes said, watching Rico ascend the stairs.

"I can't recall, exactly. We must not have spoken long, otherwise I'm sure I would remember."

"I hear all those Italians carry knives," said Ffoulkes. "He looks the type."

"If he is, then he's our man," said Dewhurst. "St. Just is a bit too delicate for our sort of work. That chap looks like he might be handy in a pinch. I don't envy him having to stay in Paris, though."

"Well, better him than either one of us," said Ffoulkes. "Paris is a nice place to visit, but I'd hate to have to live there." He sniffed. "Too many of those French girls never wash."

Andre entered the room and softly closed the door behind her. She worked her jaw around in an irritated fashion. "I hate this damn beard," she said. "I don't see how you men can eat with them. The hairs trap all the food."

"That's so you won't grow hungry later on," Finn said with a chuckle. "Relax, you'll be able to take it off as soon as we're away from Ffoulkes and Dewhurst. We'd better leave your hair dark, though. Fitzroy hasn't seen you more than once or twice, but I don't want to take any chances."

"I'll make certain that he won't see me at all," said Andre. "I still can't believe that he might actually be Mongoose."

"Well, we don't know for sure," said Finn, "but if you

knew Mongoose, the whole thing would actually make a crazy kind of sense. Fitzroy's the last person we would have suspected, so of course that makes him the logical candidate.''

"But Fitzroy was the one who clocked back to Plus Time and reported Mongoose. We know he did that because Cobra is here with his team of investigators.''

"And an assassin or two,'' added Finn. He nodded. "You're absolutely right. If Mongoose has assumed Fitzroy's identity, he could have done so afterward. Even if he didn't, it would appeal to his sense of sportsmanship to clock back to Plus Time and report himself to the one man who would want to get his hands on him more than anybody else.''

"But the new director of the TIA didn't even know about the altered records until Fitzroy brought the whole thing to his attention by telling him about the fake Observer, what was his name?''

"Jack Carnehan.''

"That's it. If Carnehan was Mongoose, then how could Fitzroy—''

"We only have Fitzroy's *word* that there was ever such a person as Captain Jack Carnehan. Remember, we never saw him.''

"But that doesn't mean that there was no Carnehan,'' said Andre.

"No, it doesn't. Which is why you're going to Paris, to find out for sure. The really funny thing is that Jack Carnehan really does exist. There's no open file on him as a member of the Observers or the Temporal Corps, which is why the new director drew a blank, but there *is* a classified dossier on a Lt. Col. Carnehan. Jack Carnehan is Mongoose's real name.''

Andre looked at him with astonishment. "But that's impossible! The new agency director would have known that. He had access to Mongoose's records—''

"Which Mongoose had altered,'' Finn said, pointedly.

Andre frowned. "Yes, all right, it could have worked that way, but then the old director, the one who resigned—''

"Darrow.''

"He would have known because he knew the old dossier. He would have recognized Carnehan's name!''

Finn nodded. "I'm sure he did.''

"Then, why . . . ?''

"Because Darrow's title as Director of the TIA was a cover.

He really *was* the administrative director of the agency before he resigned, but he was also the head of covert operations, the agency within the agency."

Andre sat down, shaking her head. "I yield," she said. "It's all too much for me."

"Lucas and I felt the same way when Cobra laid it out for us," said Finn. "Consider the fact that Darrow resigned his post as agency director. The official reason for his resignation was that the covert agency's attempt to take over adjustment jurisdiction from the Temporal Corps failed. He took the fall for it and he also resigned in protest over the Referee Corps assigning control of the TIA to the Observer Corps because the agency had gotten out of hand. However, the fact that he resigned served to protect him from the investigation being conducted by the new administration. The director's post is primarily an administrative job. When the new administration took over, they found out that the director had been little more than a figurehead for years. If it's a known fact within the agency that the director doesn't really run things, where's the best place to hide the person who *really* gives the orders?" Finn spread his hands out. "In the director's office, naturally."

Andre blinked several times and gave her head several quick, jerky shakes. "So the director who doesn't really run things is actually the man—"

"Who really *does* run things," said Finn.

"What worries me is that I think I'm beginning to understand all this," Andre said.

"Cobra realized that Darrow had to be the head man in covert operations, or one of the head men, when he found out that Darrow didn't say anything when he found out about Jack Carnehan. Carnehan was a code-named agent and the head of field operations to boot. Darrow had to have access to his dossier when he was in the director's office and he had to know his real name."

"But then he would know that Cobra would also know—"

"No, he wouldn't," Finn said. "Spooks are ultraparanoid. Agents are supposed to know each other only by their designated code-names. Mongoose and Cobra worked very closely together and developed a special relationship. As a gesture of trust, they broke regulations and privately told each other their real names."

"It seems to have backfired on Carnehan," said Andre.

Finn shook his head. "No, it didn't. How do we know about Carnehan? That was the name he gave Fitzroy, assuming that Fitzroy is genuine. Otherwise, it was the name Fitzroy gave us when he made up this fictitious pseudo-Observer. Either way, Mongoose or Carnehan was virtually certain that Cobra would be the one sent to bring him in. By using his real name, which he knew would be passed on to Cobra, he was doing two things. He was issuing an open challenge to Cobra, his old partner, and at the same time, he was warning him to watch out for Darrow."

"But by doing that, he also gave himself away," said Andre. "If he's Fitzroy, he'd have to know that Fitzroy would be the first person Cobra would suspect."

"That's assuming he's Fitzroy," said Finn. "Even if he is, making himself the logical suspect is something that would amuse him. We're really in no position to do anything without proof and he knows that."

"If Mongoose really is Fitzroy," said Andre, "what happened to the real one?"

"Maybe Carnehan has him stashed away somewhere," said Finn. "Or maybe he's killed him. Or maybe there never was a real Fitzroy. The problem is that he's got that chronoplate. With all his years in the agency, he has to have his own contacts. Cobra might know some of them, but he wouldn't know them all. If we start to get too close and Mongoose gets wind of it, all he needs to do is to clock out, visit some cosmetic surgeon he's had an old arrangement with, get a new face, come back, and start again. You were complaining that you didn't have enough responsibility on this mission. Well, you now have the most responsible job of all. You're going to have to be the one to tell us the truth about Fitzroy."

"That boy will be the key," she said. "If he contacts Fitzroy, we'll know. What do you want me to do about the boy?"

"Don't do anything. Follow him, if you have a chance. He has a brother somewhere that he's very protective of. You find me that brother."

10 _____

"St. Just can't help us much this time," said Fitzroy.

Finn and Lucas sat at the small table in his tiny apartment, making a short meal of wine, bread, and cheese. Somewhere in that very apartment, most likely, Fitzroy kept his chronoplate. It was a tremendous temptation to overpower him then and there, ransack the apartment, find the plate, and take him prisoner. The only thing that prevented them from doing just that was the fact that Fitzroy could well be exactly what he represented himself to be. If that was the case, given the way he already felt about them, their court-martial would be a foregone conclusion. The chronoplate could also be hidden elsewhere.

"Le Comte de Tournay de Basserive has been condemned to death, along with his entire family," said Fitzroy. "The comtesse and her two children are still relatively safe. They're in Valmy, where they're being hidden by trusted friends. De Tournay, however, is still somewhere in Paris. St. Just has no idea where he is. He was sentenced in absentia and St. Just did what he could to defend him, but he's already in disfavor with the rest of the tribunal."

"How did he know where the family was?" said Lucas.

"The Tournays and the St. Justs knew each other before the Revolution," said Fitzroy. "They were hardly in the same social class, but the St. Justs were not exactly paupers. Armand St. Just sent word that the Tournays had close friends in Valmy, a merchant and his wife whose children used to go to school together with Suzanne de Tournay and the young vicomte." Fitzroy smiled. "Citizen St. Just has been a great help to us, keeping me informed as a member of the league. However, now that de Tournay has been sentenced, it's only a matter of time before the soldiers of the Republic trace his family. You must get them out first. We'll get the old man out as soon as we locate him."

"Well, at least getting them out of Valmy should be easier than getting someone out of Paris," Lucas said. "They'll still have checkpoints manned by soldiers of the Republic, but their security won't be as tight, especially since the Pimpernel hasn't been active in that area."

"That's true," Fitzroy said, "but don't allow that to make you overconfident. I don't want any mistakes this time. I've devised a plan for you to follow. I want you to pass it on to the members of the league exactly as I give it to you. If Mongoose attempts to interfere again, I'll make certain that agent Cobra will be ready for him."

"That would make a nice change of pace," said Finn.

"Your sarcasm is not appreciated, Delaney," said Fitzroy. "I'll remind you that it wasn't agent Cobra who allowed Mongoose to outfox you every time. I've made matters nice and simple for you. All you have to do is follow instructions. Leave Mongoose to those more qualified to deal with him."

"What do you think?" said Andre.

"I think it's very possible," Lucas said. "Mongoose always was a slippery customer and Fitzroy has been in the ideal position to know everything that's going on. His voice didn't tell me anything, even though I was paying very close attention to its sound, but then if Mongoose couldn't learn to disguise his voice, he never would've made head of field operations."

"It felt a little tense in there," said Finn. "I hope we didn't give anything away."

Lucas shook his head. "I think it's all right, for now. If Fitzroy and Mongoose are the same, we should have proof of that very soon."

"I was thinking that he might give me the slip by using the chronoplate to clock directly out of that apartment," Andre said.

"It's possible, but unlikely," Lucas said. "If he really was an Observer, he'd do that to go from here to, say, Calais. On the other hand, we know that Mongoose isn't working alone. He's found himself a very unusual field man and he's going to have to get in touch with him.''

"Suppose he doesn't?" Andre said. "What if he decides to act alone this time?"

"He very well might," said Finn, "but that kid gives Mongoose an advantage and I think he'll use it. His plan gives him plenty of time to allow us to get in touch with Ffoulkes and then set out for Valmy. Once we've done that, he'll probably start putting his own little plan into motion. He can use the kid to get to the comtesse and her children ahead of us while he sets things up in Cap Gris Nez. In order to do that, he'll have to give instructions to the kid. I don't think he'll risk clocking around inside Paris. It's too congested. Besides, there's no need for him to do that. He has plenty of time. He'll either go to the kid or the kid will come to him.''

"Unless he has already given Jean his instructions," Andre said.

"That's one thing he wouldn't have done," said Lucas. "He'd wait to make certain we didn't demand any changes in his plan before he told Jean what to do. That's why he allowed us enough time to get back to Cap Gris Nez and get in touch with Ffoulkes. Only we're not going to do that. We're going straight to Valmy. We're also going to Cap Gris Nez by a different route than the one we agreed upon.''

"The important thing for you to do is to wait here," said Finn, "and watch that house. Use your own judgment. If he hasn't done anything after several hours or if Jean hasn't come to see him, get over there and see if he's still inside."

"And if he's not, I will break in," said Andre.

Lucas nodded. "But be very careful. If he's clocked out from inside that apartment, it'll mean one of two things. He's either clocked out with the plate, or else he's programmed it to remain behind and clock him back the moment he activates the remote control unit. If that's the case, you can be sure he'll have taken steps to protect that room."

"There are several systems he might have used," said Finn.

"I'm familiar with them," Andre said.

"I didn't finish. You're familiar with standard equipment. The TIA uses a different system," Finn said. "Cobra gave us a brief description of it. It's a more extreme defensive system than those used by the Corps and the Observers. Now pay attention. . . .''

A little over half an hour had passed since Finn and Lucas had departed for Valmy, leaving Andre to watch the safehouse, when she saw Fitzroy leave by the front door. Despite the fact that there was no reason for him to suspect that he might be followed, Andre still took great precautions to trail him discreetly. She gave him lots of room, keeping back as far as she could, only closing the distance quickly when he turned a corner or was momentarily lost to her sight. Mongoose, if he was really Mongoose, seemed oblivious to her presence as he walked purposefully through the city street, heading toward the center of the city.

Abruptly, he turned into a side street that led into a small cul-de-sac, through an alley strewn with garbage. She quickly moved in when she saw him pass through a doorway into what turned out to be a small tobacco shop marked only with a crude wooden sign. A name had been carved into the sign and then the grooved carvings had been filled in with black paint. The sign had grown so dark that it was difficult to read the name painted there, but once she came close, she could see that it said, simply, "*Lafitte's*."

Cautiously, Andre peered through the grimy window. She saw a small room, crudely furnished with several tables and benches, where customers could sit and drink wine while they sampled tobacco from the jars upon the shelves on the left side of the room. On the other side of the room was a large workbench upon which some carving tools were scattered around. She could see some clay pipes stacked and ready for the kiln at the back of the shop, as well as several meerschaums in various stages of completion. Some wooden pipes, a novelty in Paris, had been carved from apple and cherry wood and hung by the bowls on nails driven at angles into the wall. The door was wedged open and Andre could smell the pleasant aroma of strong tobacco wafting out from the interior of the shop.

Fitzroy stood at a shelflike partition at the back of the shop, behind which was a heavy curtain that separated the shop from some back room.

"Lafitte!" he called out.

An old man with a leathery face and shaggy, unkempt gray hair pulled back the curtain and came into the shop, wiping his hands upon his dirty leather apron. A large, egg-shaped meerschaum, colored so deeply that it was almost black, was clamped between his teeth. He seemed to recognize Fitzroy.

"Where is that worthless nephew of yours?" Fitzroy said.

The old man shrugged, turned around and pulled back the curtain. *"Jean!"* he yelled, his voice sounding like a death rattle.

The boy came out after several minutes, holding a broom. Upon seeing Fitzroy, he propped the broom up against the wall and joined him at one of the tables. The old man went back behind the curtain, but Mongoose, for it was obviously he, spoke with the boy in low tones and Andre could not make out what they were saying. After a short while, Mongoose rose from the table and Andre quickly got out of sight before he came back out of the shop. She followed him back to the apartment.

She waited another half an hour to forty-five minutes, watching the house from across the street; then she went up to the door and went inside. Moving slowly and quietly, she made her way up the stairs. She paused just outside the door, her back pressed against the wall, her head cocked as she listened intently for any sound coming from within. There was none. She reached into her pocket and pulled out a length of wire. Pulling on a pair of leather gloves, she shaped it carefully, then slipped it through the crack in the door, maneuvering it so that it bent itself around the wooden bar on the other side and then poked out through on her side again. Very carefully, she grabbed both ends and slowly, using gentle, steady pressure, worked the bar back bit by bit. When she was done, she replaced the wire back into her pocket and took a deep breath. Crouching on her knees, away from the front of the door, she reached out and quickly pulled it open, then jerked back.

A beam shot out the door at about the level her chest would have been had she been standing. It began to burn its way through the thick wall opposite the door. She had perhaps a few seconds in which to act. Staying very low, she dove through the door beneath the beam, spotted the assembled chronoplate in the center of the room and quickly moved toward it. She didn't know the failsafe code for this particular unit, but it didn't matter. She didn't need it. She kicked at the control panel, then ran out the door as the defense system shut itself off. She knew she had only seconds left before the failsafe was triggered. She was at the top of the stairs when the force of the explosion picked her up and threw her into the wall just above the landing. Stunned, she managed to pick herself up and get down to the first floor, then out the door.

A crowd was beginning to gather, attracted by the noise of the explosion and the smoke pouring through the hole in the wall on the second floor. Andre pushed her way through, grateful for the fact that none of her bones seemed to have broken. Her face was bleeding from her having struck the wall and her chest and head hurt. Perhaps she had sustained a slight concussion. Mongoose, however, had more serious problems.

If he was lucky, he had not been able to react to his alarm quickly enough to activate his remote clockback unit. Otherwise, he had either been caught in the explosion when he materialized or else he would never materialize anywhere, being trapped forever in the limbo soldiers called "the dead zone." For the sake of agent Cobra, Andre hoped that Mongoose was still alive. Personally, she did not much care one way or the other.

The Comtesse de Tournay was an elegant old woman who conveyed no impression that she had narrowly escaped France with her life. To look at her, one would not think that her husband still remained behind in Paris, a hunted enemy of the state. She arrived in Dover attired in the height of fashion, carrying her elaborately coiffed white head high and sniffing with disdain at the fishy smell of the seacoast town. Her son, the young vicomte, was barely eighteen years old and, like his mother, he carried himself in a grand manner, back ramrod-straight and shoulders thrown back. He walked with a cocky swagger and kept his left hand casually resting on the pommel of his sword. Suzanne de Tournay, on the other hand, seemed markedly unaffected, by comparison. She spoke English better than either her mother or her brother. While they had been content to remain in their cabins on the *Day Dream* during the crossing, she had kept company on deck with Andrew Ffoulkes. With her hat held in her hand, she had allowed the wind to play havoc with her hair as she breathed in the salty air and gloried in their newfound freedom while, at the same time, she shared her concern for her father with Ffoulkes, her rescuer, who had become totally captivated by her.

As they entered the Fisherman's Rest together with Ffoulkes and Dewhurst, Jellyband seemed to be everywhere at once, bowing, wringing his hands anxiously, looking to their comfort and barking orders at his serving staff.

"Well," said the comtesse, speaking English with a thick French accent, "I must admit, this is not quite the hovel I imagined it to be when I saw it from the outside. Still, I trust that we will not be remaining long?"

"Only long enough to have a bite to eat and arrange for a coach to London, Madame la Comtesse," said Dewhurst.

"In that case, the sooner we can dine and be on our way, the better," she said, haughtily. "We have been subjected to quite enough indignities. Please do not misunderstand, Lord Dewhurst; I am most grateful to you and this gallant Scarlet Pimpernel for delivering us from persecution. However, if I had to spend one more night in that frightful, smelly little shack, I think I would have gone quite mad."

"It was not so bad, Mama," Suzanne said, a bit embarrassed by her mother's remark. "Anyway, all that is behind us now. We are in England! Soon we shall be meeting many others like ourselves, who have found new homes here."

"Indeed," the old woman said, adding another contemptuous sniff. "I am quite sure that it will not all be entirely uncivilized. Still, there is one recent émigré I hope that I shall never meet. Have you gentlemen ever heard of a woman named Marguerite St. Just?"

Dewhurst and Ffoulkes glanced at each other uneasily.

"Everyone in London knows Lady Blakeney," said Andrew Ffoulkes. "She and Sir Percy are the leaders of London society. Everyone admires and respects her."

"Well, *I*, for one, do not admire and respect her," said the comtesse, stiffly. "What is more, if she is the type of person you enshrine in your society, I fear that I cannot say much good about it. We knew each other, once. She and my Suzanne attended school together. However, it seems that she preferred to learn her lessons at the hands of the Revolutionary tribunal. While our world was collapsing all aorund us, she helped to pull it down."

"Really, I'm sure that Lady Blakeney—" Ffoulkes began, but the comtesse interrupted him.

"Your *Lady Blakeney* was responsible for the death of the Marquis de St. Cyr. If you prefer to forget such things here in

England, I can assure you that I recall them quite vividly. We are in England now and we are grateful for your English hospitality. We shall try not to abuse it. However, should I encounter Marguerite St. Just, I shall refuse to acknowledge her existence.''

Ffoulkes leaned close to Dewhurst and whispered in his ear. "This is a most unfortunate turn of events, Tony," he said. "Lady Blakeney is due to arrive here at any moment. Percy's ridden out to meet her coach."

Dewhurst nodded. "With any luck, we can get them upstairs to refresh themselves and then try to head Percy off. It wouldn't do to have—"

At that moment, a coach was heard pulling up outside. Seconds later, the door to the Fisherman's Rest opened and Marguerite Blakeney entered.

"Lord, I'm famished!" she said. "The air in here smells quite delicious." She saw the others and her eyes widened in surprise. "Andrew! Tony! What a delightful surprise! And is that . . . ? It *is* you, Suzanne! Whatever are you doing here in England?"

"Suzanne, I forbid you to speak to that woman," said the comtesse, pointedly looking away from Marguerite.

For a moment, Marguerite looked both stunned and hurt by this rejection; but understanding quickly dawned and she recovered, albeit a bit shakily.

"Well! What bug bit you, I wonder?" she said, attempting to sound casual.

The young vicomte stood up, drawing himself up to appear as tall as he possibly could. "My mother clearly does not wish to speak with you, madame," he said. "We have no desire to socialize with traitors!"

"See here, now," Ffoulkes began, but at that moment, the door opened once again and Finn walked in, shaking the dust off of his coat.

"Begad, what have we here?" he said, taking in the momentarily frozen tableau.

Marguerite smiled a bit crookedly. "Oh, nothing very serious, Percy," she said, lightly, "only an insult to your wife's honor."

"Odd's life, you don't say!" said Finn. "Who would be so reckless as to take you on, my dear?"

The young vicomte approached him, taking a jaunty stance

with his hand upon the pommel of his sword. "The lady is referring to my mother and myself, monsieur," he said. "As any apology would be quite out of the question, I am prepared to offer you the usual reparation between men of honor."

Finn stared down at the boy, putting a look of astonishment upon his face. "Good Lord! Where on earth did you learn to speak English? It's really quite remarkable. I wish I could speak your language as well, but I'm afraid that the proper accent is quite beyond me!"

The lad looked at him with irritation. "I am still waiting for your reply, monsieur."

Finn glanced at Ffoulkes and Dewhurst in a puzzled fashion. "My reply? What the devil is this young fellow talking about?"

"My sword, monsieur!" the vicomte said in exasperation. "I offer you my sword!"

"Begad," said Finn, "what good is your sword to me? I never wear the damned things, they're forever getting in the way and poking people. Damned nuisance, if you ask me."

"I believe the young man means a duel, my husband," Marguerite said.

"A duel! You don't say! Really?"

"Yes, a duel, monsieur," said the vicomte. "I am offering you satisfaction."

"Well, I'd be quite satisfied if you went back to your table and sat down," said Finn. "A duel, indeed! This is England, my dear chap, and we don't spill blood quite so freely here as you Frenchies do across the water. Odd's life, Ffoulkes, if this is an example of the type of goods you and that Pimpernel import, you'd be better to dump 'em off mid-Channel. A duel, indeed! How perfectly ridiculous!"

Marguerite chuckled. "Look at them, Tony. The French bantam and the English turkey. It would appear that the English turkey has won the day."

"You are wasting your time, young sir," she said to the vicomte. "My husband, as you can see, is far too sensible a man to allow an insult to his wife to make him do anything so foolish as to risk life and limb in its defense."

"Please let the matter drop, like a good fellow," Dewhurst said to the vicomte, placatingly. "After all, fighting a duel on your first day in England would hardly be the proper way to make a start in your new homeland."

Looking a bit taken aback, the vicomte looked from Finn to Dewhurst and then shrugged his shoulders. "Well, since monsieur seems disinclined to accept my offer, I will take it that honor has been satisfied."

"You may take it any way you wish," said Finn, with a wave of his handkerchief, "but take it over there somewhere. This whole incident has been frightfully annoying. It would be best for all if the entire matter were forgotten. Indeed, it's already passed from my memory."

"Come, children," said the comtesse. "We have yet to reach our final destination and we would do well to take some rest. We shall dine up in our rooms," she said to Dewhurst, "where the atmosphere might be more congenial, although I daresay that it won't be a great improvement."

Suzanne was about to speak to Marguerite, but her mother spoke a sharp command and, with an embarrassed, apologetic look, Suzanne left the room to go upstairs.

"Well, I can't say that I care much for her manner," Marguerite said. "That was quite a narrow escape for you, Percy. For a moment, I actually believed that young man would attack you."

"I daresay I would have given a good accounting of myself," said Finn. "I've raised the fists in the ring with some success on a number of occasions, although brawling in a tavern would not be my idea of sport, you know."

As they spoke, there were a number of other patrons in the Fisherman's Rest, some of whose idea of sport was precisely that; they had been watching with some interest when it appeared that there might be an altercation between the young French aristocrat and the older English dandy. When the two would-be combatants disappointed them, they went back to their meat pies and ale, all except three men who sat on the far side of the room in a dark corner. These three all wore long cloaks and huddled together, as though in private conversation, although they did not speak. Instead, they listened very closely. One of them, his black hat with its wide brim pulled low over his eyes, nodded to himself with satisfaction. When the young vicomte came back downstairs briefly to tell Ffoulkes and Dewhurst that his mother was quite tired and had elected to stay the night and travel to London the next morning, he smiled to himself.

"Excellent," he said softly, in French, to his two companions. "It would seem that several opportunities are beginning to present themselves."

One of his companions nodded. "If we strike tonight and strike quickly, we can seize the aristos and bring them back to Paris for their just desserts!"

"No, no, *mon ami*," said the first man. "Put the de Tournays out of your mind. They no longer matter. We are after bigger game. Those two have proved my theory. I am convinced that this Scarlet Pimpernel is an English nobleman and they will lead us to him. Now listen closely, this is what I want the two of you to do tonight. . . ."

Captain Briggs, skipper of the *Day Dream*, owned a small house overlooking the harbor in Dover. On this night, rather than sleeping in his own bed, he was staying aboard the *Day Dream* at Percy Blakeney's request, so that Armand St. Just and his sister could have some hours of privacy together. Finn had conducted Marguerite to the tiny, whitewashed house with its neat little garden and then returned to his room in the Fisherman's Rest. After an affectionate greeting, brother and sister sat down to the table for a few cups of tea.

"I feel as though I have snuck into England like a thief," Armand said, smiling. "I hid in Captain Briggs's cabin during the crossing, fearing to venture out. I can well imagine how the Comtesse de Tournay would have reacted upon seeing not only a St. Just, but a member of the Committee of Public Safety aboard the boat that was taking her to freedom!"

Marguerite looked at her brother and felt an overwhelming sadness. At first glance, he was still the same youthful-looking charmer, but on closer inspection, she could see that his hair was now lightly streaked with gray. There were bags under his blue eyes and his face had a tired and haggard look.

"I think Percy is being totally unreasonable, insisting upon our meeting this way," she said. "You should come and stay with us, Armand, in Richmond. This is—"

"No, no, do not blame Percy," said Armand. "He invited me to Richmond. This was at my insistence. I cannot be gone from France for long and, given the climate of opinion on these shores, it would scarce serve you and Percy well to be entertaining a member of Fouquier-Tinville's committee in your home. It would be a bit awkward for me, as well. This way, at least we have some time to spend alone together. Tell me, then, my sister, are you happy here? How is England treating you?"

"England treats me well enough," said Marguerite, "but as to being happy, I cannot recall when I have been so miserable."

"What, is Percy not treating you well? He doesn't beat you, surely!"

"Oh, no, nothing like that," said Marguerite. "Sometimes I almost wish he would. It might even be preferable to the way he treats me now. He is polite and attentive, he sees to all my needs and comforts, but he has withdrawn his love from me, Armand. He has heard the gossip, the stories about the Marquis de St. Cyr—"

"Haven't you told him the truth?" Armand said. "Haven't you explained that you struck out at St. Cyr on my account?"

"What good would that do?" said Marguerite. "It would not change what I have done. What am I to tell him, that I spoke carelessly in a group of what I believed to be trusted friends, accusing a man of treason because he had my brother caned for having the effrontery to express his plebeian love for St. Cyr's aristocratic daughter? Would that excuse my actions?"

"You oversimplify the situation, Marguerite. St. Cyr *was* a traitor. We both knew he had written letters to Austria, seeking help to put down the Revolution. He did not merely have me caned when he learned of my seeing Juliette. I was nearly beaten to death. Surely Percy would understand what you did under the circumstances. You also do not mention the lengths to which you went to try to save him after his arrest. St. Cyr was a monster who represented the worst in the old system, a decadent aristocrat who flogged his servants regularly, who ran down people with his coach when they were not quick enough to get out of his way, who—"

"What difference does all that make?" said Marguerite. "It does not change the fact that I informed upon the man and sent him to his death, along with his whole family. It does not change the fact that in doing so, I became a part of what Percy so abhors about the Revolution. I can well imagine how he must feel now, having had you brought here so that we could see each other once again. He has a wife who was an informer and a brother-in-law who sits upon a committee of ruthless murderers whose thirst for blood is infamous. Why, Armand?

Why continue with it? Stay here, with me. At least give me the peace of mind in knowing that you are no longer a part of all that savagery!''

Armand shook his head. "No, my dear sister, I cannot. That we have acted savagely, I cannot dispute. Yet, there must be a voice speaking out for reason in the tribunal. I'll grant that my lonely voice has, for the most part, been lost upon the wind, but it is a wind that must soon blow itself out. The Revolution is a force for good. It has brought about a rebirth in our country and it gives the people hope. But the abuses of the aristocracy will not be easily or quickly forgotten. The beaten dogs have turned upon their former brutal masters and they must growl and rend and tear until they've had their fill. This is the way of things, for better or for worse. Until the hate of the people for the aristos burns itself out, these executions will continue. I find it loathsome, but it is a fact of life. Hard to believe though it may seem, good will come of it all in the end and the Revolution will stand in history as a terrible monument to what can happen when people are pushed too far. Meanwhile, I must remain in France and do what I can, what little that may be, to bring an end to all of it so that we may get on about the business of rebuilding and leave behind the tearing down. And just as the people's hate will burn itself out one day, so will Percy come to understand why you did what you have done and he will forgive you for it.''

Marguerite shook her head. "I wish I could believe that.''

"You must believe it, Marguerite. Percy loves you. It is the strongest of emotions and it soon defeats all others.''

"I wonder,'' she said. "I know he loves me, Armand, I can see it in his eyes. Yet, though we live together, we remain apart. We almost never speak, except when necessary, and the only true friend that I had at Richmond, one of the servants, a girl named Andre, was sent away by Percy and now I have no one left to talk to.''

"Then you must talk to Percy,'' said Armand. "You must resolve matters between you.''

"Believe me, Armand, there is nothing I want more, but I am frightened. Percy frightens me. I do not know him anymore. I think sometimes that I must be going mad. You have seen him, you have spoken with him. Have you not found him changed?''

Armand frowned. "I'm not certain what you mean. He has,

perhaps, put on a few more airs since last I saw him; other than that, he seems the same.''

"I tell you, he is a different man," said Marguerite. "I cannot explain it, but I half believe that he is not Percy Blakeney, but some impostor who looks and speaks just like him. I am living with some stranger and what frightens me even more is that I seem to find this stranger even more compelling than my husband.''

Armand smiled. "From what you tell me, it seems that Percy is at odds with his ideals. He loves you, yet he hates what you have done, what he thinks you believe. Such a state of affairs might well affect a man so deeply that he would seem a stranger, not only to you, but to himself, as well.''

"Perhaps that is what it is," said Marguerite. "Still, I cannot help but think that—''

"I'm certain that is all it is," Armand said, taking his sister's hand. "These are trying times for all of us, Marguerite. We shall simply have to persevere.''

She smiled halfheartedly. "Look at me," she said, "crying on your shoulder when you have troubles ever so much greater than my own.''

"They, too, shall pass," Armand said, patting her hand.

"Must you leave so soon?" she said. "I've missed you so!''

Armand nodded. "Yes, I'm afraid I must. I sail in the morning. Captain Briggs has been good enough to promise to take me back across. I should not have come, but I missed you, too. Still, there is much needing to be done in Paris.''

"Then I shall come to visit you in Paris soon!''

"That would not be wise," Armand said. "Things are unstable in the government right now. I would feel far happier knowing you were safe in England, where a threat to you could not be used against me.''

"Is it as bad as that?" she said, her face grave with concern.

"Yes, and I fear it will grow worse before it's over,'' Armand said. "You mark my words, those doing the chopping now may one day soon find their own necks on the block.''

"Then don't go back, Armand," said Marguerite. "Why place yourself in danger needlessly?''

"Because it is not needless, my dear. I said that there must be a voice for reason and there is precious little reason in

France these days. If those who feel as I do were to abdicate their responsibility, there would be no reason at all.''

It was late when Marguerite returned to the Fisherman's Rest. Finn had left the coach with her, but because the inn was not far away, she had sent the coachman back to eat his supper earlier, saying she preferred to walk in the cool night air. As she was about to pass through the door of the inn, she heard a soft voice behind her say, ''I always find a walk before bedtime relaxing, too, Citoyenne St. Just.''

Startled, she quickly turned around to see a little, foxlike man dressed all in black approaching her. He was about forty years old and slender. He held a tiny pewter snuffbox in his left hand and beneath his wide-brimmed black hat his sharp features were set in a look of friendly affection.

''*Chauvelin?*'' said Marguerite.

''It's so nice to be remembered, Citoyenne St. Just,'' he said, with a slight bow.

''Not Citoyenne St. Just, but Lady Blakeney now,'' said Marguerite.

''Ah, yes, of course. I stand corrected. How fares the leading light of the *Comédie Française*?''

''The former leading light of the *Comédie Française* is frightfully bored these days, my dear Chauvelin. And what brings you to England?''

''Matters of state,'' said Chauvelin, taking a pinch of snuff. ''I am to present my credentials to Mr. Pitt in London tomorrow as the official representative of the Republican government to England.''

''You may find your reception a trifle cool, my dear Chauvelin,'' said Marguerite. ''The English are not very sympathetic to the government in France these days.''

Chauvelin smiled. ''I am quite aware of that,'' he said. ''If anything, you understate the case. Still, I must do my duty. Besides, I also have other responsibilities. You mentioned that you were bored, Citoyenne. I may have just the remedy for that. It is called work.''

Marguerite raised her eyebrows. ''Work? Are you saying that you would employ me, Chauvelin?''

The Frenchman shrugged. ''In a manner of speaking, perhaps. Tell me, have you ever heard of the Scarlet Pimpernel?''

''Heard of the Scarlet Pimpernel?'' said Marguerite, with a

chuckle. "My dear Chauvelin, all of England has heard of the Scarlet Pimpernel! We talk of nothing else. We have hats à la Scarlet Pimpernel; our horses are called Scarlet Pimpernel; at the Prince of Wales's party the other night, we had a soufflé à la Scarlet Pimpernel."

"Yes, well, he has become rather well known in France, as well," said Chauvelin. "In fact, as I have said, I have several responsibilities on my mission here. One of my duties is to learn about this League of the Scarlet Pimpernel. Aristocratic French émigrés have been arousing feeling abroad against the Republic. I need to find this Scarlet Pimpernel and bring to an end his criminal activities. I am certain that he is a young buck in English society. I would like you to help me find him."

"Me?" said Marguerite. "Why, what could *I* do?"

"You could watch, Citoyenne, and you could listen. You move in the same circles as he does."

"Understand me, Chauvelin," she said, "even if I could do anything to aid your cause, I would not do so. I could never betray so brave a man, whoever he may be."

"You would prefer to be insulted by every French aristocrat that comes to this country?" Chauvelin said. "Yes, I observed that little drama earlier this evening. If this Scarlet Pimpernel is not brought to justice, I can assure you that it will be re-played time and time again, with each new arrival who recalls your part in the trial of the *ci-devant* Marquis de St. Cyr."

Marguerite stiffened. "Be that as it may, Chauvelin," she said, "I will not help you."

"I see," said Chauvelin. "Well, I am not a man to be easily dissuaded, Citoyenne." He pointedly ignored her correction of him as to her proper title. "I think that we shall meet again in London."

Irritated, Marguerite gave him a curt nod of dismissal and entered the Fisherman's Rest without saying anything further to the little Frenchman. Since they had last seen each other in Paris, he had developed an oily officiousness she did not care for at all.

There were still several patrons sitting at the tables, despite the lateness of the hour, among them Ffoulkes and Dewhurst. Marguerite said a brief good night to them and went upstairs, only to find that her husband was not in. For a moment, she wondered if she had really expected him to be. She also wondered about the pretty blonde girl in Jellyband's employ. If

Percy was not coming to her bed, perhaps he was going to someone else's.

As she prepared to go to bed, alone as usual, Marguerite contemplated all her recent disappointments. The fact that Armand was only able to spend so brief a period of time with her was only one more disappointment added to the list. She understood why he had to go back to Paris and why it would be unseemly for him to mingle in the Blakeneys' social circle. Still, she felt that she had not really been able to tell him half the things she meant to say to him. Some things, she thought, one cannot speak of, even with a brother. She had only been able to hint at what was really bothering her. She missed her confidant.

As Chauvelin quietly entered the small firelit room, he saw Ffoulkes and Dewhurst lying unconscious on the floor, his two agents going through their pockets. He closed the door behind him softly.

"Did either of them see you?" he whispered.

One of the men shook his head. "No, Citizen. We took them from behind."

Chauvelin nodded. "Excellent. Quickly now, let me see what you have found."

They passed over the two men's purses and several papers they had found on Andrew Ffoulkes. Chauvelin quickly glanced over them.

"Anything?" said one of the men.

Chauvelin made a wry face. "Several drafts of what appears to be a love poem," he said. "It seems that we have wasted our . . . one moment." He unfolded a letter and read silently to himself, then looked up at his accomplices with a broad smile. "Correction, we have *not* wasted our efforts. Quite the contrary."

"Have you discovered a clue to the Pimpernel's identity?" one of the men said, anxiously.

"No, but something just as interesting. A letter to the Pimpernel, from a member of the Committee of Public Safety, no less, clearly implicating himself."

Chauvelin carefully folded the letter and put it in his pocket. "Tear the rest of these papers up and throw them in the fire but take care to leave some scraps lying on the floor, as if they missed the hearth. Let them think the robbers went through all their pockets destroying anything of no value to them and making off with what they wanted. Remove their watches and their rings and take these two purses. The fools will never be the wiser." He smiled.

"I think, my friends, that we may now count on Citoyenne St. Just's complete cooperation."

11 ━━━━━━━━━━━━━━━━━━━━━━

The two men stood upon the bluffs overlooking the Channel, the strong wind plucking at their cloaks. In the moonlight, Finn could see that Cobra was furious.

"Better not get too close, Delaney," said the agent. "I just might take it in my head to toss you off the goddamn cliff!"

"Go ahead and try, if it'll make you feel better," Finn said, lightly. "Personally, I wouldn't recommend it."

"I can almost understand why Mongoose had it in for you," said Cobra. "I'm real tempted to take you on myself. Whose idea was it to blow the plate?"

"Mine, actually," said Finn, "although to tell the truth, I had my doubts that Andre would get the chance. Did a damn good job for a rookie, didn't she?"

"Why, Finn? I broke regulations to be straight with you. Why turn around and stab me in the back?"

"For one thing, don't take it so damn personally," said Finn. "It wasn't personal, you know. We both have our orders and I told you before that my mission comes first. I've never liked the TIA and you know why. For some reason, I find that I actually like you. Maybe because you understand the craziness of it all and try to work around it. I respect that. I'm also grateful to you for working with me on this thing. I know you didn't have to."

"Then why in the name of—"

"Because, to use your own words, it was a calculated risk.

In fact, there were several risk factors involved, but Lucas and I both felt we had to go ahead in spite of them. For Andre to attempt breaking into the safehouse was a risk. We could have lost her. Blowing the plate was another risk. It might have added yet another element of disruption to the scenario. Fortunately, it didn't. No one was killed.''

"What about Mongoose?" said the agent.

"I was just getting to that. In a way, that was the biggest risk of all. If he clocked in before Andre had time to blow the plate, I might have lost a valuable member of our team. If he tried clocking in while the plate was being blown, we might have lost him. I didn't want to do that, partly for your sake and partly because I want him brought in alive.''

"The trouble is, we don't know—"

"That's right, we don't," said Finn. "We might've lost him, but then, I'm not entirely unfamiliar with the way he thinks. I don't believe we have lost him. You know Mongoose. Put yourself in his place. Your remote unit has just given you the alarm, telling you that someone's broken in. It's either some local burglar or it's one of us. What are you going to do?''

Cobra remained silent for a moment, then nodded. "I see," he said. "If it's a local, then chances are the defensive system's taken him out. If it's a member of the adjustment team, then they might've gotten by the system and if I try clocking back immediately, I may get caught in the failsafe detonation or wind up in the dead zone if the plate blows while I'm in transit. I'd wait about five minutes, then try the remote unit. If it didn't work, I'd know the plate was gone.''

"There, you see?" said Finn. "You *can* reason these things out if you really try.''

Cobra took a deep breath. "All right. Don't rub my nose in it. I should have thought of that, but I was just so furious with you that I couldn't think straight. While I was waiting for you, I actually considered eliminating you, you know.''

Finn nodded. "I figured you would. Consider it, I mean. The reason I was certain that you wouldn't do it is that you're a pro.''

"Well, thanks for that, at least," said Cobra. He stuck his hands in his pockets and hunched over slightly from the chill. "I'll accept that the odds are very much in favor of Mon-

goose's still being alive. Your having blown the plate elimi-
nates a large degree of the threat to this adjustment and it'll
make Mongoose easier to track down. However, that still
leaves me with a major problem. My people know about the
plate having been blown. I can't account for the whereabouts
of two of them.''

"Darrow's soldiers?''

Cobra nodded.

"Well, at least now you know who they are," said Finn.

"I know who two of them are, anyway," said Cobra.
"Something might've gone down in Plus Time and Darrow
sent one or more of his people back to contact them and tell
them that the hit was on. Otherwise, they might have had
standing orders to move the moment they knew where Mongoose was. They know who he is now.''

"I want him apprehended just as much as you do," Finn
said. "If he can't be taken alive, so be it, but I'd rather have
him that way. If it wasn't for you, we wouldn't have been able
to take that plate out, so we owe you. How can we help?''

"At this point, I honestly don't know," said Cobra. "With
his chronoplate destroyed, it's just a matter of who gets to him
first. I've still got three people I know I can depend on: one in
Paris, two in Calais. If Mongoose goes underground, we may
never find him. If he's smart, that's what he'll do." He grimaced. "However, I don't think he's that smart. He's just wild
enough to take it as a challenge to his abilities.''

"That's what I'm counting on," said Finn. "I've got a
problem, too. Now that his cover as Fitzroy's been blown, I
don't have an Observer to pass on intelligence. He might've
been a phony, but at least he played straight with me so far as
that went.''

"He had to," Cobra said. "Since the information came
from the agency field office, his cover would have been blown
immediately if he gave you faulty intelligence. I'd have known
about it, the field office would have known about it, *and* it
might have meant an irreparable disruption. Don't worry
about it. I'll take over that function for you.''

"It will interfere with your trying to track Mongoose
down," said Finn.

"I know. It can't be helped. I've got my loyal operatives
looking for him; I'll just hitch up with your team and hope he

makes a move toward you. I'll need a cover.''

"We'll work something out," said Finn. "By the way, I've got some information that should interest you. It's about the boy.''

"You found him?''

"Andre did. He wasn't completely honest with us, it seems. He is an orphan, but he's got an uncle who runs a small tobacco shop in a cul-de-sac off the Rue de Vaugirard. Know what his name is? Lafitte.''

"Jean Lafitte?"

"Interesting, isn't it? You think he'll grow up to be a pirate?''

"I don't know," said Cobra.

"That Lafitte was born in 1780, in France. That would make him twelve years old right now. The boy's about the right age. When he ran his small fleet of pirate ships out of Grande Terre Island in the Gulf of Mexico, his second in command was his brother, Pierre. I'd say it adds up to a hell of a coincidence, wouldn't you?''

"Too much of a coincidence to be ignored," said Cobra. "Christ! I don't even know how to begin to handle this.''

"You don't," said Finn. "Adjustments are *my* territory. We're already working on it. Just stay away from the boy. Pass the word on to your people.''

"I will," the agent said. "What are you going to do?''

"The first thing we're going to do is get that kid under control," said Finn. "Andre was a little hurt in that explosion, but she still managed to get back to that tobacco shop and entice Pierre Lafitte away. She said she came with a summons from his brother, that the 'gentleman' who hired him had work for both of them.''

"Where is he now?''

"At Richmond.''

"So now you've turned to kidnapping.''

"I use whatever works," said Finn. "I've got to get that kid away from Mongoose.''

Cobra nodded. "Good luck. Meanwhile, I've got some information you can use. The Republican government has sent a representative to England. His name is Chauvelin.''

"Our spy.''

"That's right. We'll have to be very careful about him.''

"We, huh?"

Cobra grinned. "How about that? Looks like we're working together after all."

Finn made a wry face. "Well, it's about time something on this mission started making sense," he said.

Most of London society turned out to attend the premiere of Glück's *Orpheus* at Covent Garden. Among those attending the opera were several notable recent émigrés from France, none of whom failed to notice the slight, black-clad man seated beside Lord Grenville in his box. Citizen Chauvelin was not unknown to them. The infamous right hand of Public Prosecutor Fouquier-Tinville met the baleful glances of his former countrymen and women with a slight smile and a small inclination of his head. This gesture so infuriated them that they immediately looked away and ignored him for the remainder of the evening, a reaction Chauvelin found somewhat amusing.

"It would seem that you are not entirely unknown in London," Lord Grenville said to him as the curtain was about to go up on the performance.

"Only because I was not entirely unknown in France," said Chauvelin. "I see a good number of familiar faces here tonight, French men and women enjoying the hospitality of your government."

"We try to be equally hospitable to everyone," Lord Grenville said, "regardless of their class."

"Yes, we, too, have no regard for class," said Chauvelin. "You will recall our slogan, 'Liberty, fraternity *and* equality.' " He smiled. "Only in England, it seems that some people are more equal than others."

Grenville's reply was cut short by the start of the performance and he turned his attention to the stage. Chauvelin, however, had not the slightest interest in the opera. His attention was upon the box adjacent to theirs, where Lady Marguerite Blakeney sat with her husband. Chauvelin's hand, as if of its own volition, fluttered up to pat his jacket pocket, feeling the letter hidden there, and he smiled. During the intermission, he excused himself and made his way to the Blakeneys' box. Sir Percy had stepped out and Lady Blakeney was alone. It was an ideal opportunity.

"Good evening, Citoyenne," he said, slipping into the chair next to hers. "I told you that we would meet again in London."

"So you did," said Marguerite. "How are you enjoying the performance, Chauvelin?"

The little Frenchman shrugged. "To be quite honest, I have no ear for music, although I find the pageantry of some slight interest."

"Well, I am glad that we have been able to interest you at least to some degree," said Marguerite.

Chauvelin smiled. "Yes, well, perhaps *I* may interest *you*, Citoyenne. You will recall the discussion that we had in Dover?"

"If you recall our discussion," Marguerite said, "then you shall also recall my answer."

"Indeed," said Chauvelin. "I was hoping that I could persuade you to change your mind."

"My answer still remains the same," said Marguerite, stiffly.

Chauvelin's smile became even wider. "Yet I remain confident that I can prevail upon you to reconsider," he said. "I have here a letter which I think will greatly interest you." He reached into his pocket and passed the paper over to her. "It is a copy, of course. I retain the original. I am not greatly skilled in these matters, but I have made an effort to reproduce the hand as exactly as I could, along with the signature, to which I would draw your attention in particular. I trust you will recognize it."

Marguerite grew pale as she read the letter. *"Where did you get this?"*

"From two young gentlemen named Ffoulkes and Dewhurst," Chauvelin said. "I knew them to be members of this League of the Scarlet Pimpernel, you see, so I thought it prudent to have my men . . . how shall I say it? . . . *incapacitate* them temporarily so that I might examine them for clues. This letter was quite interesting, I thought, but folded together with it was another note, from which I learned that there would be a meeting between Andrew Ffoulkes and the Scarlet Pimpernel at Lord Grenville's ball at the Foreign Office. I trust that you will be in attendance?"

"Yes," said Marguerite, in a low voice. She couldn't tear her eyes away from the paper. It wasn't Armand's handwriting, but it was a copy close enough to tell her that Chauvelin had worked from a sample of the original. "We have been invited." She swallowed hard and made an effort to compose herself. "You are indeed quite bold, Chauvelin, to assault Englishmen in their own country like a common bandit."

"I had uncommon cause," said Chauvelin, taking the paper from her hands and replacing it in his pocket. "You see, I know that the English, above all, insist on the proper form in all things. As an accredited representative of my government, I could hardly be accused of doing such a thing without conclusive proof. Your word would carry weight, I'm sure, but under the circumstances, I feel confident that you will keep my little secret."

"What do you want?" said Marguerite, her voice barely above a whisper.

"I thought that I had made that quite clear," said Chauvelin. "I merely want you to listen and observe. Your brother has, quite foolishly, aligned himself with these criminals and has seriously compromised himself, as you can see. You can well imagine what his fate would be if this letter fell into the hands of Citoyen Fouquier-Tinville. However, I have no wish to see any ill befall Armand St. Just. I am satisfied that he is not a criminal, only misguided in his idealism. Still, people have lost their heads for far less than what he has done."

"Chauvelin, please—"

"Do not plead with me," said Chauvelin. "It would be to no avail. I will make you a promise, however, on my honor. The day I know the identity of the Scarlet Pimpernel, your brother's self-incriminating letter will be in your hands and this copy I have made will have been destroyed. Help me to discover the Scarlet Pimpernel's true identity and I will forget all about Armand's involvement in this affair."

"You are asking me to murder a man to save my brother," Marguerite said.

"Consider the alternative," said Chauvelin. "It is a question of bringing a criminal to justice or seeing your brother lose his head for his foolishness when you could have prevented it. You see?"

"I see that I have no choice."

"We all do what we must," said Chauvelin. "When you are at Lord Grenville's ball, watch Andrew Ffoulkes. See who he comes in contact with. One of them will be the Pimpernel."

At that moment, Finn returned to his seat. Seeing Chauvelin sitting in his place, beginning to rise at his entrance, he said, "No, no, do not let me interrupt your conversation. Chauvelin, isn't it? The French representative?"

Feeling slightly faint, Marguerite performed the introductions. The curtain was about to go up again and Chauvelin excused himself, saying that he looked forward to seeing them again at Lord Grenville's ball. "It promises to be a memorable occasion," he said.

Lord Grenville's ball was, indeed, a memorable occasion. It was the highlight of the season. The grand rooms of the Foreign Office were exquisitely decorated with plants and artworks for the evening and there was a full orchestra on hand to play throughout the night. The Prince of Wales arrived together with the Blakeneys. On seeing the Comtesse de Tournay approaching with her children, Marguerite detached herself from the company, anxious to avoid another scene. She needn't have worried. The comtesse totally ignored her as she swept past to pay her respects to the Prince of Wales.

"Ah, good evening to you, Comtesse," the Prince of Wales said. "Allow me to express my joy at seeing you and your children safely in England."

"You are most kind, Your Highness," said the comtesse. "I only pray that my husband will soon be able to join us here."

"I am sure that all here will join in that prayer," the Prince of Wales said, somberly.

"Not all, Your Highness," the comtesse said, as Chauvelin approached. She gave him an acid look.

"Your Highness," said Chauvelin, bowing very slightly from the waist. "You are looking very well, Comtesse. The climate here seems to agree with you. I see that there is color in your cheeks."

The comtesse ignored him. Lord Grenville looked ill at ease.

"Welcome, Citizen Chauvelin," the Prince of Wales said, breaking the awkward silence. "I trust that our English climate will agree with you, as well. Though we may not be in sympathy with the government you represent, nevertheless you are as welcome here as are our friends, the Comtesse de Tournay and her two children, whose presence here pleases us immensely."

"We owe our presence here to that gallant English gentleman, the Scarlet Pimpernel,'' said the young vicomte loudly, with a pointed look at Chauvelin.

"Please," said Lord Grenville, touching the boy on the elbow. "Let us try to remember that this evening is—''

"Do not concern yourself, Lord Grenville," said Chauvelin. "I can quite understand the young man's attitude for your fellow Englishman. The Scarlet Pimpernel is a name well known in France. We have as great an interest in this man of mystery as you English seem to have.''

"Everyone seems to be fascinated by this fellow," Finn said. "He has become quite the rage on both sides of the Channel. I heard Sheridan say that he was thinking of writing a play about him. Perhaps he could use a bit of doggerel I've composed upon the subject. You might recommend it to him, Your Highness, if you find it amusing:

> "We seek him here, we seek him there,
> Those Frenchies seek him everywhere.
> Is he in heaven? Is he in hell?
> That demmed elusive Pimpernel.''

Grenville looked pained, but the Prince of Wales chuckled and slapped Finn on the back. "Excellent!" he said. "You must tell me how that goes again, Percy! What was it? We seek him here, we seek him there. . . .''

Within moments, everyone was repeating it. The Blakeneyites were chanting it like a Greek chorus. Marguerite might have wondered at the imbecility of it all, but she had spotted Andrew Ffoulkes talking with Suzanne de Tournay and she felt a sudden tightness in her stomach.

Sometime during the evening, Ffoulkes would meet the Scarlet Pimpernel. If she did not help Chauvelin unmask this man, Armand was lost. If only she had been able to convince him to remain with her in England! He would now be safe and she would not be helpless in Chauvelin's power. She would not have to betray a man whom all of England admired and respected. She watched Andrew Ffoulkes and felt that everyone could see that she was watching him. What if she could not help Chauvelin? How could she save her brother then?

Ffoulkes spoke with Suzanne for several minutes more, then parted company with her and started across the room. Marguerite's gaze was riveted to him. As Ffoulkes crossed the ballroon, he passed Lord Hastings, who shook his hand and slapped him on the back before moving on. Marguerite stiffened. For a moment, she thought that she had seen Hastings give something to Ffoulkes. Yes, there it was, a note! Ffoulkes was putting it into his pocket, unaware that she had witnessed the brief exchange. Feeling lightheaded, Marguerite followed him. Could it be Lord Hastings? Was *he* the Pimpernel?

She followed Ffoulkes as he left the ballroom and entered a small drawing room which was, for the moment, empty. He closed the door behind him. Marguerite felt terrible. She was on the verge of being sick, but for Armand's sake, she had to know what was written on that piece of paper. She waited a moment, then opened the door and entered the room. Ffoulkes was reading the note. He glanced up quickly, fearfully, then recovered and quickly lowered the note, attempting to make the gesture seem casual and inconsequential. He failed.

"Andrew! Goodness, you gave me a start," she said. "I thought this room was empty. I simply had to get away from that throng for a short while. I was feeling a bit faint." She sat down on the couch beside which he stood.

"Are you quite all right, Lady Blakeney?" he said. "Should I call Percy?"

"Goodness, no. Don't make a fuss, I'm sure that I will be all right in just a moment." She glanced around at him and saw that he was putting the note to the flame of a candle in a standing brass candelabra. She snatched it away from him before he realized what she intended.

"How thoughtful of you, Andrew," she said, bringing the piece of paper up to her nose. "Surely your grandmother must have taught you that the smell of burnt paper was a sovereign remedy for giddiness."

Ffoulkes looked aghast. He reached for the paper, but she held it away from him.

"You seem quite anxious to have it back," she said, coyly. "What is it, I wonder? A note from some paramour?"

"Whatever it may be, Lady Blakeney," Ffoulkes said, "it *is* mine. Please give it back to me."

She gave him an arch look. "Why, Andrew, I do believe I've found you out! Shame on you for toying with little Suzanne's affections while carrying on some secret flirtation on the side!" She stood up, holding the piece of paper close to her. "I have a mind to warn her about you before you break her heart."

"That note does not concern Suzanne," said Ffoulkes, "nor does it concern you. It is my own private business. I will thank you to give it back to me at once."

He stepped forward quickly, trying to grab the note from her, but she backed away and, as if by accident, knocked over a candle stand.

"Oh! Andrew, the candles! Quick, before the drapes catch fire!"

The bottom of the drapes did begin to burn, but Ffoulkes moved quickly and smothered the flames. While he did so, she quickly glanced at the note. Part of it had been burned away, but she could read:

> "I start myself tomorrow. If you wish to speak with me again, I shall be in the supper room at one o'clock, precisely."

It was signed with a small red flower.

She quickly lowered the note before Ffoulkes turned around.

"I'm sorry, Andrew," she said. "My playful foolishness almost caused an accident. Here, have your note back and forgive me for teasing you about it."

She held it out to him and he took it quickly, putting it to the flame once more and this time burning it completely.

"Think nothing of it," he said. He smiled. "I should not have reacted as strongly as I did and it's of no importance. No harm's been done." He smiled at her and then his look changed to one of concern. "I say, you really don't look well."

"It's nothing, I'm just a little dizzy," she said. "I think perhaps I should step outside and get a little air. Don't bother about me, Andrew, I will be fine."

"You're quite certain?"

"Oh, yes, it's really nothing. You go on, enjoy yourself. I will return presently."

She left the drawing room and started toward the exit, making sure to catch Chauvelin's eye on her way. He raised his eyebrows and she nodded. He returned her nod, then turned to talk to someone. Marguerite went outside.

Well, in a few moments, it will be done, she thought. Chauvelin will have the information that will help him learn the true identity of the Scarlet Pimpernel and Armand will be saved. And I will have sent another man to his death. She heard a step behind her and turned to face Chauvelin.

"You're being uncharacteristically silent tonight," Finn said to Marguerite as they drove back to Richmond in their coach. He had resolved to face his feelings for her head-on and deal with the situation as best he could. The relationship between them had warmed over the past several days, but now it was Marguerite who was acting withdrawn. "Is something wrong?"

She hesitated for a moment, then the words all came out in a torrent.

"It's Armand," she said. "He is in terrible danger and I don't know what I can do to save him. I fear for his life."

Finn frowned. "You seem quite friendly with the French representative, Chauvelin. Perhaps he can do something?"

She shook her head. "It is Chauvelin who holds Armand's life in the palm of his hand," she said. "He has put a terrible price upon it. To save Armand, I would have to condemn another man. I fear that I have already done so. I could not live with the death of yet another on my conscience!"

"Ah," said Finn, softly. "I see. You mean the Marquis de St. Cyr."

Marguerite began to weep. The stress of the past two days finally took its toll and she began to shake uncontrollably, unable to hold anything back.

"I never meant for him to die," she said, her fingers clutching spasmodically at her dress. "In anger, I spoke out against him, wanting to hurt him because he had hurt Armand. You should have seen him! When I found him that day, beaten nearly beyond recognition. . . . Yes, I wanted to hurt St. Cyr, God help me, but I did not want him to die!"

"Marguerite—"

"After the trial, I did everything I could to try to save him and his family. I begged and pleaded, I humbled myself before the tribunal, I went to all my influential friends, but it was all to no avail. As if the burden of the guilt were not enough, I have had to live with all the gossip and the scorn, hated by my old friends, distrusted by others who believed me to be an informer. Then I met you. I thought that with you, I had another chance. A chance for a new life in England, where no one knew me and perhaps I could forget what I had done, but no, my infamy followed me to London. I never had that chance. I see loathing in the faces of the French aristocrats who have come here. I know your friends speak about me behind my back and I know that you have heard all of the stories and despise me for what I have done. When all of this is over, you will despise me more!''

Finn leaned over and took Marguerite by the shoulders. "I do not despise you, Marguerite. Whatever else you may think of me, I want you to believe that. I am not without some influence in France and I have powerful friends in London. I will do what I can."

"How could you possibly—"

"I said that I would help," said Finn, "and I will. Trust in me. Armand will be safe. I promise."

"If I could only believe that!"

"Believe it." He pressed her close to him and she put her arms around him. "I know that it's been very hard for you," said Finn. "I know that I've been terribly unkind. I will make it up to you, I swear it. Look, we are home now. If I'm to try to help Armand, there are some matters I must see to. You must get some sleep. Try not to worry. Things will look better in the morning, you'll see."

The coach pulled up to the entrance of the mansion and Finn helped Marguerite out. She was unsteady on her feet. As the coachman drove the rig down to the stables, Finn hugged Marguerite and stroked her hair reassuringly. She clung to him tightly, desperately. After a moment, Finn held her away, wiping the tears from her cheeks with the knuckle of his index finger. Later, he wasn't sure which of them initiated the kiss, but it lasted for a long time. When it was over, she gazed at him with an expression that was a mixture of happiness and confusion. She started to say something, but Finn put a finger against her lips.

"Tomorrow," he said. "Get some rest now. Leave everything to me."

12 _____

In the morning, Marguerite awoke with a cry from a nightmare. She had been standing in the Place de la Révolution, all alone. It was dusk. The city was as quiet as a deserted forest clearing as she stared at the platform upon which stood the guillotine, its blade raised and ready to descend. From the distance, she could hear the creaking sound of wooden wheels and the slow clip-clop of a horse's hooves upon the cobblestones. A soft breeze began to blow, gaining in strength as the sound of the approaching tumbrel grew closer. Then the wooden cart entered the empty square. The wind was fierce now and she had to lean into it to stand upright. The tumbrel had no driver. The tired-looking horse moved slowly, ponderously, as though it found the load that it was pulling unbearably heavy.

Armand stood in the tumbrel, dressed simply in black britches and a white shirt that was open at the neck. His hands were bound behind him and his eyes were glazed. It was rapidly growing darker in the deserted square. The horse came to a stop almost in front of her and Armand, moving slowly, regally, stepped out of the tumbrel and began to climb the steps up to the platform. She wanted to say something, to call out to him, to run to him and stop him, but she was unable to move or speak. Armand stopped. He kneeled, then slowly bent over, putting his head down. . . .

She spun around, turning her back upon the sight, and was confronted with a crowd of people. The entire square was filled with people holding torches, hundreds, thousands of them, all looking at her. She recognized Chauvelin. He smiled, then pushed another man forward. The man stepped up to her, holding out a paper. She looked down at the paper he held out to her and saw that it was Armand's letter. As she looked up, she saw that the man holding out the letter to her was the Marquis de St. Cyr. At that moment, she heard the sound of the blade descending. She covered her eyes. Something bumped against her feet. She opened her eyes and saw Armand's head lying at her feet. His eyes were open and looking straight at her, accusingly. As she stared down in horror, his mouth opened and he said, "Why, Marguerite? Why did you not help me?"

She cried out and sat bolt upright in bed, clutching at her throat. She jumped out of bed and threw on a dressing gown, then ran downstairs. One of the servants started to approach her, but she ran past him into the dining room. Percy was not there. From the dining room, she ran to Percy's den and flung open the door. The room was empty. She came into the den, looking around wildly, as though he might be hidden somewhere. He was an early riser, surely he could not still be sleeping! He had promised that he would . . . she looked down at the desk. She had leaned upon it and knocked over an inkwell. The ink was red. Lying on the surface of the desk was a signet ring. She picked it up. It was a design in the shape of a flower. She dipped the ring into the ink and pressed it down upon a piece of paper lying on the desktop. The imprint was the same as that she briefly saw on the note burned by Andrew Ffoulkes. It was the sign of the Scarlet Pimpernel.

The door to the den opened a little and the servant who had tried to speak with her moments earlier stuck his head in.

"Excuse me, Lady Blakeney, but there is a gentleman—"

"Come in," Marguerite said, dully, not having heard him.

"Milady, there is a gentleman, a messenger to see you. He insists upon speaking to you. I've left him waiting in the reception . . . Oh, dear, I see you've had a slight mishap. Allow me, my lady. . . ."

He pulled out a handkerchief and began wiping up the spilled ink.

"A gentleman, you said?" said Marguerite, feeling numb.

"Yes, my lady. He was most insistent upon speaking only to you. I told him that you had not risen yet, but he said that he would wait."

He picked up the signet ring which she had dropped upon the desk and began to wipe at it.

"Tell him that I will see him," Marguerite said.

"Very well, mi— *ouch!*"

"What is it?"

"I seem to have pricked myself," the servant said. He held up the ring. "There's a tiny needle—" He collapsed onto the floor.

"Giles!" Marguerite was down by his side in an instant. She listened for his heartbeat. He was not dead. He seemed to be asleep. Carefully, she picked up the ring and looked at it. The top of the ring seemed to have been moved very slightly off center and now there was a small needle protruding from it. Cautiously, she tried pressing on the sides of the ring. When her finger touched one point, the top of the ring slid back into position and the needle disappeared. She wrapped the ring inside a handkerchief and put it in her pocket, then left the room, closing the door behind her. She called for a servant.

"Have you seen my husband?" she said.

"Yes, milady. He left early this morning, shortly before dawn."

"Before dawn! Did he say where he was going?"

"He did not tell me, milady. Perhaps the grooms might know?"

"Go and find out immediately," she said. She hurried into the reception hall. A swarthy-looking man rose to his feet as she entered.

"Lady Blakeney?"

"Yes, what is it that you want?"

"I have been instructed to give you this from a gentleman named Chauvelin, a Frenchman—"

"Yes, I know him, give it to me!"

He handed her a letter. She quickly broke the seal. It was a note from Chauvelin and along with it was Armand's letter. Chauvelin's note read: *You have discharged your service, Citoyenne St. Just. Your brother will be safe. I leave for Dover this morning. Adieu. Chauvelin.*

She continued staring at the note, oblivious now to the man's presence.

"I have already been paid for my service, Lady Blakeney," he said after a moment. "I will see myself out."

He hesitated and, when she did not respond, gave her a slight bow and left. He passed the servant she had sent out to question the grooms as he left.

"Milady, the grooms report that your husband left for Dover, along with Master Lucas and Miss Andre."

She crumpled the letter in her hand. So they are all in it together, she thought. Ffoulkes and Dewhurst, Hastings, Lucas, Andre, all of them. The League of the Scarlet Pimpernel—and she had betrayed them. She had told Chauvelin of the meeting Ffoulkes had had with the Pimpernel in the supper room at the Foreign Office, long after most of the guests had left and those few remaining were gathered in the parlor. Chauvelin had seen Ffoulkes meet the Pimpernel and now he was on his way to apprehend him the moment he set foot in France. They were riding directly into a trap and she had set it.

"Tell the grooms to have my horse saddled at once," she said.

"Your horse, milady? Would not the coach be—"

"Yes, my horse, damn you! Be quick about it!"

With Cobra's chronoplate, they didn't have to waste time sailing across the English Channel or riding to Paris. They clocked from Dover, where the agent had set up a temporary safehouse, directly to Calais.

"All right, here's how it stands right now," said Cobra. "I've got one of my men stationed at Lafitte's tobacco shop, just in case Mongoose or the boy returns there. There's been no sign of the boy since we took his brother. What's more, there's been no sign of the old man, either."

"What, the tobacconist?" said Lucas. "Jean's uncle?"

Cobra nodded. "He may be working with Mongoose, as well. Something that you don't know is that before he became head of field operations, Mongoose was section chief in Paris in this time period. I'm only making a wild guess, but it's possible that Lafitte might have been one of his indigenous field men."

Finn threw up his hands. "Jesus, this is getting nuttier all the time!"

"But it makes sense," said Lucas. "I was wondering how

Mongoose was able to dress up as an old woman and make off with Leforte and still have time to get back to the safehouse and meet us as Fitzroy some ten minutes later. I had thought that he might have taken Leforte directly to the safehouse and hidden him from sight after tranquilizing him, but that would still have been cutting it extremely close. In fact, considering everything that he's been able to accomplish, it would make sense that he was getting help from more than just a 12-year-old boy.''

"Wait a minute," Finn said. "If Mongoose used to be the section chief here, wouldn't the man who came in to replace him know the—''

"Allow me to anticipate you," Cobra said. "No, not necessarily. Remember, we're still dealing with a practice that is technically illegal. As a result, section chiefs tend to be extremely secretive about such things. Besides, no one would like to inherit somebody else's field personnel. They'd prefer to pick their own. The old contacts would simply dry up and new ones would be made. Except in this case, it looks like the old contacts have been reestablished. The problem is, I have no idea *how many* of them there might be.''

"You're saying that Mongoose has an indefinite number of indigenous personnel dancing to his tune?" said Finn.

"I don't know," said Cobra, "but it's entirely possible. Probable, in fact. He likes to have an edge.''

"Terrific," Finn said. "I'm sure glad you save these little tidbits until they become germane.''

"Delaney, you just don't seem to understand," said Cobra, in exasperation. "I'm disclosing top-secret information to you here! You guys aren't supposed to know any of this!''

"What worries me is not what we're not supposed to know that you've already told us," Finn said, "but what we're not supposed to know that you haven't told us yet.''

Lucas looked at him and frowned. "You want to run that by me again?''

"No, I'm not sure I understand what I just said, either," said Delaney.

"Never mind," said Cobra. "It doesn't really matter. There's nothing I can do about it anyway. I'm way out of line in telling you as much as I have already. You could do a great deal of damage to the agency with what you know now.''

"What about the damage the agency has done?" said Finn.

"In spite of what you may want to believe," said Cobra, "the agency is the only thing keeping—"

"Let's not get into this, all right?" said Lucas. "We've got enough problems. The question is, what do we do about St. Just, now that he's been compromised?"

"We get him out," said Cobra, "and we take the Comte de Tournay on this trip, as well."

"When did you have time to locate him?" said Finn.

"I didn't. The local section chief did."

"How many people does the TIA have back here, anyway?" said Finn.

"I can't tell you that."

"Where are St. Just and the Comte de Tournay now?" said Lucas.

"At this moment, they should be somewhere between Paris and Cap Gris Nez," said Cobra. "They're going by road because by the time they get there, Ffoulkes should arrive in time to receive them. You don't want them rescued before the Pimpernel could have had time in which to do it, do you? He's due to arrive in Calais tomorrow, right? By then, the section chief's people should have them here and if Ffoulkes is surprised at the speed with which you got them out, you can tell him that the Pimpernel's agents in Paris were in on it. It'll almost be the truth."

"So what's our next move going to be?" said Andre, who had been silently smoking a pipe all through the discussion, having developed a liking for it.

"First of all, is Pierre Lafitte going to be safe alone at Richmond?" said Cobra.

"He'll be fine," said Andre. "I've got him in the gamekeeper's cottage."

"What did you tell the gamekeeper?" Cobra said, surprised.

"The truth," said Andre.

"The truth?" they all asked, in unison.

"Well, something fairly close to it, anyway," she said. "I told him that I was having an affair with Andrew Ffoulkes, that Ffoulkes was a member of the League of the Scarlet Pimpernel and that the league had kidnapped the boy because he's the son of a French spy we wanted to put pressure on. Ffoulkes needed a safe place to keep the boy for a week or so and I thought I could help."

"And he bought that?" Cobra said, incredulously.

"Why not? Who'd make up a lie like that?"

"Amazing."

"What's amazing is that in all the excitement, I actually forgot about that kid," said Finn.

"Believe it or not, so did I," said Lucas. "This mission has me going in so many directions at the same time, I can't even keep track of what's happening anymore."

"Well, in that case, you'll be pleased to know that it's almost over," Cobra said. "The Scarlet Pimpernel ended his career after rescuing the Comte de Tournay and St. Just. It was a brief career, but a flamboyant one."

"You mean that's it?" said Finn. "It's over?"

"Not quite," said Cobra. "This will be your last trip to France, but there's still the matter of Percy Blakeney to consider. Chances are there's going to be a relocation and you'll be relieved, but that can't happen until the adjustment has been reported as complete and I can't clock to Plus Time to do that so long as Mongoose is at liberty. You're just going to have to stay here until he's found and apprehended."

"Hold on," said Finn. "Maybe you can't clock forward, but any one of the agency people here can."

"True, but with Mongoose still loose and Darrow's people hunting him, I'm not in a position to spare anybody. I'm not even completely certain which of the agency people back here I can trust."

"That's not my problem," Finn said.

"You're wrong," said Cobra. "It *is* your problem, because as long as Mongoose is still free, you're staying right here."

"The hell you say! Suppose he decides to go underground? I don't see what else he *can* do. You might never find him!"

"My job is to stay here until I do," said Cobra.

"And what about us?"

Cobra shrugged.

Jellyband was slightly disapproving as he served them. He knew who they were and it appeared to him that Lady Marguerite Blakeney and Andrew Ffoulkes were running away together. The fact that they both traveled on horseback and had obviously ridden hard from London to Dover seemed to confirm his suspicions. It wasn't his place to say or do anything, but he seemed somewhat scandalized.

"I feel so damn *helpless*!" Marguerite said. "We rode hard all this way and now we can't cross because of bad weather!"

"Take heart," said Ffoulkes. "If *we* can't cross, then no one else can, either. If Chauvelin left London for Dover only this morning, then he could not have had time to sail yet. No boats have left for Calais since last night. He's somewhere here, in Dover, waiting for a change in the weather, just as we are. Had I known about this, I would have taken the time to gather some of the others together and we could have taken him here and taught him a lesson. Unfortunately, I know for a fact that Chauvelin has other agents with him and I cannot risk going after him alone. If anything happened to me, you would be unprotected and Percy might not be warned in time."

"I've been an awful fool," said Marguerite. "I've placed my own husband's life in jeopardy."

"You could not have known," said Andrew, kindly.

She shook her head. "He had become so changed, so distant and secretive that I had actually convinced myself that something incredible had happened to Percy and that his place had been taken by some impostor who was his twin!" She laughed, feeling herself to be on the edge of hysteria. "Small wonder he seemed a different man to me! He was living a secret life, not daring to tell me he was the Pimpernel because he knew I had informed upon St. Cyr. Poor Percy! How it must have tortured him!"

"What matters is that now he knows the truth of the St. Cyr affair," said Ffoulkes. "He doesn't blame you. No one would. I can't understand why you didn't tell him what really happened earlier."

"How could I? After what he must have heard, it would sound as though I were making feeble excuses. I was afraid that he might not believe me and . . . no, that isn't true. I'm lying to myself. It was pride, Andrew, foolish, stubborn, damnable pride! When I realized that he must have heard the stories, I was furious with him for not coming to me at once and asking to hear my side of it. I was too proud to go to him and offer an explanation; I thought that he should come to me. As a result, it has come to this. I have no one but myself to blame."

"That isn't true," said Ffoulkes. "You could not help the fact that Chauvelin's agents attacked us and stole Armand's

letter to the Pimpernel. Nor could you help giving aid to
Chauvelin when your brother's life hung in the balance. Have
faith, we shall reach Percy in time. Chauvelin will not be certain where to look for him, while we know where he can be
found."

"That may be," said Marguerite, "but there is still the matter of the Comte de Tournay and my brother."

"If I know Percy," Andrew Ffoulkes said, "he will see the
matter through and rescue both of them."

"That is exactly what I mean," said Marguerite. "That will
be dangerous enough, but now that Chauvelin is on his trail,
how can he possibly hope to succeed?"

Ffoulkes smiled. "Don't forget one thing," he said. "In
Percy's own words, that Pimpernel is 'demmed elusive.' "

"You promised!" said the old man, angrily. "You promised that we would be safe, that there would be no reprisals!"

"In this world, no one is ever safe, Lafitte," said Mongoose.

They were in a small house on the outskirts of Calais which
Mongoose had purchased in his days as section chief of 18th-
century France. Along with several other properties he owned,
spread out across the globe and throughout time, it was one of
the places he used to get away from it all when he was given
leave. It was one of several places where Lafitte knew he could
find him or leave word for him in the unusual event that their
regular procedure had to be abandoned and Lafitte had to get
in touch with him, rather than the other way around. It was a
simple house, with a slate roof and planked flooring that
showed signs of age. It was sparsely yet comfortably furnished
and, in the absence of its owner, it was kept up by an old
woman whose husband had been lost at sea ten years ago. She
was reliable and fiercely loyal, as were all of Mongoose's indigenous employees, for he paid them very well and saw to it
that their needs were taken care of in his absence. There was
nothing about the house to set it apart from any other in
Calais, save for the fact that it had one room in the cellar that
was impregnable. It contained a number of items not native to
that time; among them a chronoplate, which Mongoose kept
for emergencies.

"They have Pierre!" said the old man.

"I know," said Mongoose, whom the old man knew only as

Monsieur l'Avenir. "I told you, there is no cause for concern. They will not harm him."

"How can you know?"

"I give you my word that Pierre will not be harmed in any way. Have I ever let you down before, Lafitte?"

"No, Monsieur l'Avenir, but—"

"Then trust me. There is only one reason why they took Pierre and that is so they will have a hold on you. They do not want you or Jean helping me."

"Then there is nothing you can do?" the old man said, crestfallen.

"For the moment, nothing. But only for the moment. However, rest assured that I will restore Pierre to you. I am certain that I know where he is. They will not harm him. They only mean to frighten you."

The old man shook his head, miserably. "It is all my fault. I should never have allowed you to bring Jean into this. He is just a child."

"But a remarkable child, you will admit," said Mongoose. "He is most resourceful. Already, at twelve, he is an accomplished liar, a gifted thief, an excellent marksman, and he is utterly without scruples. He has a brilliant future ahead of him."

"You have perverted him," Lafitte said, glumly.

"No. I have only helped him to discover himself. You are an old man, Lafitte. Face it, my friend, you are not long for this earth. You should be grateful to me for having helped Jean discover the innate abilities that he possessed. When it is time for you to die, you can do so knowing that the boys will not go hungry or uncared for. They will be quite able to fend for themselves."

"I have served you faithfully, Monsieur l'Avenir," said Lafitte. "Even though I do not understand these secret dealings of yours, I have done everything you asked me to do without question. If you can assure me of their safety, I shall do anything you ask, even give up my life, what little of it there is left to me."

Mongoose smiled. "I can assure you not only of their safety, but of their prosperity," he said. "They will both become very famous men. Jean, especially, will make his mark upon the world."

"Where *is* Jean? I had hoped he was with you, but—"

"Jean was with me," said Mongoose. "He does not know about Pierre and it is very important that you do not tell him, should you see him. He will not be able to think clearly if he is concerned about his brother. At this moment, he is performing a service for me. I also have work for you to do, as well."

"Say it and it shall be done."

The weather cleared and Marguerite Blakeney and Andrew Ffoulkes were able to sail to Calais that afternoon. They knew that Chauvelin would be sailing at the same time, although they would probably beat him to Calais upon the *Day Dream*.

"A lucky break for us," said Ffoulkes. "Percy and the others must have sailed on another boat, leaving the *Day Dream* in Dover. Perhaps he suspects that someone is on his trail and is being extra cautious. I certainly hope so."

"Do you think that we shall reach them in time?" Marguerite said, anxiously.

"I have no doubt of it," said Ffoulkes, although privately he was not so certain. He knew that Percy was to meet with him at Brogard's inn in Cap Gris Nez; however, he was arriving a day early. He had left word for Tony Dewhurst to gather the others together and proceed on to Calais as soon as possible, but he had no way of knowing when Dewhurst would get the message. He knew that Percy was very secretive about his plans and chances were that he and the others might have gone on to Paris. If that would be the case, then there was little he and Marguerite could do, other than to wait for their return and try to get to him before Chauvelin could. Unfortunately, that would give Chauvelin all the time he needed to gather his forces together and by the time Percy and the others returned to Cap Gris Nez, it could well be crawling with soldiers. The advantage that they had was that they knew that Percy would go to Cap Gris Nez, rather than Calais. Chauvelin would waste valuable time searching for him in Calais. Still, it would not take very long for him to conduct his investigation and ascertain that no one had seen a party of English citizens loitering about. Once he came to the conclusion that Blakeney wasn't in Calais, Cap Gris Nez would be the next logical place in which to search for him.

When they arrived at Calais, they quickly made their way to Cap Gris Nez and the Chat Gris. Brogard received them in his usual surly manner and, when questioned, replied that "the

English aristo" had, indeed, been there, but that he had left. He did not say exactly when he would return, but he had kept the rooms that he had taken, as usual, so that it would seem that he would not be gone for long. Brogard then began to sound Ffoulkes out as to the possibility of selling him some wine. He did so with little enthusiasm, as though he felt guilty for being forced to do business with English aristocrats. Having established their cover as oenophiles, the members of the league now had to carry on with the deception, which meant that they were forced to buy wine every time they came to Cap Gris Nez. To curry favor with Brogard, they had bought some wine from him on several occasions. Evidently, he received some sort of a commission from whoever he got it from and he thus profited by playing the middleman. Undoubtedly, he cheated both parties involved. Ffoulkes didn't mind that so much, but the wine he sold them was terrible. They usually dumped it off mid-Channel, because not even Briggs would drink it.

Marguerite fidgeted throughout Ffoulkes's conversation with Brogard, but she managed to keep silent until he left them.

"How can you discuss buying wine at a time like this?" she said. "We should be looking for them, instead of—"

"Please," Ffoulkes kept her from going on. "Lower your voice. There may be spies about, one never knows. Brogard believes us to be wine merchants to our well-heeled friends and it is necessary to keep up appearances. As for looking for Percy, there may be little we can do now. I think it would be best if you remained here while I scouted around. Have something to eat, you must be starving. The food here actually isn't so bad. It will fill you up, at least. Then go upstairs and stay in the room. Do not come out under any circumstances until I return. Please, for all our sakes, you must do as I ask."

She nodded.

"Remember that there may be spies about," said Ffoulkes. "Stay out of sight and speak to no one. Do not admit anyone into your room for any reason, not even Brogard. Trust no one. Percy's life may depend upon it."

Ffoulkes gulped the rest of his wine, grimacing. Brogard insisted upon serving him the awful stuff and he could hardly claim that he didn't like it, since they were buying so much of it. He then ordered some food for Marguerite and hurriedly departed to search the streets of Cap Gris Nez for Percy. There was also a chance that he could be at Père Blanchard's cottage and therefore Ffoulkes had to look there, as well. There was a great deal of ground to cover and not much time to do it in. Before he left, he once again reminded Marguerite to remain inside her room, no matter what.

Marguerite made a somewhat halfhearted attempt to eat something, but she was unable to do much more than pick at her food. She purchased a bottle of wine from Brogard, deciding that even the swill he served was better than nothing, and went upstairs. She closed the door and bolted it, sat down on the bed and took a healthy swig from the bottle. The taste was horrible, but at least it was wet. Her mouth and throat felt very dry. She thought to herself, the waiting will be the worst part.

The waiting *was* the worst part. Hours went by that seemed like days. There was no sign of Ffoulkes. It was beginning to grow dark. *Where can he be?* She thought that surely Ffoulkes would have returned by now. All sorts of possibilities occurred to her. Ffoulkes had been captured by Chauvelin. Ffoulkes had injured himself somehow and was lying outside somewhere in the growing darkness. Ffoulkes had found Percy and they had both been captured. She brought the bottle to her lips once more and was astonished to discover that she had emptied it. Yet, she did not feel drunk. She had always joked with Percy that her capacity for wine was much greater than his, but never before had she finished a whole bottle by herself. The room suddenly seemed oppressively hot. She started to get up to cross the room and open the window, but sat back down upon the bed, involuntarily. The floor seemed to be tilting of its own accord.

Fool, you fool, she thought, *you're drunk!*

Of all the stupid things to do and at a time like this! Furiously, she threw the bottle at the wall and it shattered, sending shards of glass flying in all directions. The window, she thought, I must open the window. Some fresh air will help to clear my head. With deliberate effort, she rose to her feet unsteadily and took several tentative steps. All right, it was not too bad. She was inebriated, but at least she still had some semblance of control. She was not falling down drunk.

Andrew will be furious with me, she thought. She staggered over to the night table, where stood a bowl of water for washing up. She emptied it over her head. Dripping wet, she walked over to the window, feeling her way along the wall and using it for support. The water combined with the chill air outside will do it, she told herself. She made it to the window and opened it, taking in deep gulps of air. Her room was on the far end of the inn, the window opening out onto the street. The entrance to the Chat Gris was just below and to her left. She heard the sounds of hoofbeats rapidly approaching and, remembering what Ffoulkes had said, she ducked back out of sight, pressing herself against the wall beside the open window. The horses stopped in front of the inn and she held her breath.

"Percy!" she whispered. "It *must* be!"

"You men start at the other end of town, I'll interrogate the innkeeper here myself. Besides, you've had a chance to eat your supper and I haven't. I'm told this inn has the only decent food in all of Cap Gris Nez."

Chauvelin!

She heard the horses galloping away; then a moment later, she heard the door downstairs open and Chauvelin call out for the innkeeper. My God, she thought, he mustn't come here now, he mustn't! She managed to get to the door of her room and she opened it, ignoring Ffoulkes's instructions. She was still feeling lightheaded, but the wine didn't seem to be affecting her as much now. She closed her eyes and tried to fight off the dizziness. She could hear Chauvelin and Brogard talking downstairs, but she could not clearly make out what was being said. Opening the door all the way, she stepped outside into the hall and went to the top of the stairs. She looked down to the first floor and she could just see the table at which Chauvelin sat. His back was to her. Brogard was standing before him, she could see the innkeeper from about the shoulders down.

"He was *here*, you say?" said Chauvelin. *"When?"*

She quickly backed away without waiting to hear Brogard's reply. The window! It looked out onto the street. If either Ffoulkes or Percy came now, she could shout down to them and warn them of the trap. She went back to her room and stood by the open window, staring outside, up and down the street. She saw a number of other people enter the inn, but none of them was Ffoulkes or Percy. Could Percy be disguised? Ffoulkes had told her that he had become quite an actor, often resorting to elaborate disguises to effect his rescues. If he slipped into the inn in such a costume, perhaps he would not be recognized, but surely he would recognize Chauvelin and realize the danger. How long would it be before the soldiers returned to the Chat Gris?

A hand covered her mouth and another pinned her arms behind her back. She was pulled away from the window.

"Not a sound, Lady Blakeney, please."

Whoever it was spoke to her in English, but he did not sound English. Too late, she realized that she had left her door open. She could not see who was holding her. She began to fight against her unknown assailant.

"Struggling is useless, Lady Blakeney. I'm much stronger than you are."

She was forced face-down onto the bed. She tried to fight, but her attacker's claim was no idle boast. He was immensely powerful. She tried kicking at him, but it was to no avail.

"Jean, hand me that rope, will you?"

She felt her hands being bound moments later. The man holding her had uncovered her mouth to do the job and she opened it to scream, but instead found a cloth being jammed into it. She was astonished to see that the person who had gagged her so expertly and now stood there grinning at her was a mere boy. In seconds, she was immobilized, her mouth gagged, her hands tied, and her feet and knees bound together. Suddenly, she remembered Percy's ring. Working her fingers madly, she managed to move the top of the signet ring so that the tiny needle was exposed. Now if she only had a chance to—

"All right, Lady Blakeney, let's see if we can't sit you up and try to make you a bit more comfortable. At least, as comfortable as possible, under the circumstances."

As she felt his hands on her, she gave a convulsive jerk and thrashed toward him, trying to swipe at him with her hands tied behind her back.

"What the . . . *ow*! Damn bitch scratched me. She. . . ." The voice trailed off. Then her hands were seized and she felt the ring being wrenched off her finger.

For several moments, nothing happened. Then she heard a clearly audible sigh of relief.

"Christ, for a moment there, I thought I'd had it."

She felt herself being turned over and she looked up at the face of her assailant. He was of medium height, not as tall as

Percy, and he was dark-haired. He had the build of an athlete, he was clean-shaven, and he was good-looking in a menacing sort of way. He smiled and it was an amazingly charming smile. He held up the ring.

"You gave me quite a turn there," Mongoose said. "It certainly would have been ironic if I'd had this thing turned against me. However, if he gave it to you, which I doubt, he didn't show you how to load it. Fortunately for me, the cartridge has been spent." He put the ring in his pocket. "You have no idea what I'm talking about, do you? I suppose it's just as well. Jean, get over by the window there and let me know if you see anybody coming."

The boy complied.

"You needn't stare at me so malevolently," he told her. "Believe it or not, I'm trying to save his life."

"Three men approaching," Jean said from the other side of the room.

"It's getting awful crowded down there, isn't it?" said Mongoose.

"They are coming inside."

"I rather thought they would. This is beginning to get interesting." He went over to the window. "I estimate that it should take the soldiers at least another half an hour, maybe a little less, to work their way through town. That's if they're efficient."

Marguerite was looking around to see if there was anything that she could knock over or use to free herself when her gaze fell upon the door. The boy had shut and bolted it before and now something was *burning its way through the wooden bolt from the other side!* Her eyes widened as she saw the tiny wisps of smoke curling up from the bolt. It was as though someone was using a very fine saw on it, but she could see no blade and there was no sound whatsoever.

"More people coming," Mongoose said. "It's getting to be quite a—"

The door swung open silently, revealing a tall man holding a small metal tube in his right hand.

"Watch out!" the boy said and, in the same instant, drew a slim knife from behind his neck and hurled it at the tall man holding the tube. It struck him in the chest and he fell, but whatever sound he made in striking the floor was drowned out by the noise of all the customers downstairs. There were two other men behind him, but all Marguerite saw was a thin, brilliant shaft of light that seemed to appear and disappear all in one second. She did not know how it happened, but suddenly the two other men were on the floor as well, having fallen out of her line of sight.

Mongoose closed the door quickly. He looked at Jean and grinned. "You're just full of surprises, aren't you?" he said. "I didn't even know you carried a knife."

Jean bent down over the first man, the one he had killed. "I thought it was a pistol," he said. "What is—"

"Don't touch it!"

The boy froze.

"It's all right," said Mongoose.

Marguerite saw that the man held an identical tube in his right hand. He bent down and took the other tube from the dead man, then removed two others from the other men.

"What is it?" Jean said. "I have never seen a weapon like that before." He stared at the tubes Mongoose held. "How can they kill so . . . so. . . ."

"Never mind," said Mongoose. "Here, take your blade back. And thanks. You saved my life."

"You would have done the same for me," Jean said, gallantly. He was obviously proud.

"Yes, but what you just did is a great deal more important. Much more important than you could possibly believe or understand. Here, help me drag these bodies out of the way. Over in the corner, there."

"Who were these men?" said Jean, dragging one of them by the legs across the room.

"You might say that they were colleagues of mine, in a way," Mongoose said, with a chuckle. "A very unusual way."

"I don't understand."

"It doesn't matter."

"They were not the same three men I saw enter the inn just now," said Jean. "They are dressed differently. Besides, they would not have had the time to get upstairs so quickly."

"You're right," said Mongoose. "You don't miss a thing. These characters were already here. My guess is that they were coming upstairs to take up their positions and they overheard us in here. All this means that we have very little time. No time for any more questions. From now on, you just listen well and keep your eyes open and your mouth shut. Whatever happens next is going to happen very fast.''

He looked at Marguerite. ''Lady Blakeney, you'll excuse us, won't you? Don't try to get free; you won't be able to. If you roll off the bed and onto the floor, you'll only succeed in making yourself more uncomfortable and you might hurt yourself.''

He opened the door and stepped outside, with Jean following him. The door swung shut and Marguerite, finally succumbing to the shock of what she had just experienced and the effect of all the wine she had drunk, passed out.

They ran into Andrew Ffoulkes as they were approaching the inn. Ffoulkes had been out to Père Blanchard's cottage and, not having found them there, had hurried back to town as quickly as he could. He caught up to them when they were within a block of Brogard's inn.

''Ffoulkes!'' said Lucas. ''Where are you coming from? What's happened?''

''Thank God I've found you,'' Ffoulkes said, dismounting from his horse. ''I've just been out to the cottage and, not finding you there, I thought that all was lost! I came with Marguerite—''

''Marguerite!'' said Finn. ''*Here?* What the hell is she—''

''She's waiting upstairs in the Chat Gris,'' said Ffoulkes. ''I told her not to venture forth from her room under any circumstances. We are all in great danger. We came to warn you.'' He saw Cobra, registering his presence for the first time. ''Who's this?''

''It's all right,'' said Finn. ''This is Collins. He's one of us, one of our agents in France. Speak quickly, man, what danger? Warn us about what?''

''It's Chauvelin,'' said Ffoulkes.

''The French representative?'' said Finn.

''The French spy. He knows everything. He knows you are the Scarlet Pimpernel. He has come to France to set a trap for you. He cannot be far behind.''

''Then we'll have to move quickly,'' Cobra said, taking over. ''The Comte de Tournay and St. Just will be arriving any moment. Ffoulkes, you'd best get back to the cottage and wait for them. We'll send them on to you. Meanwhile, we must go and take Lady Blakeney from the inn. It is a dangerous place for her to be.''

Ffoulkes glanced at Finn for confirmation. "Do as he says," said Finn. "Quickly!"

Ffoulkes swung up into the saddle. "Good luck, Percy. God speed!"

As he galloped off, Finn turned to Cobra and said, "That was quick thinking."

"We'll have to move even quicker," Cobra said. "Lucas, you and Andre take up positions at opposite ends of the street. I'll cover the inn from the outside while Finn goes in and gets Marguerite. If you see any soldiers coming, fire your pistols. That'll warn us and it may give the soldiers pause, since they won't know what they'll be riding into. The moment Finn's got Marguerite safely out of the inn, you all get to Père Blanchard's hut as quickly as you can. I'll stay behind to redirect the Comte de Tournay and St. Just."

"Alone?" said Lucas.

"Chauvelin doesn't know me," Cobra said. "I'll be safe enough. Besides, without someone to guide them, they'll miss that footpath down to the cottage in the dark. Now get going."

Lucas and Andre split up, each of them running to take up their positions at opposite ends of the street, where they would have a good view of any soldiers approaching. Even if they didn't see them in the darkness, they would hear the approach of mounted men and have enough time to fire their warning shots and run for it.

"How the hell did Marguerite find out—" Finn began, but Cobra interrupted him.

"You can ask her later. Right now, let's get her out of there before Chauvelin shows up. We can worry about the fine points once we're all safely out of France."

They ran to the inn.

"Don't waste any time," said Cobra.

"You don't have to tell me twice," said Finn. He opened the door and entered the Chat Gris. He noticed that Brogard wasn't doing as badly as he usually did. At first glance, he estimated that there were perhaps fifteen or twenty customers seated at the tables. Perhaps it was his imagination, but the moment that he entered the inn, it seemed to him that there was a brief lull in the undertone of conversation. Standing there, he felt suddenly very vulnerable.

Pull yourself together, Delaney, he thought. This is no time to have an attack of paranoia.

He put an expression of vague boredom on his face and started walking casually across the room, heading for the stairs leading up to the second floor. He was about halfway across the room when he heard someone call out Blakeney's name. For a moment, he froze, then turned around to see Chauvelin rising from a table about twenty feet away.

"It *is* you," said Chauvelin, beaming. "What a pleasant surprise! Whatever are you doing in France, Sir Percy?"

It was with an effort that Finn kept himself from glancing toward the door. He would simply have to brazen it out. He hoped that Cobra was on the ball. With difficulty, he put a smile on his face and started walking toward Chauvelin's table.

"Odd's life!" he said. "Chauvelin, isn't it?"

"I am so pleased that you remembered," said Chauvelin.

"Imagine running into you again in a place like this," Finn said. "I thought I'd just pop over and pick up some of your excellent French wine." He extended his hand.

Chauvelin also extended his hand. There was a pistol in it.

"I think not," said Chauvelin. His smile disappeared. "I am afraid that your diet will consist of bread and water from now on. However, you shall not have to put up with such an inconvenience for long. The guillotine has long been waiting for the Scarlet Pimpernel!"

There was total silence in the inn.

"I am sure you've got a pistol," Chauvelin said. "Throw it down onto the floor. Carefully."

Moving slowly, Finn pulled out his pistol, holding it gingerly with two fingers, and dropped it onto the floor.

"Now kick it away," said Chauvelin.

Finn complied. Where the hell are you, Cobra? he thought, furiously. If Chauvelin had only allowed him to get a little closer. . . .

"Drop your pistol, Chauvelin!"

The Frenchman's eyes grew wide as he saw the man two tables away stand up and level a pistol at his head. Finn stared with amazement at Fitzroy. Looking suddenly frightened, Chauvelin dropped his pistol down onto the table. Before Finn had a chance to say anything to his rescuer, another voice said, "Now you drop yours, Mongoose."

Cobra was standing in the doorway, holding a laser.

"You haven't got a chance, Cobra," said Fitzroy. "Take a good look around you. I've got men all around. . . ." His voice trailed off. Every single customer in the inn held a laser and they were all suddenly pointing them at each other.

Cobra fired, his shot catching Fitzroy squarely in the chest. As Fitzroy fell, Finn dropped to the floor and rolled as the inn became a violent crisscross of laser fire. He retrieved his totally inadequate pistol and hid under a table, trying to become part of the floor. It lasted perhaps a second or two; then Finn heard somebody moan. Finn looked up to see that Chauvelin, miraculously, stood unscathed, his jaw hanging open. Finn started to get up, cautiously. There were dead bodies all around the room.

"Shoot him, damn you!"

Cobra was on his knees. One arm was gone from the shoulder down and there was a hole in the side of his face.

Bewildered, Finn stared from him to Chauvelin. The Frenchman stared in horror as Cobra lurched to his feet.

"Shoot him! Shoot him or you're a dead man, Chauvelin! Shoot! Shoot!"

Even as it dawned on Finn that Cobra was shouting at the Frenchman, Chauvelin moved as if in a trance. His eyes were unfocused as he reached for the pistol he had dropped upon the table. As he picked it up, a thin shaft of light lanced out across the room and neatly sliced his head off. Chauvelin's headless corpse remained standing for an instant, then it toppled to the floor, upsetting the table.

"NO!"

Cobra lunged forward, bending down to pick up a fallen laser. As his fingers closed around it, a knife struck him in the chest. At the same instant, Cobra screamed and vanished. The knife which had been sticking in his chest clattered to the floor. There wasn't even any blood on it.

Finn heard a soft gasp and turned to see Jean Lafitte, staring slackjawed at the spot where Cobra had been an instant ago. His own eyes bulged when he saw Mongoose standing on the stairs, holding a laser in his hand as he casually leaned on the railing. Finn quickly looked to his left, seeing Fitzroy's body sprawled over a table. Then he looked back in disbelief at Fitzroy's double, who was standing on the stairs. The double grinned.

"Hello, Finn," he said. "Long time, no see. By the way, we're even."

EPILOGUE ⸻

The five of them sat in the living room of Forrester's suite in the Bachelor Officers' Quarters section of the TAC-HQ building. Forrester had broken out several bottles of a fine Napoleon brandy and Mongoose was swirling his around absently in his snifter as he spoke.

"Darrow wanted to prove to the Referee Corps that the agency should remain independent of the Observers," he was saying. "We had accumulated so much power over the years that neither the Observers nor the Referee Corps suspected just how far out of line we were. A good number of us, myself included and Darrow in particular, were using agency resources to enrich ourselves. It's not all that uncommon a practice, really. The temptation to clock back a short way and take advantage of market trends, for example, is particularly hard to resist. Right, Forrester?"

Forrester gave him a surly look.

"It's all highly illegal, of course, but it's one of those things that don't present much of a threat of instability so long as you're very careful and act conservatively. It also helps not to get caught. Obviously, the temptation is especially hard to resist for highly placed officials and Darrow was no exception. I knew Darrow very well and I knew that he was incredibly wealthy, but I had no idea just how heavily involved he was in temporal speculation until it all came out into the open during the past few days. Art treasures stolen by the Nazis that were thought to have been destroyed, gold liberated from pirates who had liberated it from the Spaniards, 20th-century stock portfolios—''

"They really found the Maltese Falcon in his library?" Lucas said.

Mongoose nodded. "Not only that," he said. "What wasn't released as part of the official inquiry was the fact that he had three adolescent girls in his house whom he had purchased in various time periods on the white slave market." He shook his head. "And I always thought they were his daughters."

"Nice people you work for," Finn said.

"Look, whatever you might think," said Mongoose, "if I had suspected any of this, I would have turned him in myself. A little short-range temporal speculation is one thing, but he went way too far. Beyond the point of no return. He had to protect himself and his interests, which was part of the reason why he wanted to take control of temporal adjustments away from the First Division. What seemed like an ideal opportunity presented itself when an unstable Temporal Corps recruit named Alex Corderro caused a disruption that resulted in the death of Sir Percy Blakeney.

"You'll never see it in any official report because no one has the guts to admit to what really happened. Your mission was an adjustment of an adjustment. The first attempt, with a different cast of characters, came about as a result of what you would call TIA interference," he said, looking at Forrester and smiling mirthlessly. "Purely by accident, there were a couple of agents on the scene when Blakeney was killed. Being good company men, they quickly took control of the situation, but instead of reporting a disruption to the Observer Corps, they reported it to Darrow. Darrow had a brainstorm. Why not let the agency handle the adjustment? Leave the Observer Corps, the Referee Corps and the First Division out of it entirely. Let the TIA take care of it and when it was done, he could come up with some sort of an excuse as to why the agency had to move in quickly, without being able to contact the proper authorities. Then, with the adjustment completed, he could present the case to the Referee Corps as proof that we were more than qualified to handle such tasks. The whole thing would have been facilitated by the fact that we . . . shall we say, had some not inconsiderable influence with several members of the Referee Corps. The plan was made possible by the fact that our people were on the scene first and by the fact that Corderro had been shot a number of times. One of the musket balls took out his implant and there was no termination signal. It would be interesting to speculate what would have happened if no one had been on the scene when Blakeney was killed. With no termination signal to alert the Observers, would Corderro's death ever have been discovered? Would Blakeney's death have been discovered in time to effect an adjustment? Would Marguerite Blakeney have died of her wound?''

"What *did* happen?'' Forrester said.

"Darrow put a team together and clocked them out,'' said Mongoose. "One of them, like Finn, was given the full treatment so that he could become Sir Percy Blakeney. The substitution was made, as we now know, and the adjustment proceeded. However, none of those people ever made it back. They simply vanished. When they did not clock back in on schedule, Darrow started getting nervous and he dispatched several agents back to see what went wrong. They didn't come back, either. At that point, Darrow panicked. It was possible that the first team completed their adjustment and got lost in transit while clocking back to Plus time. Possible, but highly unlikely. They were using the personal chronoplates, which meant that they would be in transit one at a time. One or two of them lost in the dead zone, maybe. But the entire team? For the whole team to disappear, as well as those sent after them, the unthinkable had to have happened.

"To cover himself, Darrow made a big show of resigning the directorship, ostensibly in protest over the agency's being placed under the jurisdiction of the Observer Corps. By that time, I had returned to active duty and was working in the evaluations section as a result of screwing up on the Timekeeper case.''

"Never thought I'd hear you admit it,'' said Delaney.

"Be quiet, Finn,'' said Forrester. "Go on.''

"Darrow's last act before resigning was to reinstate me, clandestinely, as a field operative once again. He needed his most experienced agent, otherwise I'd still be sitting at a console. Darrow was afraid to try sending anyone else back. He was on the verge of a nervous breakdown because, quite clearly, the team he had sent back messed up somehow and a timestream split had occurred. We put our heads together with a member of the Referee Corps who shall remain anonymous. This ref had long been sympathetic to the agency and could be trusted not to reveal what had happened to his colleagues, mainly because Darrow had something on him. If Darrow went down, *he* went down. So, together we reasoned that the original disruption had set up what Mensinger referred to as a 'ripple' and that, at some point, the TIA adjustment team had failed in their task and caused an event or a series of events to occur that overcame temporal inertia. Instead of the ripple being smoothed out, it branched off into another timeline. The main problem was that we had no way of knowing exactly when that had occurred or what specific incident or incidents had triggered it.

"Obviously, having caused the split, whichever members of the team survived the incident wound up in the alternate timeline, which they had created. When Darrow sent people back after them, they may have wound up in the second timeline, as well. We're not sure why, exactly. Nothing like this had ever happened before. Maybe they were lost in transit or caught in some kind of zone of instability and ceased to exist. That's one for the refs to work on. Frankly, I doubt anyone will ever know the answer.

"Anyway, if we were to assume that Blakeney was the focal point of the scenario, then the point at which the original disruption occurred was not the split point because we had been able to get our man in and there was still, at that point, a Blakeney in existence, even if it was a bogus one. Naturally, this was all guesswork on our part. We know what happened now, but at the time, if we hadn't acted on that assumption, we might as well have not done anything at all. We figured that the split point had to have occurred within the boundaries of the ripple. Either the death of our man and our inability to compensate for it or something he and the team had done or failed to do had been the direct cause. Only what *was* that, specifically?"

He shrugged. "There was no way on earth that we could tell unless we had been there. Yet, we had to do something. Darrow was practically hysterical with fear that the timelines would rejoin before we could do something to remedy the situation."

"The only way that you could remedy the situation once it

had occurred,'' said Forrester, ''would be to wipe out that alternate timeline.''

''Precisely,'' Mongoose said. ''Now you see why it had to be, why it *has* to be kept secret. Frankly, we didn't know what would be worse, failing or succeeding. There was, however, no alternative.

''In order for anyone to be able to clock back safely, they would have to be sent back to a point *before* the split occurred. Since we had no way of knowing when that was, we decided to make certain that whoever was sent back would arrive moments before the actual disruption occurred.''

''You mean that when I arrived in Minus Time, the original Blakeney was still alive?'' said Finn.

Mongoose nodded. ''It all required careful timing. First it was necessary for the disruption to be reported, as it should have been right from the beginning. Then it had to be arranged for the adjustment team to arrive upon the scene just before the actual disruption was to occur, not too terribly difficult because we had the connivance of a referee and we'd already been through it once. I underwent cosmetic surgery to become Major Fitzroy. The real Fitzroy, the one whom Cobra killed in the Chat Gris, was a genuine member of the Observer Corps, but he was also a TIA agent. The reason for there being two Fitzroys was that our man in the Referee Corps raised the unpleasant possibility of interference from the alternate timeline.

''It was possible that all the members of the first team and the agents we sent after them had died, but it was also possible that, having caused the split, they then tried to clock back to Plus Time. It would have explained their having disappeared. They clocked forward several centuries, but they arrived in the 27th century of the *alternate timeline*.

''We began playing with scenarios for what might have happened. If the 27th century they arrived in was significantly, which is to say, obviously different from the one that they had left, they might have realized what had occurred. They might have had the presence of mind to keep their mouths shut and try to find a place for themselves, if that was possible. On the other hand, suppose they did not immediately recognize that they were in a different timeline? What if there was an *alternate* Darrow heading an *alternate* TIA and so forth? We could not afford to dismiss that possibility, because the moment that they reported in, our counterparts in the alternate timeline would realize that they were the result of a timestream split. We had to ask ourselves how we would react if we were in their place.

"Once the shock wore off, we would realize that we'd have to take steps to protect our own existence. We'd have to send people back to make certain that events in that particular scenario occurred exactly according to *our* history. And we would have the advantage in that the people in the original timeline would have no way of knowing what our history was."

He paused to take a drink and there was dead silence in the room.

"If it was me, living in the alternate timeline," Mongoose said, "I would have put that TIA team through an exhaustive interrogation. I would have wrung them dry. I would have had to know *everything* they knew, because my existence would depend upon that information. As it turned out, that was exactly what Cobra must have done. He was good. He was *really* good. He knew who our top field operative was, yours truly, and he realized that the people in the original timeline would bring in their best people. What he didn't learn from our agents, he inferred. What he didn't infer, he got straight from the source. Meaning, he came to us.

"Finn, you arrived somewhat earlier than you thought you did. You presented a slight problem. Andre and Lucas were clocked back and immediately sent on to Richmond, which got them out of the way. You had to be stalled long enough for us to make certain of several things. The moment you materialized, I had to get to you fast, before the aftereffects wore off and you were fully cognizant of your surroundings. Fortunately, I was able to time it just right. Just as you materialized, I injected you with a tranquilizing drug similar to the one we used on Lady Blakeney. Then, while you were out, I clocked you about an hour into the past with a fugue program sequence."

Finn nodded. "Clever. I was in limbo for an hour, which allowed the disruption to occur and gave you time to do what you had to do. You must have timed the dose real well, because I materialized just as I was coming out of it, thinking I had just arrived. Nice piece of work."

"What I don't understand," said Andre, "is that if we were

all clocked back to a point prior to the disruption, then that means that the team you had originally sent back would have been arriving after us. What happened to them?''

"Fitzroy and I killed them," Mongoose said.

"Your own people?"

"We had no choice. During the hour that Finn was in fugue, Blakeney died, our first team arrived to make their substitution and as they arrived, we had to take them out so Finn could then step into the role of Blakeney. It was the only way. They had to die back in that time period."

"But . . . but then if *you* killed them," said Andre, "how could they possibly have gone on to cause the split in the first place? It just doesn't make sense!"

Mongoose smiled. "It does, but it's a bit of a brain-bender for a rookie. No offense meant."

"They disrupted the adjustment of a disruption," Lucas said to Andre. She looked at him blankly.

"Blakeney died," said Lucas. "That was the disruption. The TIA team went back to adjust for it, taking advantage of temporal inertia to substitute another Blakeney for the real one. At some point thereafter, temporal inertia was overcome and the split occurred. In order to negate that, they had to go back and cause yet *another* disruption. However, in this case, the people who would have to adjust that second disruption would come from the alternate timeline, since it was now *their* history that was disrupted. We thought that we were adjusting a disruption, which we were, but while we were doing that, we were being a disruption ourselves. All things considered," he said to Mongoose, "you were putting one hell of a strain on temporal inertia."

"They had no choice, considering what was at stake," said Forrester.

"The real game began when Finn stepped into the role of Percy Blakeney," Mongoose said. "Since we had no way of knowing what event had caused the split, Fitzroy and I had to make certain that events proceeded according to *our* history. We couldn't clock back to see what had caused the split because we didn't know when that happened. We might have clocked back beyond the point at which it happened and disappeared just like the others. So we had to replay the whole scenario with a different cast of characters and make sure that we controlled the plot. The moment Cobra showed up, we knew he was the agent from the alternate timeline, sent back to make certain that the split occurred."

"How did you know?" said Andre.

"We knew because Cobra, *our* Cobra, couldn't possibly have clocked back to join us. I had been removed from active temporal field duty for a time while Cobra stayed on as a field agent. During that time, he was sent on a mission from which he never returned. He was killed by Indians in the American Revolutionary War and his death was witnessed. Unless he had somehow come back from the dead, this Cobra had to be from an alternate timeline in which events had proceeded almost exactly parallel to ours. Who knows, perhaps in the alternate timeline, I was the one who was killed instead of Cobra. He certainly knew 'me' well enough."

"But if you knew he was from the other timeline, why couldn't you move against him?" Andre said. "Why couldn't you tell *us*?"

"Because we were meant to be the judas goats," said Finn, grimly.

"That's part of it," said Mongoose. "The other part is the fact that I couldn't do anything against him because he was the only one I knew about. I had no idea how many other people from that timeline came back with him. At least I knew who Cobra was. At first, I was so paranoid that I began to think that there was a possibility that he could have pulled a substitution of his own and brought in an alternate Finn Delaney. However, Finn disproved that for me most emphatically." He smiled and felt his left side, where Delaney's sword had grazed him. "It was necessary for you to think that it was nothing more than an ordinary temporal adjustment mission. Kowing the truth about Cobra would certainly have affected your performance."

"But he had plenty of opportunities to move against us," said Andre. "Why didn't he?"

Mongoose glanced at Finn.

"Because he couldn't," Finn said. "He didn't dare to act until the actual split point. His timeline came about as a result of the first adjustment team's interaction with an historical event. That's why Mongoose had to snatch all the aristocrats away from us. He didn't know when the actual split point was and he had to protect the historical events of our timeline."

"Exactly," Mongoose said. "Fortunately, the Cobra from the other timeline didn't know that our Cobra had died prior to this mission. However, he figured that out quickly enough. It took a lot of nerve to play it the way he did. He had to improvise like crazy, but he really had you going. We might have been stalemated if I hadn't doubled Fitzroy. That's the one thing he didn't anticipate. Just the same, it was pretty close right there at the end."

"I had a feeling something strange was going on when I walked through the door of the Chat Gris," said Finn. "Talk about your Mexican standoffs. Everybody in that place with the exception of Chauvelin, Brogard, and Lady Blakeney was from another time. And from two different timelines."

Mongoose grinned. "You should have seen your face when they all pulled out their weapons."

Finn shook his head. "I imagine it was something like Brogard's expression when he came up from the cellar to find his inn full of dead bodies. If he had come up several moments sooner, he would have seen twice as many corpses, half of which would have disappeared before his eyes. He was shocked enough as it was; I don't think he could've handled that."

"What happened to Chauvelin's soldiers?" Forrester said. "You decoyed them away?"

Mongoose nodded. "That's where old Lafitte came in. He met them as they were approaching and told them he was one of Chauvelin's agents and that Blakeney had ridden out of town, trying to escape, with Chauvelin hot on his heels. The soldiers took off down the road to Amiens at full gallop. Chauvelin was to lose his head in Paris. He just died a little sooner."

"Whatever became of old Lafitte?" said Lucas.

"I never saw him again," said Mongoose. "I told him that he would have one final service to perform for me and then he would be on his own. He died soon afterward. He was an old man."

"That still left you with some cleaning up to do," said Forrester.

"Not much, really. We had to bring Pierre Lafitte back from England. Simple enough. Then we had to take care of Jean and Lady Blakeney. Pierre and his uncle never knew anything that would be a threat to temporal continuity, but

Brogard, Jean, and Marguerite had seen things they should not have seen. They had to be conditioned to forget that they had seen them. A man from Relocation was sent back to take Finn's place as Percy Blakeney and I imagine that they lived happily ever after. The relocation assignment was about as easy and pleasant as they come. Life in the upper crust of London society as an extremely wealthy man with a beautiful and adoring wife. We should all be so lucky.''

Andre glanced at Finn and their eyes met for a second; then he dropped his gaze, staring down into his glass. He did not look up again for a long time.

"As for Jean," Mongoose smiled, "I was almost sorry that he had to undergo conditioning. I really developed quite a liking for that kid."

"How extensive was the conditioning?" said Forrester.

"In Jean's case, fairly minor. He would remember Monsieur l'Avenir and his peripheral involvement with the League of the Scarlet Pimpernel, but he would forget all about the . . . *untimely* things that he had seen. After that, well, it seems he had always hated Paris. He and his brother used to dream of going to sea and becoming sailors. After their uncle died, they signed onto a merchant ship as cabin boys. They had a fascinating future ahead of them."

"What actually happened to create the split?" said Andre.

Mongoose shook his head. "I can only guess. Perhaps Blakeney, *our* Blakeney, was killed by Chauvelin in the Chat Gris and the fact that it was a substitute Blakeney, which already worked against temporal inertia, was enough to cause the split. But then, Armand St. Just and the Comte de Tournay were due to arrive shortly. They would have been arrested, in spite of Chauvelin's promise to Marguerite, no doubt. Possibly Ffoulkes and several other members of the league would have been caught as well. Whatever it was, that one moment in the inn was obviously the catalyst, because when it occurred or rather, when it *did not occur*, the alternate timeline ceased to exist."

"Having never existed in the first place," Forrester said.

"But of course it existed," Andre said, frowning. "Why else was all this—"

"*It never existed in the first place*," Forrester said, emphatically. "It was a shadow, a dream. What happened to the bodies of those agents from the alternate timeline? They disappeared, because they were never really there."

Andre stared at him, perplexed.

"What he means," said Mongoose, gently, "is that we changed reality. For a time, our reality was that which we knew, prior to the split. Then, we were dealing with another reality altogether. We changed that. We restored reality to the way it should have been, the way it was, the way it *is*. At this moment, as we sit here now, the incident that created the alternate timeline never occurred. That timeline, along with everyone in it, never existed. It was like a dream."

"A nightmare," said Forrester, drinking deeply.

Andre shook her head. "No, you can't play tricks with logic to change what was. For a time, however brief a time from where we sit now, that timeline existed. Those people were real. There was another world, another universe!"

"If we accept that," Forrester said, "then we must also accept that you helped kill them all." He held her gaze. "You understand?"

She remained silent. She glanced at Finn and Lucas, but they wouldn't meet her gaze. Both men stared down at the floor.

"I need another drink," said Finn.

"So do I," said Lucas.

Forrester refilled their glasses.

MORE SCIENCE FICTION! ADVENTURE